# Young Jesus ...the missing years

## or

## A Young Jew Called Jesus

## A fictional biography of Jesus of Nazareth from age 13 to 30

### by Joseph H. Radder

ISBN: 1-4033-4866-9 (e-book)
ISBN: 1-4033-4867-7 (Paperback)

This book is printed on acid free paper.

1stBooks – rev. 07/31/02

# ACKNOWLEDGMENTS

I will forever be indebted to the people who read YOUNG JESUS in manuscript form and provided invaluable criticism and input.

Dr. Gerhard Falk, author and professor at the State University of New York at Buffalo, and retired business executive, Marvin Wolfish, read the book from Jewish points of view and saved me from some grave errors.

The Reverend Paul Henderson, Episcopal priest, and Father Alfons Ossiander, a professor at Christ the King Roman Catholic Seminary, gave me valuable suggestions from theological Christian viewpoints.

Rebecca Fasanello, an actor and business person, gave me the wonderful idea which became the several chapters about Jesus' travels with the trade mission. Playing the role of the typical reader, she also made numerous suggestions for change, holding nothing back; and for that I will ever be grateful.

My dear friend Catharine Fasanello was the most tireless critic of all. Her education as an English major saved me from dozens of errors in grammar and syntax. She read the manuscript at least three times and never let our friendship stand in the way of frank and valuable criticism.

My son Jon and my grandson Aaron saved my life when computer glitches overwhelmed me. I will be ever grateful for the countless hours they spent correcting the first floppy disc.

Finally, I am extremely grateful to Helen Slobuc, one of very few people who can read my handwriting, for her laborious typing, retyping, and retyping the manuscript on her word processor.

Without these people, YOUNG JESUS could never have seen the light of day.

To Catharine

Thank you for your tireless support
and frank criticism. Without your
help this book would not
have been possible.

## PREFACE

None of the New Testament Gospels really gives us Jesus' full life story. Matthew tells us about Jesus' birth, but then jumps to the teaching of John the Baptist. Mark skips Jesus' birth and youth entirely and begins with the Baptist's story. Luke is the most complete of the four Gospels as far as Jesus' biography is concerned, telling more about the adolescent years (e.g., the story of the child Jesus with the teachers in the Temple). John is of little help, omitting the Nativity and Jesus' childhood. In other words, the Gospels tell us nothing about Jesus' life from about age 12, when he was found with the teachers in the Temple, until his baptism by John ...probably about age 30. The only clue is in Luke (2:40), "The child grew and became strong, filled with wisdom and the favor of God upon him." In "The Hidden Jesus", author Donald Spoto says, "The construction of a biography (of Jesus) in the modern sense of the word invariably fails precisely because the Gospels were not written with that modern sense of history in mind." we agree. That is, we believe that if one is to attempt a biography, including Jesus' adolescent and young adult years, it must be drawn from the imagination; or in other words, it is a piece of fiction.

This is not an attempt to write "the missing Gospel". It is simply the product of the author's imagination ...a <u>fictional</u> account of what might have been Jesus' experience from adolescence through young manhood.

The pages which follow trace what Jesus and his family <u>might</u> have done, what he could have taught the teachers in the synagogue. How he might have questioned and elaborated on the law and the prophesies.

Jesus' teachings about such subjects as the evolution of man, life after death, human sexuality, the violence of man, singing and laughter versus the solemnity of the Pharisees, and other issues are also <u>fictional</u>. There is no biblical authority for any of this.

The idea that Jesus was the Messiah (The Christ) is not addressed in this story except to relate Mary and Joseph's belief that he was indeed the Son of God. In the time period covered by this novel, nobody but Mary and Joseph had believed or accepted Jesus' divinity. Some of those close to Jesus suspected he was the Messiah, but he never admitted it until the very end, when he was baptized by John.

We trust there will be nothing in these pages to disturb or offend Christians, Jews, or people of other religious persuasions. There is no intent to blaspheme here.

Read it, please, as you would any novel. You may well believe that the characters in this story did indeed exist, but please understand that their thoughts, words, and actions, as told here, are simply the product of the author's imagination.

x

## CHAPTER 1 — REMEMBERING

Peter, deeply disturbed by some of the things Jesus had said at supper, stayed behind in the upper room to have a private word with him. The other 11 had left with solemn faces and subdued voices. This group was never known for decorum, and even though this was Passover, their talk and laughter had been anything but religious in tone until Jesus had spoken those sobering words..."From this time on I shall not drink of the fruit of the vine until the kingdom of God comes." (Luke 22:18)

As the 11 descended the stairs, they gave each other puzzled looks. And when they went out the door to the street, James asked: "What did he mean, one of us will betray him? What would be the reason for any of us to betray the master?"

"You're his cousin, James," Philip said. "Has he told you anything he hasn't told the rest of us?"

"Not a word."

"And what about that business with the bread and wine?" Matthew asked. "This is not the first time he has talked as if he were about to die. What kind of talk is that for a man who's only 30 years old?"

And so the conversation went as they made their way to the Mount of Olives. It was actually more debate than conversation.

Before the 11 left the upper room, it had been a colorful scene. It seemed that each tried to outdo the other in the wearing of brilliantly—hued garments. Only Peter wore brown flax. And now that he and Jesus were alone, the room took on a sombre, almost foreboding appearance, with its stark whitewashed walls, the white linen covered table, and Jesus' plain white robe.

"I want to thank you, Master," Peter said. "And I want to apologize for my brothers who were too thoughtless to do so. Thank you for this fine Passover supper; but most of all, we are grateful for the symbolic gift you gave us."

"Symbolic?"

"Yes, the gift of bread and wine as a symbol of your body and blood."[1]

"It will soon be more than a symbol, my dear Peter. This very night, as I said at table, I will be betrayed by one of our number.[2] And you yourself, Peter, will deny me three times before the cock crows."

"How can you say that, Jesus? It hurts me that you question my loyalty. I would die for you, or with you. Don't you know that?"

"I know you really mean that, dear Peter. But the prophecy must be fulfilled. One who sat with us a few minutes ago will betray me, and you will deny me. Wait and see."

Peter was angry now. "Tell me! Tell me who the betrayer is. I'll kill him!"

---

[1] Luke 22:19,20 — "This is my body which will be given for you. Do this in memory of me. This cup is the new covenant in my blood which will be shed for you."
[2] Mark 14:18 — "One of you will betray me."

3

Jesus laughed quietly. "No you won't Peter. You wouldn't kill anybody. You're a good Jew, and good Jews don't kill people."

"All right, I might not kill him, but I certainly will deal with him and give him what he deserves. Please tell me who it is."

"I can't. You'll know soon enough. — Go now, Peter. I must have a few minutes alone before the time comes. I will see you at the Garden of Gethsemane."

And so, reluctantly, Peter left Jesus after asking anxiously, "Are you sure you'll be safe here alone?"

"Yes. Go now."

And so Peter obeyed, taking a long sorrowful look at Jesus before he descended the stairs.

As Jesus sat alone at the center of the table, sipping the last of the wine that remained in the chalice, the bitter hours to come were, for the moment, obliterated by memories of his short but happy life on earth.

Youthful days, special events, and happiness stood out clearly in his mind ...the thought of the time his parents took him to Jerusalem at about age 12 for the Passover feast when he had wandered away from them at the Temple and had come upon some teachers engaged in a fascinating discussion. Apparently he had stood there for over an hour listening, losing all track of time. Meanwhile, as the caravan moved northward, Mary and Joseph assumed he had joined his cousins James and John and other friends, and would be with them in the caravan. Thus the caravan was well on its way back to Nazareth before Mary and Joseph realized that Jesus was not in the group at all. Leaving the caravan, Mary and Joseph went back to the Temple and found the boy listening to the teachers. When his parents reprimanded him, Jesus said something about being about his Father's business. Joseph was puzzled by this statement, but said nothing. Now 18 years later Jesus realized that it was very wrong to speak to his father and mother so rudely. "I'm sorry, dear parents," he murmured aloud, as he remembered his happy life with his earthly family.

His next vivid recollection was of his 13th birthday about eight months later.

An angry rain was lashing at the window. The sky was dark and gloomy. His father had just spoken sternly to him about spending so little time in the carpenter shop. But there was joy in Jesus' heart. In a few weeks it would be his 13th birthday and time for the ceremony signifying his right to participate fully in religious services. [1]

It was early in the month of Tevet. The first rains of autumn, the olive harvest, the planting of grain for the new season, and the feast of Hanukkah were pleasant memories of the season just past. The heavy rains of early winter had begun, and the days were dark and gloomy.

---

[1] Today this ceremony is known as Bar Mitzvah. However, the term Bar Mitzvah did not come into use until the 16th century AD.

Jesus had an idea for a magnificent way to celebrate his birthday. He was bursting to ask his parents the all—important question, but felt he should wait until the proper time.

Now, at last, it seemed the time was right. And so, after prayers for the afternoon meal, with the wind whistling and the rain pouring down outside, Jesus asked his mother and father, "Do you suppose it would be possible to go to the Temple in Jerusalem for my birthday ceremony?" Joseph almost spilled the spoonful of soup he had halfway to his mouth. He and Mary looked at each other in amazement. There was a long silence. Jesus feared he had asked a forbidden question.

Finally Joseph spoke. "I know how much you love the Temple, Jesus. But that would be impossible." Mary nodded in agreement. Jesus couldn't conceal his deep disappointment. But he was an obedient son and knew better than to question his father's judgment.

The meal continued in silence, but the little room was alive with thoughts. What a dream, thought Joseph ...a 13th birthday celebration in the Temple in Jerusalem. What a thrill for Jesus, but so unrealistic. Truly an impossible dream. Oh to be rich enough to own a pair of camels to ease the long hard journey to Jerusalem. But with just one donkey, it was difficult enough to make the trip once a year for Passover.

Then too there was the matter of money. It would be necessary to stay at inns at least four nights. Not to mention the loss of almost a week's work in the carpenter shop. But why was he even thinking about it? Indeed he had given Jesus the only possible answer under the circumstances.

Mary's thoughts, on the other hand, were of an entirely different nature. If there was some way to go to Jerusalem for Jesus' birthday, perhaps he could meet the famous Rabbi Hillel. Of course there was also Rabbi Shammai at the Temple School, equally famous. But Hillel's reputation as a

8

liberal gave Mary a strange feeling that he would be the one most sympathetic to Jesus' thinking. Shammai, on the other hand was a conservative. Actually, Mary believed the truth to be somewhere in between the liberal and conservative views. But Jesus had already revealed that his thinking leaned toward the liberal. And so it was her goal to have Jesus meet Hillel...if not now, perhaps next year at Passover time.

Jesus' thoughts meanwhile were more prayerful. As he absent—mindedly broke Mary's barley loaf and dipped it in the stew, he silently asked his Heavenly Father's forgiveness for being so selfish. How could he have been so thoughtless as not to realize what a burden an extra trip to Jerusalem would have placed on his parents? Jesus also prayed for God's strength to assume the duties and responsibilities that were about to become his

And so he prayed that he could deliver his first address at the Nazareth synagogue, so his parents would be proud of him.

Finally Jesus broke the silence by saying, "Please don't be sad. I understand you and I love you."

A week or two later, the preparations for Jesus' birthday began in earnest. First, preparation for Jesus' participation in the Sabbath service. Second, the celebration to follow.

Jesus had already begun to study the Tfflin[1]...the scriptures which he would address in the synagogue service.

Mary, meanwhile, wove a beautiful shawl which Jesus would wear over his head in the synagogue and during prayers at home. Lovingly she had shorn the soft wool from the lamb, washed it thoroughly, and when it had dried she dyed it beautifully. The brilliant reds were from the juices of beets and berries. The deep rich blue from a special indigo

---

[1] Tfflin or Teffilin, also called by the Greek name, Phylacteries, are actually two leather boxes containing scriptures, which are attached to the forehead of the maturing male by a leather strap placed upon the skull and another leather strap placed on the left forearm.

dye purchased from the bazaar, brilliant yellow came from almond leaves, green from pressed grape skins, and the rich black from the bark of the pomegranate tree. These different—colored wools would then be painstakingly woven into the most beautiful shawl anyone in Nazareth had ever seen.

Then there were the preparations for the feast to follow. Since many Nazarenes lived in one—room houses, it was necessary to rent rooms at the inn for their sons' 13th birthday celebrations. Joseph and Mary were fortunate, however. Thanks to Joseph's skill and his recent prosperity, they had built a new home large enough to accommodate many friends at the feast.

The centerpiece of this house was a large cedar table with six chairs. Joseph had spent all of his spare time for over two years working on it. He had skillfully carved the curved legs for the table and chairs, and fashioned and beveled the oval table top. Patiently he had rubbed each piece with a porous cloth bag filled with sand until the wood was as smooth as glass. Finally he rubbed the pieces with several coats of oil until they had a fine patina. After he assembled the pieces, both Jesus and Mary were in awe of Joseph's skill. They were lucky. Indeed, many homes in Galilee had no chairs, to say nothing of a fine table. Local families sat on the floor around a rough wooden table standing only two hands from the floor.

The house of Joseph Ben David was made of clay and stones. But Joseph's skills had also incorporated beautifully polished wood in many places like the door and window frames. Unlike most houses in Galilee, which had dirt floors, the Ben David house had wooden floors held together with wooden pegs. Along the east side were three small chambers, one for each of the family members. Into these, Joseph had built shelves for scrolls, garments, and bed coverings. Beds were simple straw mats covered with woolen pads, raised off the floor by wooden bed frames, also fashioned by Joseph in the early years of his marriage to Mary. Facing the

Temple to the south in Jerusalem, was the front entrance with its Mezuzah[1], and an entrance hall which opened into the main room. Here was the hearth, used mostly for cooking. It seldom got cold enough during the daytime in Nazareth, to need anything other than the sun for warmth. During winter nights, woolen garments and bed covers kept the family warm. In the center of the main room stood Joseph's pride and joy, the well—polished cedar table and chairs. Along the wall next to the hearth were more shelves for Mary's cooking pots and serving dishes. on the opposite wall was a special shelf for Joseph's precious scrolls ...all of the five hand—copied books of the Torah which he had purchased one at a time as he was able. Jesus loved to hear his father read from these scrolls each evening... the stories of their ancestors back to King David. Joseph often pointed out to Jesus

---

[1] Mezuzah — a case containing a small parchment scroll inscribed with Deut. 6:4—9 and 11:13—21 and the name Shaddai, fixed to the door post.

that, after his birthday, he too would be called Ben David.

Behind the main room was the relatively large walled courtyard, where the donkey, a few sheep, goats, ducks and chickens were kept. This is where Jesus had played as a young child. Off the courtyard was Joseph's carpenter shop, a small stable for the mule, a chicken coop, and a storage shed—all in all a fine house for a family of modest means.

It was Joseph's job to go to market to buy the foods needed for the feast. And so he headed for the center of the city.

Joseph never ceased to admire the town where they lived. While smaller than Jerusalem, where life teemed in the maze of streets and alleys, Nazareth was indeed a city.

The common people, like Joseph's small family, were the mainstay of Nazareth. These were the artisans, craftsmen, and tradesmen who lived in the middle class section near the outskirts of the city. Joseph was one of several carpenters who lived there.

As he passed through the poor part of town, he pitied the beggars, the crippled, the diseased, the blind, the many unloved and hopeless, all living amid squalor in flimsy shacks. These people relied entirely on the charity and kindness of people like the Ben Davids for their existence.

Jesus often took a basket of Mary's bread, dried fish, and dried fruits to this part of town; but the grabbing hands of the poor would snatch everything away long before all the needy were satisfied. Helping the poor was a time—honored Jewish tradition.

Like all cities and towns in Galilee, Nazareth had a marketplace ...a bazaar where all sorts of goods and foods were sold and bartered. When he was younger, Joseph used to take his products to the bazaar... tables, chairs, shelving, and cabinets. Soon, however, he had earned an enviable reputation, and people came to him... to the little shop in the corner of his home.

There was continuous and lively trade in staple foods at the marketplace ...barley, nuts, olives, onions, cucumbers, dried fruits, and salted fish. Meat, being reserved mostly for feast days, was available only from the farmers outside the city. often, however, families maintained their own small herds of lambs and goats in the courtyards of their homes. For feast days they would slaughter and dress one of these animals. They seldom slaughtered goats, however, because the goats' milk was used to drink and for cheese—making.

A stroll through the bazaar would be a treat to the nostrils, or an ordeal, depending on one's viewpoint. The sight of a potential customer would set off a barrage of merchants' shouts and claims for their wares. A dyer, wearing a brightly colored shawl, might shout: "See this? Bring me your wool, and I can make it beautiful. I can dye it any color of the rainbow!" A tailor, with a large bone needle in his robe, might cry, "You could look better than you do if you'd let me make your clothes."

Numerous linen—makers dominated the Nazareth bazaar, because Galilee was the center of the flax country. The competition among the linen—makers was fierce as they shouted claims like: "No finer linen in the world! Buy from me, or you'll be sorry."

Perfumers were among the few who conducted their business quietly. Their customers were usually women of questionable reputation who would haggle with the perfumers about prices in whispered tones. Sometimes, it was said, these women would exchange sexual favors for the purchased wares behind the flimsy curtain hung at the back of the stall.

Just before the great festivals, the farmers would arrive at the bazaar with wagon—loads of doves in cages, sheep, and fatted calves to be sold to the pilgrims who would take them to the Temple in Jerusalem for sacrifices.

Each merchant's stall usually had an older man or woman assisted by a younger and, if there was

17

heavy work to do, a slave. Apprenticeship within families was the tradition. A boy would learn his father's skills as a girl would learn her mother's.. There was never any question about it, just as it was always understood that Jesus would be a carpenter like his father Joseph.

Over the years, Jewish law had protected tradesmen and laborers, and even slaves, from unfair practices.[1]

Slavery was an ancient custom in Galilee, Samaria, and Judea. The slave market in Nazareth was hard by the bazaar. Here too there was much shouting and haggling. After considerable bargaining, a healthy gentile slave would fetch as much as 2,000 denarii.[2]

When Joseph reached the bazaar, he walked quickly past the tables of chickens, dried fish,

---

[1] Deuteronomy 24:14 — "You shall not defraud a poor and needy servant, whether he be one of your countrymen or one of the aliens who live in your communities."

[2] Denarius (plural denarii) - A silver Roman coin, about the size of a dime, and probably worth about a penny by late 20th century standards.

and vegetables, heading directly to the fruit vendors' tables and the stall of his favorite young woman. Today she had dried figs, dates, currants, and raisins to offer — as well as fresh oranges, lemons, and bananas.

After negotiating the price, Joseph took a good supply of each and put them into two bags which he had brought with him. Mary would be pleased to get fresh fruits as well as dried, he thought as he tied the two bags together and slung them over his back.

Heading home, Joseph was in a happy mood, as he thought about his son who was about to become "of age". He had had doubts, at times, about Jesus' divinity, and he asked God to forgive him for that. But as the boy grew older it became more and more clear that Jesus was indeed getting to be more and more a man of God. Was he really the Son of God as Mary continued to insist, and as an angel had told Joseph in a dream?

Jesus' preparation for his participation at the synagogue was, of course, to study as hard as he could. While he and the other 13—year—old boys at the school had spent over a year learning to read the Torah[1] and Haftorah[2] lessons in Hebrew, there was still much to learn. All five books of the Torah were to be studied, as well as the Haftorah, biblical selections which were read at the conclusion of each synagogue service. Jesus had made extensive notes over the past year. He would also be expected to be well—versed in Jewish history, the Bible, prayers, customs, ceremonies, and the Hebrew language. And here, only a few days away from the day when he would be accepted as an adult, he felt lacking in confidence and so, he prayed to God the Father for help. In a dream that night God spoke to him and said: "Fear not. You have worked hard. And you are well prepared. You will make me proud of you at the ceremony celebrating your coming of age."

[1] The Pentateuch or the Law.
[2] The teachings of the Prophets.

Finally the long—awaited day arrived. Jesus rose before sunrise, said special prayers, and bathed more thoroughly than he ever had before. Dressed in his special birthday clothing which Mary had made for him, he finally appeared in the doorway of the central room. Joseph and Mary were already dressed in their Sabbath best and waiting for him. "How fine you look, son," Joseph said.

"I hope my readings and my address do my garments justice," Jesus said.

"I know they will," Mary said. "You're standing on the threshold of a new life, dear Jesus. And I know you are as thankful to God as we are."

As Joseph attached the Tfflin to Jesus' forehead and forearm and placed the beautiful Tallith over his shoulders, he said: "Come now. We want to be early. The services begin in less than an hour."

The short walk to the synagogue took even less time than usual. The excitement quickened their steps. On entering the synagogue, they said the

21

ancient prayer pleading for worthiness to be in the House of God.

The synagogue at Nazareth could not compare with the Temple at Jerusalem, but it was one of the larger and more ornate of the Galilean synagogues. It had a flagstone floor, a beautifully carved ark to house the Torah scrolls, and stately menorahs. The front entrance had an arched window above it, and stone pillars framed the porch. Inside, was a large hall between two colonnades; its pillars were repeated from the front entrance to the dais to support the high roof in the main sanctuary. Windows were large so the Torah could be read in full light. An elaborate frieze along the top of each wall repeated a pattern of the star of David, roses, and barley sheaves. Inside benches were placed in rows facing the dais.

Because of the occasion, they were required to sit on the front bench. As Jesus gazed at the ark and Torah, he prayed fervently that he might do well. Finally the cantor began the familiar chant and the leader appointed for the day, a Nazarene named Joathim, took his place at the reading desk on the dais. The service proceeded as usual until Joathim said in his clearly Galilean dialect of Aramaic: "Today we are pleased to honor Jesus, son of Joseph Ben David, who on this day will become Jesus Ben David (Jesus, Son of David) and assume all the rights and responsibilities of an adult member of the Jewish faith. Will you please step forward, Jesus."

At this point the cantor led the assembled congregation, now crowding the benches and the aisles, in a chant of thanksgiving. The leader took the scroll from the ark and placed it in Jesus' hands. Jesus then surprised all present, including his parents, with his ability to read so beautifully. When Jesus had completed the assigned passage from Exodus, a man named Ahaz stepped forward to interpret the passage, as was the custom.

Now Joseph stepped to the reading desk to recite aloud the ancient statement of release of responsibility ..."Blessed be he who releases me from the responsibility of the child." Joathim then spoke of the drama of this moment signifying that Jesus was no longer dependent on his father, that his moral conduct would henceforth become his own responsibility. "Now," Joathim said, "Jesus Ben David is eligible for the religious privileges enjoyed by all male adults. And with these privileges come new responsibilities. For example, he is now allowed to become part of the Minyan (the Quorum of Ten mandatory for holding public worship). He may also now serve as one of three male adults whose presence is required for grace after meals. The Tfflin he wears today will now be required to be worn at morning prayer. Congratulations, Jesus, we are pleased to have you as a full member of our congregation"

At this point in time it was Jesus' choice to deliver a discourse on the Law, or postpone it to later in the day at the home celebration. Thinking of others, as always, Jesus felt it would be less boring to his friends and neighbors to hear it now, instead of in the middle of the home festivity.

Here again Jesus demonstrated his unique insight into the Law as he said: "I feel fortunate that my assigned passage of scripture was the 20th Chapter of Exodus, which is the portion of the Torah in which Moses delivers God's Ten Commandments to the people. In these few short sentences, I learn everything I need to know about pleasing God or bringing his wrath down upon me. I believe, however, that the Law, as given to us in the 34th Chapter of Exodus is beautifully summed up in the sixth Chapter of Deuteronomy...'Hear, O Israel! The Lord is our God, The Lord alone. Therefore you shall love the Lord Your God with all your heart and with all your soul and with all your mind and with all your strength. Take to heart these words ...drill them into your children, speak of them at home and abroad ...bind them at your wrist as a sign and let them be as a pendant on your forehead. Write them on the doorposts of your houses and on your gates."' And so Jesus ended his discourse, saying in conclusion, "I pray to God that I may keep these commandments every day of my life." As he took his seat, Jesus sensed a pent—up feeling of approval throughout the synagogue. Actually, the entire assembly felt the urge to burst into applause for this astounding young man. But, applause was not acceptable in the synagogue.

After the closing chants and Benediction the crowd became extremely animated, speaking to each other of how well Jesus had read and interpreted his assigned lesson. This continued on the porch as Mary wondered how she could accommodate so many people. She and her cousin Elizabeth had made only 300 of the tiny tarts, and Joseph had only four large jardinieres of wine prepared. But there must be 200 people here. "Don't worry; God will provide," Elizabeth assured her.

And surely God did provide. When the family arrived home they were delighted to discover that many of the neighbors had preceded them, bearing gifts of food and wine. Joseph's sturdy cedar table would groan under the load of delicacies this day.

Jesus, of course, was the center of attention at the celebration. He scarcely got any food or wine himself as he shook hands with neighbor after neighbor, friend after friend, relative after relative. Finally after the last guests had left, Jesus, Mary, and Joseph were alone in the house which had been spotless earlier in the day, but now bore all the signs of the aftermath of a very good celebration.

"Let's join hands to thank God for this day," Jesus said as the family collapsed wearily into their chairs.

Jesus and Joseph both insisted on helping Mary clean up, even though it was the duty of women to do so, while men were exempt from such chores. She protested, but she was secretly grateful for their

27

help. Finally they said good night, each retiring to their chambers for bedtime prayers. Needless to say, Mary, Joseph, and Jesus Ben David slept well that night.

## CHAPTER 2 — CARPENTER'S APPRENTICE OR

## RELIGIOUS SCHOLAR?

Things were back to normal soon after the birthday celebration. The day after that memorable Sabbath, Mary and Joseph fell into the usual routine.

For Jesus it was a change. School was finished now, and that meant he would be expected to spend a full day, each day except the Sabbath, as an apprentice in Joseph's carpenter shop. Joseph was grateful for this because he had a constant backlog of work. His reputation as a fine woodworker had spread throughout Galilee, and even into Samaria. More than one Samaritan had risked his life in hostile Galilean territory to bring a project to Joseph.

And now, more work than ever was coming to the shop. Many of the Galilean carpenters had gone south to Judea to work on King Herod's gigantic project, known as Herodium, which was to be one of a line of fortresses protecting Judea's southern and eastern borders.

Joseph was proud to be a carpenter; but more than that, he was a fine cabinet—maker. It was his dream to pass on this God—given skill to Jesus, as he had learned it from his father. And, of course, he welcomed Jesus' full—time help, enabling the filling of customers' orders without making them wait so long. But Jesus did not have Joseph's inborn aptitude. When Joseph would fit two boards together, not even a pinpoint of light could be seen between them. Try as he might, Jesus couldn't do that, not yet anyway. Meanwhile however, Jesus could help a great deal, preparing the wood for Joseph to finish, bringing in the rough lumber from the courtyard, cutting it, and planing it until it was ready to become part of a cabinet, a chair, a table, a set of shelves, or a tool handle.

Joseph's prosperity permitted him to equip his shop better than most. In addition to the tools inherited from his father, he had acquired several fine hatchets, an adze for shaping wood, planes, iron saws, an ax, a stone—headed hammer, iron chisels, awls, and a bow drill and bits. His measuring tools included a rule, a compass, a plumb line, a chalk line, and pencil markers. All of them were beautifully kept, and arranged within his reach.

During his half—day apprenticeship with Joseph, each day since his tenth birthday, Jesus had learned to identify all of these tools and was able to fetch them for Joseph when asked; but there were many of them that he was not yet able to use with an acceptable degree of skill. This was something Joseph looked forward to teaching his son.

Meanwhile, Mary's routine revolved around the homely age—old chores of clothing and feeding her family and keeping the house clean. These tasks would begin each morning at first light with the baking of the daily bread. Mary would take handfuls of wheat and barley and place the kernels in a hollowed—out stone mortar, and then grind them with another stone until they became a coarse flour. Then she mixed this flour with goat's milk and salt in a clay bowl. Except at Passover time, she would add leaven (a culture of fermented and sour dough saved from an earlier batch). After mixing, she would knead the mixture, let it rise, and finally shape the dough into loaves and bake them in a clay oven. While the dough was rising, Mary would attend to her other tasks ...sweeping out the rooms, mending clothing, working on a new garment, and preparing the first meal of the day, to be served at midmorning. During this busy time each day, Mary would dye thread and cloth; sew and weave; and tend to the chickens, sheep, and goats (the donkey was Jesus' responsibility). Her day was indeed much like that of any other Galilean housewife.

It was not all work and no pleasure, however. In the evenings, Joseph would read to the family from his precious scrolls, and lively discussions would follow. It was during these exchanges of ideas that Joseph became even more convinced that Jesus was different. No boy of 13 years could possibly have this kind of understanding of the Torah without a unique gift from God. For example, Jesus saw more in the Exodus story of Moses' parting of the Red Sea[1] than a colorful legend. In this passage of scripture he saw proof that the Jews were indeed God's chosen people.

Because oil for lamps was expensive, most Galileans followed an early—to—bed, early—to—rise schedule. The birds singing at first light would awaken them in the morning. Then, not long after sunset, it would be time to go to bed again. On the Sabbath day no work was permitted. However, after synagogue services, there was always some activity to make life enjoyable.

On the hottest summer days, Jesus, Mary, and Joseph would travel to the Sea of Galilee, where they enjoyed the cool, refreshing waters. Jesus and Joseph would swim, and Mary would wade along the

---

[1] Exodus 14:10—16.

shore, digging her toes into the soft, wet sand at the foamy water's edge.

After a while, she would lay a clean white cloth on the sand, and put down bowls of fruit and a basket of fresh bread for the mid—morning meal. This always brought Jesus and Joseph back to shore with the keen appetite only outdoor exercise can impart.

On cool winter days they would take long walks in the country, and perhaps spend a few convivial hours trading news of the day with friends and relatives who lived in nearby towns. Occasionally the family would be invited to stay for the afternoon meal. As the conversation went around the table, the people who had not seen Jesus for some time always marveled at the thoughts he would express.

By the time Jesus reached the age of 15, work in the carpenter shop was going smoothly. One day, out of the blue, Joseph announced that they would soon be able to take a day off now and then ...a day other than the Sabbath. This was welcome news because there were many activities not permitted on the Sabbath.

"Let's plan to go somewhere and do something together. Just the two of us," Joseph said. "Where would you like to go?" Without hesitating, Jesus answered, "To the Sea of Galilee."

"Ah, yes, I know how you love to swim."

"No, not this time, father," Jesus answered. "This time I'd like to go fishing."

And so, at dawn on the appointed day, they gathered their nets and the lunch of bread and cheese Mary had packed; and started down the dusty, winding road through the hill country toward the sea.

They found a cheerful bait vendor who also had boats and nets for rent. "We needn't have brought these heavy nets from home," Jesus said.

But Joseph, being frugal, said, "It would have cost a pretty shekel to rent all we need. He wants too much for the boat as it is."

By mid—morning, the two had cast off from the shore, tied some bait fish to the nets, and cast the nets into the sea.

Hours went by before the nets moved. Joseph said, "We should have been here at dawn. Next time we'll bring a tent and stay overnight. Just then the net pulled away from the boat. There was a large fish in it. Jesus took his position at the stern end, Joseph at the bow. It was all they could do to pull the fish and net aboard. Their catch was still flopping around wildly, trying to escape from the net.

"It's a tilapia," Joseph said.

"Praise God!" Jesus had never caught such a fish before.

The two were especially grateful because the tilapia was a fish permitted by the dietary laws. The rest of the day yielded several more, as well as three or four forbidden fish, which were immediately thrown back into the sea. The tilapia were kept fresh in a rough iron bucket loaned to them by the boatman.

Jesus was glad for this opportunity to be alone with Joseph. There was something he had to tell him. But he knew better than to spoil the day by making Joseph angry. So he held back until they were almost home. The sun was setting in the west when Jesus said, "Father, I have something to tell you. You remember, when we were in Jerusalem for Passover, how I spent time with the temple teachers, and you thought I was with the caravan?"

"How could I ever forget it? Your mother and I were worried sick."

"Yes, I know, and again I say I'm truly sorry that I caused you such grief."

"That's behind us now. Forget it!" said Joseph. "But why do you bring it up now?"

"That event, father, was probably the happiest of my life. I learned more, and felt closer to God than I ever have."

"But," Joseph knew what was coming, "we won't be going to Jerusalem again until Passover."

"I know, but each day at the synagogue, in Nazareth, the teachers spend the afternoon in discussion. I feel a strong pull to join the teachers at the synagogue."

"So what do you propose?"

"If I work for you six hours every morning in the carpenter shop (every day except the Sabbath of course) and work as hard as I possibly can, could you let me have the afternoons to go to the synagogue?" Jesus half—expected an angry outburst, but it didn't come.

Instead, Joseph, while taken aback, simply reacted with a frown. Finally he said, "Let me think about it."

Soon, the fishermen arrived home. Mary was delighted when she saw the fine catch of tilapia. "I wish we could keep them for the Sabbath, but they'll never last. We'll have them tomorrow," she said, putting them in a bucket of cool water fresh from the village well. "But there are more here than we can eat. I'll give the rest to Elizabeth."

The next afternoon, the delightful aroma of fish baking on the hearth filled the house of Joseph Ben David. Finally Mary called her family for the afternoon meal. To begin, Joseph said the ancient Shema..."Hear, O Israel, the Lord our God is one Lord." And each said silently a prayer of thanksgiving and a plea for blessing of the food about to be shared. Mary had prepared the fish with egg and bread crumbs and served it with fresh barley bread, clay ramekins of olive oil, and a stew of mixed vegetables. At the end of the meal, Mary brought out a bowl of golden honey and a pitcher of rich goat's milk. The barley bread, dipped into the honey gave a delightfully sweet finishing touch to the meal.

When they had finished, Joseph reminded Jesus that it was time to feed the donkey. When the boy had left the room, Joseph told Mary of their son's proposal.

39

"Yes I think we should be pleased, for the time has come," Mary said. "And after all, you only had him half days before his birthday, and you managed. If need be, I'll help in the carpenter shop."

Joseph laughed, saying, "As if you don't have enough to do. Don't worry, we'll manage somehow." When Jesus returned to the table, Joseph said, "Your mother and I have some good news for you, Jesus. We've decided to let you go to the synagogue in the afternoons, provided the teachers are willing and you do indeed work extra hard each morning in the carpenter shop."

Jesus was, of course, overjoyed; and in an unusual display of emotion, he jumped up and threw his arms around his father and then his mother, saying: "Thank you. Thank you. You won't be sorry." While he was feeding the donkey, Jesus had prayed to his Heavenly Father that this would be his parents' decision. And now he said a silent prayer of thanks.

The next afternoon Joseph visited the synagogue and told the teachers of Jesus' request.

A teacher named Jacob seemed to be the leader of the group. "Why yes, let him come," Jacob said. Addressing the other three teachers present, he added, "If you attended his birthday celebration, you know what a gifted lad he is."

"I disagree," said a mean-spirited old teacher named Achim. "This has always been a council of elders. If we admit one young person, we'll have to admit them all."

"Do we not say that a young man has become of age when he is 13 years old... that he has reached his religious adulthood?" asked teacher Manasseh.

The fourth teacher, Josiah, remained silent. Finally, Jacob proposed that they put it to a vote and asked Joseph to leave the room while they did so. As Joseph waited in the courtyard, he could hear loud voices in a heated discussion coming from the teachers' council room. After what seemed to Joseph to be an unreasonably long time, Jacob stepped out the door. Smiling, he said: "We've agreed to let your son join us here in the afternoons for a while until we see how things work out. But, mind you, this will only be a trial."

"Thank you, thank you," said Joseph gratefully. "Jesus will be so pleased. And remember, I'll expect to hear from you immediately if things don't work out."

Jacob nodded and Joseph knelt, as was the custom to show respect for Holy Men, and embraced Jacob's knees, saying, "May the Lord bless you."

"And also you," Jacob answered.

Joseph walked home quickly, anxious to tell the good news.

It had been agreed that Jesus would begin his synagogue studies on the first day of the month of Shevat. And finally the happy day arrived. He proudly put on his new prayer shawl and yarmulke as he left home for the synagogue. Jesus was greeted warmly in the council room by Jacob, Josiah, and

Manasseh. Achim, on the other hand, did not greet him at all, but looked away, scowling.

"Sit down, Jesus," said Jacob. "It's good you are joining us today. After many months of studying the five books of the Torah, we're about to begin at the beginning again ...with Genesis."

It was the custom of the teachers to take turns reading and then discuss what had been read.

This day, before the discussion began, Jacob explained to Jesus: "We seldom agree on anything here. Sometimes our discussions can be very spirited. But there is one thing we do agree upon. This sacred history which we study was indeed given to us by Moses, guided by God. It was sung beside the desert campfires, it has been commemorated at liturgical feasts through the ages, and it was transmitted by word of mouth from generation to generation, long before it was ever inscribed on scrolls. It is for this reason that we believe there could very well be errors in the Pentateuch we study today. That's why we discuss each portion of the Torah after we read it. Each of us has his own interpretation. And if that interpretation varies radically from the original text, all four of us must agree on the radical departure. If that happens, and it never has so far, we would take our opinion to the Rabbis in Jerusalem and then they would discuss it at great length. Only after years of study would the Law be revised. In other words, revision of the Law in our lifetime is highly unlikely."

With that introduction, the readings began. Achim read the Primeval History from Genesis, including the two stories of Creation. Josiah took his turn reading about the Fall of Man, and the births of Cain and Abel.

Josiah read about the descendants of Adam and Eve and the generations which followed. And finally Jacob read of the Great Flood, of Noah and the Ark, and the sons of Noah.

The discussions on this day centered around the two stories of Creation. In the first story of

Creation (Genesis chapter 1) we are told that God brought an orderly universe out of chaos...the Earth, the seas, the bodies of fresh water, the wind, and abundance of living creatures; and then man, male and female, was created in God's image.

In the second story of Creation (Genesis chapters 2 and 3) the emphasis is on man. We hear the story of Adam and Eve and the Garden of Eden. The teachers believe this to be an older story than Genesis 1. In Genesis 2 man comes before the rest of God's creatures. In Genesis 1, the creatures come first.

In their many years of discussing this first book of the Torah, the teachers at the Nazareth synagogue. had never been able to agree which story of creation was the more accurate. Finally, after much heated discussion, as had happened many times over the years, the teachers reached the conclusion that further arguing was useless. Jacob turned to Jesus and asked, "And what is your opinion, young man?"

Jesus had come to listen. He had planned to remain silent this first time with the teachers. But he did have a strong opinion on this subject and, after all, he had been asked. So after a long pause he ventured to say..."I'm inclined to believe the first story of Creation is more accurate." Quoting from memory he continued: "Let the water teem with an abundance of living creatures. And let birds fly beneath the dome of the sky. God created the great sea monsters and all kinds of swimming creatures ...and all kinds of winged birds ...then God said, let the Earth bring forth all kinds of living creatures, cattle, creeping things, and wild animals of all kinds ...then God said, let us make Man in our image ...male and female he created them" Jacob and Manasseh smiled. Jesus had taken up their side of the argument. But it seemed Achim's characteristic scowl grew deeper than ever. Josiah was neutral, as usual.

Jacob was about to take back the lead of the discussion when Jesus said, "I believe that someday, perhaps hundreds of years hence, wise naturalists and scientists will expand on this text and explain that Adam and Eve did, in fact, evolve from the earlier species. If you were to study the anatomy of man and some early mammals, for example, you would find that they are both constructed on the same general model. God, the Creator, was the great designer. He not only designed the many beautiful birds and fishes, all the animals and beasts of the wild, but he designed what will one day be known as the the antecedents of the first male and female persons...Adam and Eve. These scientists and naturalists will, I believe, one day prove that there is conclusive evidence in favor of gradual evolution and that man differs less from the higher apes than the apes do from their own antecedents."

Achim interrupted by slamming his fist on the table. "I've never heard such drivel!" he shouted. "If I had known we'd be sitting here listening to such nonsense from a juvenile, I never would have agreed to admitting him." Jesus blushed. He had no desire to create conflict among the teachers.

"Now hold on Achim," Jacob said. "What the boy said makes a great deal of sense. And when a lad, not yet 16 years of age can articulate it so clearly, I must believe that his words are divinely inspired." Josiah and Manasseh nodded in agreement.

"Your liberal thinking will be the ruination of this synagogue," Achim growled. And with that he pulled his things together and stormed out of the room.

"Well, I guess that ends our session for today," Jacob said.

"I'm terribly sorry if I said something blasphemous," Jesus said.

"You didn't," Jacob answered. "All of us question the Law repeatedly. That's what we're here for. Achim resents you because you are so young. But Josiah and Manasseh are your friends. So feel free to come back tomorrow."

"Thank you, I would be most grateful," Jesus said, as he picked up his outer garment and prepared to leave.

"The Lord be with you," intoned Jacob.

"The Lord be with you," the others repeated.

"And also with you," Jesus answered as he bowed deeply before them and then left the room.

He was already having second thoughts. Perhaps he didn't belong at the synagogue. On the way home Jesus was sad. He hadn't anticipated Achim's hostility, although perhaps he should have. Going over the experience, he couldn't quite explain to himself his discourse on the subject of creation. He hadn't had those thoughts before. He was simply thinking out loud. Surely it was God the Father speaking through him. In a few minutes he felt much better, and a new feeling of peace came over him.

As he walked, he said a prayer of thanksgiving... for the opportunity to meet with the teachers and for his clear insight into the Genesis story of Creation. Strangely, he now had absolutely no guilt feelings or regrets about what he had said. Truly it was the will of the Father that he say these things. Perhaps someday even Achim would believe the truth. Jesus was so absorbed in his prayer and thoughts that he almost walked by his own house.

When he entered the courtyard, his mother was hanging clothing on a rope stretched from the corners of the courtyard. "Well, my son the scholar," Mary said, "how did it go?"

"It's a long story," Jesus answered as he kissed his mother on the cheek. "I'll tell you and father at mealtime. Right now I'd just like to bathe and take a short nap."

"A good idea, son, you do that," Mary said. "I'll call you when it's time to eat."

Jesus pushed aside the cloth hanging of his chamber door, and turned to smile at his mother. What a wonderful mother she is, he thought. I truly love her more than I can say.

At the afternoon meal, Jesus went over the events of the day at the synagogue. Finally he said, "At first I felt I shouldn't go back again, but on the way home I got this strong feeling that God wants me to continue." "Yes!" exclaimed Mary in an unusual display of emotion. "It's clearly God's will that you meet with them and express your thoughts. And I'm convinced those ideas you're expressing are coming direct from the Father."

"I couldn't agree more," Joseph said. "You shouldn't let a cranky old man like Achim stop you. Achim was a cantankerous 'old man' even when he was young. He'll never change. And you shouldn't expect him to accept your ideas."

"After all," Mary said, "three of the four teachers seem to be on your side."

"Well, two anyway," Jesus responded. "I never know where Josiah stands. He never says anything. But Jacob is wonderful. And Manasseh has been supportive too."

"Then what more do you want?" Mary asked. "Go tomorrow as planned and try to forget Achim. Our prayers are with you. I'm sure you know that."

"I do. Your support is all I need," Jesus said. "I really can't wait to go back tomorrow."

The next day Jesus half expected to find Achim missing from the group, but there he was, sitting sullenly at the end of the table. The other three seemed to go out of their way to greet Jesus warmly. And so, the discussion of Genesis continued. Jesus had no trouble accepting what was said about Cain and Abel and their descendants down to Noah. However, when it came to the story of the Great Flood, Noah, and the Ark, Jesus felt he must again express his views. "I think it's important to remember," he began "that when this story was first told, people thought the entire world began at the Dead Sea on the east and the Great Sea[1] on the north and west. Today we know that the world is much much larger, extending north through Rome and

---

[1] Later called the Mediterranean.

Gaul to Britain, east to the China Sea, west to Spain, and south far beyond the Dead Sea. I believe the story of Noah. But I can't believe that the entire world as we know it today was flooded. Therefore, there must have been thousands, perhaps millions of humans and beasts alike who were not touched by the flood. In other words, I see the story of Noah as a beautiful legend, but no more."

Surprisingly, Achim had nothing to say.

"Interesting idea," said Jacob. He and the other two friendly teachers found themselves in awe of a 15—year—old boy who had a perception of the Torah which was far beyond anything they had ever thought about or discussed. Furthermore, he had a unique way of articulating these ideas. Indeed he was more eloquent than anybody who had ever spoken in the synagogue in their lifetime. For the rest of that year the meetings progressed smoothly. No agreement was forthcoming from Achim, but no more outbursts either. And for that, the others were grateful.

## CHAPTER 3 — PASSOVER PILGRIMAGE

At age 16 Jesus felt like an old hand at going on pilgrimages. This would be the fifth time he would accompany his parents on the trip to Jerusalem. It was a four—day journey, and, as always, it would be made with Nazarenes from all walks of life ...wealthy families who would travel in fancy carriages attended by slaves and pulled by two or more horses or camels; working—class people like the Ben Davids who would take turns riding in a donkey cart; and the poor, who would have to walk with heavy packs on their backs or, at best, push a two—wheeled cart.

Joseph would frequently get angry at Jesus because he would want to let a poor person take his turn in the donkey cart. "There are hundreds of them, Jesus. If we give one of them a ride, they'll all be around us asking for the same treatment. Joseph never explained why his reasoning didn't apply when he shared food with the poor along the road.

Jesus would often try to get his mother to take his turn. When she refused adamantly, Jesus would reluctantly take the seat in the little cart.

Preparations for the trip were always exciting. First, there would be a large meeting of the male household heads in the town square. All except the favored rich, whose preferred positions were guaranteed by cash payment to the caravan master, would draw lots to see who would get the second—best positions in the center of the caravan or the more dangerous positions at the head or the rear. This time Joseph drew position number 11, not the best, but not the worst either.

At home, the aromas from Mary's kitchen would reassure Jesus and Joseph that she was baking unleavened bread and preparing dried fruits in abundance. It was her custom to prepare enough food to feed the poor around them as well as her own little family.

In the days approaching the caravan departure, Mary would be washing and mending clothes, packing them tightly with camel hair blankets in saddle bags to be carried on the donkey's back and in the little cart.

Meanwhile, Joseph would be preparing the cart with Jesus' help, tightening loose boards, greasing the wheels and axles, sorting out the harness, softening its leather with oil, and cleaning the straw debris from the bottom of the cart. After washing the cart floor thoroughly, fresh straw would be put in to be prepared for possible cold weather along the way.

Finally, the much—anticipated day would come. — At dawn, Jesus, Mary, and Joseph would load the goatskin bags (one of them filled with fresh, cool water), and lead the donkey to their assigned place in the town square.

Joseph's friend, Eleazar, who was the cantor at the synagogue, had been elected caravan master for this year's pilgrimage. His symbol of office was the shofar he carried. As the brilliant red sun came over the horizon, he sounded this historic horn, signalling the lead camel to start down the road to Jerusalem.

The Romans had built good roads on the main trade routes, and the road from Cana to Jerusalem, which passed through Nazareth, was a good one. The Galilean roads, however, were not paved with stone, and so the way was often dusty or muddy. Fortunately, the spring rains were, for the most part, finished by the beginning of the month of Nisan. Not long after Passover, the summer dry season would begin.

The principal purpose of these roads was to supply the Roman army and provide routes for its movement. The southbound Jewish pilgrims would often pass northbound trade caravans accompanied by helmeted centurions and soldiers with gleaming swords and breastplates riding their beautiful horses. There were no greetings exchanged, because the Romans looked with scorn on the Jewish people, and the Jews likewise hated the Romans. Jesus was an exception. He often nodded and smiled at the Romans, but they returned his friendliness with scowls, wondering who this insolent young Jew was who was bold enough to smile at them.

Not far behind the Ben Davids' donkey cart was a heavy four—wheeled wagon pulled by a pair of mules. Rented from the Nazareth livery, this wagon was used to carry the lambs that would be offered for the Passover sacrifice. Jesus was always saddened by the bleating of the lambs and wondered why it was necessary to offer their blood at the altar, and their fat and their entrails to the Temple holocaust. Someday when he was older he would confront the teachers at the synagogue with this question.

At the forward end of the center of the caravan were the wealthy in their carriages, with servant slaves trudging along behind. During overnight stops, Jesus would surreptitiously admire these carriages. Some were fitted with roofs and curtains or elaborately decorated wooden walls to hide the passengers from view. on one of these carriage inspections, even though he was some distance away, Jesus was caught looking by the young daughter of a rich Nazareth merchant. As she peeked from behind the curtain at him, she mischievously shook her finger, laughed, and then retreated behind the curtain. Red—faced, Jesus hastily escaped to his family's place in the caravanserie.

This particular inn, just one day's journey south of Nazareth, was a large one. There was no large town or city nearby to offer overnight accommodations, and so the travellers had no other choice.

Its sun—dried brick walls were the color of sand, with three buildings joined together around a courtyard and walled in on the fourth side. There was an arched opening in the wall high enough for a camel and driver to pass through and wide enough for a large wagon.

This opening would be closed and barred at night with heavy wooden gates. In the center of the courtyard was a well where the travellers watered their animals and filled their waterbags. The poor slept in the courtyard with their animals. The working—class people took shelter in the stables around the courtyard, and the wealthy had rooms on the second level, above the stables. If there were not enough wealthy to fill the rooms above, the working class would draw lots to determine who would occupy the unused rooms. On this first night out, Joseph had been lucky and had won the privilege of sharing one of these upper rooms with his family. Jesus was uncomfortable about this while there were poor sleeping in the open courtyard. "What if it should rain, father?" But again, Joseph laughed off Jesus' suggestion that he change places with a poor and very pregnant woman he saw trying to make a bed near the well.

Jesus was restless following supper, taken later in the day than it would have been at home. In his restlessness, he ventured out for a walk along the balcony that ran around three sides of the caravanserie. Standing in the doorway of a room in the choice center section of the building was the young girl who had flirtatiously shaken her finger at Jesus earlier in the day.

Her cheeks were as pink as a rose. Her brown eyes sparkled like gemstones in the moonlight and, smiling, she revealed teeth as white as the alyssum edging his mother's garden.

"Looking for more wagons to inspect?" she asked teasingly, with more than a hint of sarcasm. Even so, her voice was soft and sweet, not unlike his mother Mary's.

"No, but I must say yours is a beauty. I've never seen a carriage like that before."

"You should see the inside. My father has had it lined with gold—colored silks, red and blue pillows, and beautifully woven carpets from the east. If you'd like to see it, I'll take you down."

Jesus had a feeling this was the wrong thing to do; but he was bursting with curiosity about the wagon, and thought it might be a pleasant experience to spend some time in the company of this charming young girl.

As they descended the stone stairway to the courtyard, the girl took his hand, ostensibly to keep from falling on the stairs. Jesus found her skin to be soft and smooth as velvet.

"My name is Maryamne. What's yours?" she asked.

"Jesus. Jesus Ben David."

When they reached the carriage, Jesus noted there was a slave guarding it, sitting on a wooden step stool. When the man saw Maryamne, he jumped up and said: "Good evening, Mistress. Can I help you?"

Close up, the carriage was even more magnificent than Jesus had imagined from his distant vantage point earlier in the day. Its roof was apparently fashioned from dried camel skins, symmetrically scalloped all around, dyed a rich royal blue, and edged with gold piping. The body of the carriage was a shiny deep red, and its doors and windows were trimmed in the same royal blue as the roof ...with gold edges. Each window had white curtains trimmed with delicate lace and pulled back by royal blue rope ties. The ornate door handles, if not real gold, were of a metal that resembled gold quite accurately. The carriage's wheels were white with royal blue and red spokes, and the hubs were the same gold color as the body trim.

Bedded down nearby were two beautiful white horses that pulled the carriage by day. Their gold—trimmed polished brown leather harnesses were hung neatly between two poles. Maryamne laughed at Jesus. It was obvious he was in awe of her father's carriage.

"This young man wants to see our carriage," the girl said to the slave. Hearing this, he placed the step stool at the door, took her arm, and helped her into the vehicle. Maryamne beckoned for Jesus to follow. Declining the slave's help, he stepped into the vehicle.

*Joseph Radder*

Maryamne had not exaggerated. The interior of the wagon was as luxuriously appointed as the castles of kings Jesus had read about. In addition to the furnishings the girl had described, there was a highly polished table, apparently for eating or writing enroute, and a gold lamp hanging from the center of the white satin—draped ceiling.

"How old are you?" the girl asked.

"Sixteen."

"I'm seventeen." Was Maryamne telling the truth? Jesus suspected not. Eighteen or nineteen was probably more accurate.

"Come, sit down," she beckoned.

Maryamne pulled the leather side curtains closed. "Why are you doing that?" Jesus asked.

"So we can have some privacy."

"I have to leave," Jesus said, and without further explanation he stood up in the carriage.

Maryamne pouted, but opened the door for him. Jesus stepped down first, offering his hand to the

64

girl, who took it eagerly as she shooed the slave away with her other hand.

The two parted at Maryamne's doorway. Her father was standing just inside, scowling. The girl knew better than to introduce Jesus. Her father would be furious about her association with a young man beneath her station. As the door closed, Jesus could hear muffled, but clearly angry voices.

When Jesus got back to his room, he found Joseph reading a scroll, but his mother was absent. "Where's mother?" he asked.

"She's down in the courtyard at the public hearth, baking bread for tomorrow." Jesus' anticipation of the fresh bread, even though unleavened, made him quickly forget Maryamne.

Jesus did not encounter the girl again. Through two more overnight stays, at Syrach and Sebaste, Maryamne tried to find Jesus, but he managed to elude her by staying close to the Ben Davids' room or place in the stable.

On the third night it was dark, before they reached Emmaus. Suddenly there were shouts, screams, the neighing of horses, and the braying of donkeys and mules. The clattering of metal on metal was a bad sign. Surely there was trouble at the head of the caravan.

Joseph immediately picked up a club, lit a torch, and headed forward. Jesus started to follow him, but Joseph ordered him to stay with the halted cart and protect his mother.

There was more noise, and finally the travellers could hear horses galloping away. After much too much time passed, Joseph returned to the wagon to say: "Thieves! Arabs! They attacked a rich man's wagon not far ahead of us. They raped and killed his young daughter. They stole everything they had with them and destroyed their beautiful carriage."

That night in the tent he had pitched in the courtyard of the inn, Jesus wept. As it turned out, the young girl was Maryamne.

The next morning, beginning at daybreak, Jesus visited every family in the caravan and asked each for a small contribution of food, clothing, or bedding for Maryamne's parents.

"We're poor! Why should we give to the rich?" was the typical reaction of most of the travellers. But Jesus was already skilled in the art of gentle persuasion. By the time he reached the victimized couple, grieving deeply over the loss of their daughter, and in despair over the theft of one of their horses and the destruction of their beautiful carriage, Jesus' donkey cart was piled high with food, clothing, and blankets. Now trudging alongside the wrecked carriage with their slaves, Maryamne's parents were moved to tears when they realized that Jesus' wagonload of gifts was for them.

"How I misjudged you, my son," the father said. "Little did I realize how rich in spirit are the poor. Indeed you and your kind friends put us to shame.

*Joseph Radder*

After helping the man and his slave transfer the gifts from the donkey cart to the wrecked, but still mobile carriage, Jesus went back to Mary and Joseph, feeling he had come close to performing a miracle. To get the poor to give to the rich, he thought, you need all the help God can give you.

Finally, as they came over the crest of the last hill, the splendid city of Jerusalem came into sight.

Gleaming in the sunshine, it was exactly as Jesus remembered, the holy city, once King David's stronghold. The Temple dominated the city; Jesus picked it out immediately among the many beautiful sun—washed buildings, and he remembered the ancient psalm: "I lift up my eyes to the hills. From whence does my help come? My help comes from the Lord, Who made heaven and earth."[1]

Along the roadside now, stood Roman soldiers spaced about 20 feet apart. Proudly they sat on their handsome horses, their silvery breastplates

[1] Psalm 121.

68

shining in the sun. During the three great religious feasts of the year — Passover, Shavout, and Succoth — the Roman army ordered its troops out to guard the four major roads into Jerusalem. Their mandate was to keep order, lest the Jews do some damage to their precious military routes.

In spite of themselves, many of these hard—bitten troops had great admiration for the tenacity of the Jewish pilgrims. Camel after camel, wagon after wagon, cart after cart, and on foot, one person after another they came ...all day long, an unending line of worshipers from every corner of Galilee and Judea.

Of the three high holidays, Passover was the greatest ...the one of all that must not be missed. Those who lived near Jerusalem could attend all three of the great religious feasts, but those who lived as far away as Nazareth would be forced to content themselves with one pilgrimage a year. Since Passover came during the spring, after the rains had ended and the roads were no longer rutted and slippery with mud, and since Passover was considered the most important of the three feasts, it attracted the largest numbers from the longest distances. Even Jews who dwelt in foreign lands came to Jerusalem for Passover.

After a time, the Nazarene caravan reached the Temple. It was possibly the largest building Jesus had ever seen, an immense structure of cream-colored limestone with gleaming marble columns and massive golden gates. The Temple courtyard was swarming with priests, pilgrims, sacrificers, and treasurers. Even at this young age, Jesus was displeased with these haggling money-changers. He loved his Temple and felt that these mercenaries defiled it. When he discussed this with Joseph, his father said, "But that is the custom, my son; it always has been, and probably always will be." Jesus never found answers like that to be acceptable, but he knew better than to argue at this point in time. Perhaps some day, when he was older, he would be able to do something about it.

It was always the goal of pilgrims to arrive in Jerusalem well ahead of the Passover feast in order to find a place to stay. With the inns and caravanseries always over—crowded, Joseph and Mary preferred to pitch a tent in one of the large fields set aside for that purpose. With the donkey and cart tethered nearby, they could survive quite comfortably until it was time for the Temple ritual, and then share the Passover feast with the other pilgrims from Nazareth.

The afternoon preceding the Passover feast, considered the most important of the sacrifices, was the group offering of the paschal lambs. Jesus and his father represented 12 Nazarenes at this ceremony, carrying the unblemished lamb to the Temple for the sacrifice. Some pilgrims bought their sacrificial lamb from the money—changers at the Temple. Joseph, however, sharing Jesus' distaste for the greed of these men, preferred to bring his group's lamb from Nazareth.

After waiting for the greater part of the afternoon for their turn for admission, Jesus and Joseph finally heard the piercing sound of the shofar, signifying their turn to pass through the golden gates.

It was the duty of each sacrificer to kill his own animal and present the fat and entrails to the priests to be burned at the Temple altar, and then to give the lamb's blood to the waiting priest who held a bowl to receive it. The rest of the lamb would be saved for the Seder feast the next day. After passing the bowls back to the altar from one priest to another, the blood of the lamb was dashed against the base of the altar, commemorating the original Passover when the Hebrews marked their doors with the blood of the lamb so their houses would be passed over and their firstborns would not be taken with those of the Egyptians. Throughout the ceremony, the voices of Levite singers chanting psalms echoed through the Temple.

Passover began with an evening feast shortly after sunset, marking the beginning of the 15th day of the month of Nisan. In the afternoon, the men would build huge fires in the center of the encampment, erecting spits of cedar logs brought along for the purpose.

The lambs for the Seder would be pierced through by the pointed spits and placed over the fires on the crossed sticks. Enough of the spit extended past the fire to enable all the men, women, and older children to take turns rotating the lambs until they were golden brown. The tantalizing aroma of the roasting lambs permeated the campsite during this ritual cooking. After a few hours, the fire would die down to embers and the lambs would need turning only occasionally to permit the final slow roasting.

To prepare for the Seder feast, Mary would set out earthenware bowls, bronze jugs of water and wine, plates of unleavened bread, and dried fruits. The men then carved up the roasted lambs and distributed succulent pieces to each member of the seven families, who reclined on straw mats around low tables. Joseph then poured the wine and recited the Kiddush, a blessing said over the meal.

It was the duty of the head of each household to punctuate the meal by reciting from the scriptures and telling the Passover story from Exodus. And so Joseph intoned, "For seven days you shall eat unleavened bread, and the seventh day shall be a festival to the Lord. Only unleavened bread may be eaten during the seven days; no leaven and nothing leavened may be found in all your territory. On this day you shall explain to your son, 'This is because of what the Lord did for me when I came out of Egypt.' It shall be as a sign on your hand and as a reminder on your forehead. Thus the law of the Lord will ever be on your lips, because with a strong hand the Lord brought you out of Egypt. Therefore you shall keep this prescribed rite at its appointed time from year to year."[1]

---

[1] Exodus 13: 6—10.

Listening intently as always, Jesus was reminded each year that Passover commemorated the Jews' deliverance from the yoke of Egypt. It was said too that Passover had an even more ancient origin, observing the spring migration of flocks.

The Passover festival would last a full week. Finally, on the last day, the pilgrims would return home, enriched spiritually, but weary and eager to return to a quieter routine.

The journey north to Nazareth, unlike the eventfilled southward journey, was quiet. As Jesus walked beside the little wagon or took his turn riding, he was able to appreciate the beautiful countryside—the purple hills along the western edge of the wilderness of Judea, then the green plains of the west. This longer route was always taken to avoid the populated parts of Samaria, following the mountainous southern edge of Galilee, and finally to Nazareth, nestled in a valley of Gaililean hills. The flowering fields in fertile Galilee were a refreshing sight after the Judean desert and

75

*Joseph Radder*

barren Samarian hills. Passover was a pleasant memory now, and already, Jesus was thinking about next year's pilgrimage.

## CHAPTER 4 — GROWTH IS PAINFUL

Strange things were happening to Jesus, and he was experiencing new feelings. His voice began to crack when he spoke ...modulating from soprano to baritone in the same syllable. Hair was beginning to grow where he had no hair before. And he had a disturbing new awareness of feminine beauty.

Up to now he had enjoyed many happy hours with his cousins and friends who lived nearby. When they weren't playing stick ball, they would sit around, usually just before sunset, talking about the mysteries of the world. James loved to imagine what it would be like to go to sea on a great ship. John felt a strong attraction to the wilderness. He often said that one day he would live among the wild beasts and share their diet of locusts and honey. Jesus, on the other hand, would tell them about his experiences with the teachers at the synagogue.

He couldn't understand why his cousins and friends seemed bored with the great writings of Genesis, Exodus, Deuteronomy, Leviticus, and Numbers.

As time went on Jesus grew more and more weary of childish pastimes, and at the same time he felt an even stronger pull to the synagogue and the challenging discussion of the teachers.

As Jesus spent less and less time with his cousins and friends, they were on the verge of being angry. Only John seemed to understand. "Jesus was born to serve God," he said. "It would be sinful of us to be jealous of God." This was something the other boys had not thought about, and it seemed to satisfy them, turning their anger back into love.

The time came when Jesus was spending all of his time in adult—like pursuits. Mornings were spent with Joseph in the carpenter shop, afternoons at the synagogue with the teachers, evenings in discussion with his parents. Mary and Joseph found these evening conversations to be the most enjoyable part of their day. Jesus was bringing them an insight into the Torah they had never before experienced. Almost overnight their roles were reversed. Jesus had become the teacher, and his parents had become pupils.

The teachers at the synagogue were also aware that Jesus was maturing. It was not only the physical changes like the beard, still fuzz upon his chin, it was an understanding of the scriptures and his ability to articulate them that they had never possessed.

One day the discussion centered on the testing of Abraham (Gen. 22).

It was Achim's turn to read: "Some time after these events, God put Abraham to the test. He called to him, 'Abraham! Take your son Isaac and go to the land of Morrah. There you shall offer him up as a holocaust on a height that I will point out to you.' Early the next morning, Abraham saddled his donkey, took with him his son Isaac and two of his servants as well, and with the wood he had cut for the holocaust, set out for the place which God had told him."

As Achim continued the tale of the innocent son, who thought they were taking a lamb for the holocaust but was puzzled because he saw no lamb, Jesus squirmed in his seat. This scripture passage had always been distasteful to him, and he always found it hard to believe.

As Achim concluded the reading: "When they came to the place of which God had told him, Abraham built an altar and arranged wood on it. Next, he tied up his son Isaac and put him on top of the wood. Then he took a knife to slaughter his son. But the Lord's messenger called to Abraham from heaven, 'Do not lay your hand on the boy. Do not do the least thing to him. I know how devoted you are to God since you did not withhold from me your own beloved son.'"

Jesus could listen no more. "Stop!" he shouted at the shocked Achim. The others looked on in amazement. "I can't listen to that reading again without saying that I cannot accept it as having happened that way."

Achim was angry now. "How dare you question the word of God? This is holy scripture and is not to be questioned, least of all by the likes of you!"

"Let the lad finish," interrupted Jacob.

"How can I?" Achim's face was red with rage. "How can I let a mere child question the word of God?"

Jesus tried to be calm. "Don't you agree, Achim, that these stories were handed down by word of mouth from one generation to another, told around campfires from memory, long before they were written down? Isn't it possible that many of these legends could have been changed in the telling from one to another?"

"Legends he calls them!" Achim was growing angrier by the minute, and it secretly distressed him that Jesus was able to stay calm.

"All right, scriptures then. Even though God spared Isaac in the end, I have never been able to believe that God would ask anybody to kill his own son."

"What do you think the scripture means, then?" asked the usually silent Josiah.

"I believe God asked Abraham, 'Would you do any thing I asked?' and Abraham replied of course he would.

'Even if I asked you to kill your own son?' And Abraham responded yes, proving his love and obedience to God above all else. But I don't believe God actually made Abraham and Isaac go through the kind of torture that this chapter of Genesis recalls."

Jacob now took up his leadership role. "I think perhaps Jesus is right." Josiah and Manasseh nodded in agreement. Achim was not ready to agree; but even though he continued scowling, he offered no further argument.

"And while we're on the subject of holocaust," Jesus said, "I believe even the burning of lambs and spilling their blood on the altar is wrong and should be abolished."

Achim's cooling period had lasted less than a minute. "I've had all I can take for one day!" he shouted, slamming his fist on the table. He got up, and left the room. The four others couldn't help but notice that he left his belongings behind. Was he so angry he'd forgotten them? Or did he intend to return?

They didn't have to wait long for their answer. Within a minute or two, Achim reappeared in the doorway. As he gathered up his things, he said, "I want you all to know that I plan to take my complaints about this young man to the Elders in Jerusalem." And with that he stormed out the door.

"I'm sorry," Jesus said. "I didn't mean to be disruptive."

Jacob reached over, and put his hand on Jesus'. "No need to apologize, my son. Achim has a closed mind. The rest of us appreciate that you've brought a breath of fresh air to this synagogue."

Jesus had a worried look on his face. "What will happen now?" he asked. "If he does complain to the Elders, they may rule that I can no longer meet with you."

"Rest easy, Jesus. We'll support you completely," Manasseh said.

"Indeed," agreed Jacob. Josiah was silent as usual, but he was smiling and nodding.

Achim had arranged for a meeting with the Elders in Jerusalem on the tenth day of Iyyar.

on that day, after hearing Achim's carefully prepared complaint, the Elder appointed to lead this investigation, a man named Sirach, said, "You must give us some time to consider your charges. Come back tomorrow at the same hour."

Achim arrived at the Temple promptly the next morning. He stood as the Elders entered the room.

"We have decided to reserve our decision until we can summon this young man, Jesus, to Jerusalem for a hearing. You'll be notified of the time and day, and will be permitted to attend and participate in that hearing, presenting your side of the argument." Having said this, Sirach sat down. The assembled court then stood and filed out.

Achim took this as his cue to leave. Thanking the Elders, he bowed deeply and left the room, not entirely satisfied with the court's decision; but at least his case was still alive.

As it turned out, Jesus' hearing in Jerusalem was postponed until after Shavout. And so, on the 20th day of Sivan, under a hot summer sun, Jesus and Jacob climbed into Joseph's donkey cart for the long four—day journey to Jerusalem.

On the way, they passed grove after grove of fig trees...a thick, rich, leafy mass as far as the eye could see. The trees were heavy with fruit, and pickers could be seen in every grove. "We must stop and buy some for your mother on the way home." Jacob was always a thoughtful person.

The next day they entered the grape country. "Look at those vineyards," Jesus said. "Soon it will be time for the vintage."

"Perhaps another month," said Jacob. "Most of the vineyards are owned by the same wealthy farmers who own the fig groves. "It's lucky for them the figs and grapes don't ripen at the same time. If they did, they'd need twice as many pickers."

This was the way they passed the time as the donkey ploddingly made his way along the dusty road southward.

As usual, they took a longer—than—necessary route to avoid the populated parts of Samaria. Finally, however, weary and dust—covered, they arrived in Jerusalem.

As they rounded the bend, putting the last hill behind them, the view of the city was breathtaking. Jesus had never seen Jerusalem in summer. All of his trips had been at Passover time.

Laid out before the two travellers were lush green gardens with the flowers of summer dressed in every color imaginable, from light pinks to deep reds, from light yellows to brilliant oranges, from light blues to deep purples, enhancing the sunlit gold of the buildings. There was the great Temple, of course, and also magnificent tombs. The mansions of the rich, even the hovels of the poor, were made of the sandstone that looked its best in sunlight. Flowering trees too, were nestled among the fig trees, the olive trees, the date palms, and the coconut palms. The hand of my Father, thought Jesus.

After they had drunk in the beauty of the great city, Jacob said: "We'll stay at the Temple residence tonight. The hearing begins in the morning."

"I hope they have plenty of water," said Jesus. "I've never felt more in need of a bath in my life." The galloping horses of the uncaring passing Roman soldiers had coated them both with dust.

As they entered the hearing room, Jesus and Jacob noted that Achim was already present. "I was

87

hoping something might keep him from being here," said Jacob.

"He doesn't worry me," said Jesus. He had prayed about this hearing, asking only that God's will be done, but he knew that his Heavenly Father was with him, represented by Jacob.

In addition to Jesus, Achim, and Jacob, there were several unknown spectators in the hearing room. There was no way of telling which side they were on, if indeed they had a position at all. It was Jacob's opinion that many came just to see a "good show".

All stood as the Rabbis and priests filed in, led by the chief priest in an impressive red robe trimmed in gold, and a matching cylindrical headpiece. He was followed by a shorter priest in blue; Sirach, the leader of the investigation, in black; and several priests and scribes in drab flax.

"Please be seated," intoned the presiding priest. "We're here today to address charges of blasphemy against a young man named Jesus Ben David of Nazareth. Is this person present?" Jesus stood to answer the question.

"Does he have representation?" Jacob stood to acknowledge his role as Jesus' defender.

"The charges have been brought by a teacher by the name of Achim at the Nazareth synagogue. Is he present?" Achim stood.

The priest continued, "All being present, I will turn the proceedings over to Elder Sirach, the leader of this investigation."

Sirach then took his place at the podium. "Teacher Achim, please state your charges."

Without looking at Jesus or Jacob, but addressing the assembled court, Achim said in a loud voice, "This young man, Jesus Ben David, has been meeting with us at the Nazareth synagogue for about a year now. I was reluctant when my brother teachers proposed admitting him to our learned council, but I finally agreed to a trial period of participation. That trial period is now coming to an end. I am here to ask you, honored sirs, to prevent further participation in our council by Jesus Ben David. Over the past year, this young man has repeatedly and persistently questioned The Law. I call it blasphemy!"

"In what way has he questioned The Law?" the high priest asked.

"May I speak, honored sir?" Jacob asked.

"Indeed."

"You should know, honored sirs, that this young man Jesus is an exceptional scholar. He has a deeper knowledge of the scriptures, even at his young age, than many of us do after years of study."

"Please answer the question," the high priest interrupted.

Jacob complied. "In what way has he questioned The Law? I'll give you a recent example. The questioning that prompted my learned colleague's charges arose out of our discussion of the Genesis account of God's testing of Abraham. Jesus finds it hard to believe that God would be so cruel as to make Abraham and Isaac suffer as Genesis tells us he did."

"I'd like to hear the young man's defense of questioning the Torah." It was the priest in blue speaking now.

Jesus stood. "It is my understanding, honored sirs, that the scriptures were handed down by word of mouth from generation to generation for many, many years before they were ever inscribed on scrolls. Therefore, I find it easy to believe that many accounts were modified, changed, yes, even distorted before they were recorded for others to read."

"You don't believe the scriptures to be the accurate word of God?" The priest's voice was louder than before.

"Not necessarily," Jesus replied.

"I vote for blasphemy!" shouted the priest in blue. Achim was smiling.

"Wait!" said the high priest.—The assembled court will make the decision through a secret ballot. Does anyone have anything else to say?" Jacob was disappointed. He had been counting on at least one of the priests to lean their way.

There was no response to the question. "In that case, we'll adjourn to the council room, and will return with our verdict after the mid—morning meal.

With that, he stood, as did the other priests and the spectators, and the court filed out of the room.

One of the more learned—looking spectators, a man named Shobach, came over and invited Jesus and Jacob to come to his home nearby for a meal. However, they did not feel much like eating, and so they thanked the man and declined his invitation. Shobach said, "I wanted you to know, I'm on your side." And with that the three shook hands and the man left.

Jesus and Jacob sat down in the hearing room to wait patiently. It seemed like days had passed before the court filed in again as the assembled principals and spectators stood. Jesus noted Shobach had returned and was smiling at him. "Could he be a guardian angel?", Jesus wondered.

His thoughts about angels were interrupted by the high priest's voice. "Have you counted the secret ballots, Sirach?"

"I have, honored sir."

"And what is the result?"

"We have two votes for guilty of blasphemy, five not guilty, one abstention."

As the verdict was announced, the crowd cheered, and Jesus and Jacob embraced. Achim had already left the room, and only a few of the spectators seemed to be disappointed.

The high priest was smiling. Apparently, in spite of his demeanor, he had been sympathetic to Jesus all along. "You will be permitted to continue meeting with the Nazareth teachers." And the group filed out.

Many of the spectators did not seem to be in a hurry to leave. They were smiling at Jesus, while he returned their smiles and nodded to thank them. Shobach waved.

"Were you worried?" asked Jacob.

"Not for a minute," said Jesus. "You see, our Heavenly Father was also present in this room."

Jacob nodded approvingly. Did he too think that Shobach was the Lord's messenger? Jesus didn't ask.

Not long after Jesus returned home, a courier arrived with a scroll. It was from Rabbi Hillel.

Jesus read it silently. "I was in the audience at your hearing last week, and I was pleased with your testimony," Hillel wrote. "As you may have heard,

I share many or your beliefs. Perhaps we can talk the next time you come to Jerusalem."

"Look, Mother, it's from Hillel himself," Jesus excitedly told Mary.

This was just one of many times Mary would be proud of her beloved son.

## CHAPTER 5 — JOHN'S VISIT

"It's been over two years since we've seen John," Mary said, beginning the evening conversation. "I wonder how he is."

"I'm sure the good Lord is watching over him," Joseph replied.

Preoccupied with thoughts of his day at the synagogue, Jesus wasn't really listening.

"Do you think we'll ever see him again, Jesus?"

"Who?"

"John! Your cousin."

"I'm sure we will. At least, I will, even if I have to go to the wilderness to find him."

"You're not going into that desert wilderness, Jesus." Joseph was stern. "At least not until you're a little older. After all, John is older than you are."

"Not much. And you forget I'm almost 18, father."

"Yes, I guess I'll always think of you as the little boy who got lost in the Temple." Joseph smiled.

"Anyway, my son," Mary added, "there will be plenty of time for you to go to the wilderness. You'll know when the time is right." Mary had a much better understanding than Joseph of God's plan for Jesus.

"I bow to your mother's wisdom," said Joseph, changing the subject. "So what happened at the synagogue today?"

"No loud arguments, at least," Jesus responded. "I thought for a minute Achim would be angry when we were talking about healing, but since the hearing in Jerusalem, he seems to have resigned himself to the fact that the council has a heretic in its midst, and there's not much he can do about it."

"What did you say today that was heretical?" Joseph asked.

"I questioned the statute that makes it unlawful for a sick person to be healed on the Sabbath. It seems to me if a person is ill and another person has the ability to cure him, the healing should take place as soon as possible, whether or not it's the Sabbath day."

"How strange you should say that, Jesus," Mary said. "I always felt that way, but feared I was wrong to question God's law."

"So, when you asked why we have that law, what did the teachers say?" Joseph asked.

"I got the usual answer ...Tradition. I say it's time to get rid of some of these traditions. I think there should be a new law, based on love. We should love one another, and laws governing our conduct should be based on love, not tradition."

"I couldn't agree more, even though what you propose is radical indeed." Mary was always supportive.

Joseph had nothing to say. He was never as ready to criticize the law as Jesus and Mary were.

Finally he spoke. "How do you see your idea for a new law in a structured form... a form that could be written down in a scroll?"

"I think the poor in spirit, those who mourn, the meek, those who hunger and thirst for righteousness, the merciful, the clean of heart, the peacemakers, those who are persecuted for the sake of righteousness, all should be blessed and should inherit the kingdom of heaven.[1]

As the evening discussion ended, Jesus thought back to his parents' concern about John. It was indeed two years since they had seen him.

Because John's parents, Elizabeth and Zechariah, were of advanced age when John was born, they had died when he was quite young. He had no home other than the Ben Davids'.

John was in Jesus' prayers every day, so he knew the Father was watching over him, but he couldn't help but wonder about his welfare.

_____

[1] Author's note: These thoughts, of course, were the basis for the beatitudes which Jesus would articulate so beautifully at a later time, in his sermon on the mount (Matthew 5:3—10).

Jesus remembered the day John left. He had tried his best to persuade him to stay in Nazareth.

"You're one of my best supporters," Jesus had said. "What am I going to do without you?"

"Come with me, then," John had suggested.

"I can't, John. My work isn't finished at the synagogue."

"Promise me, then, that you'll join me in the wilderness as soon as you can," John had replied.

Jesus smiled and took John's hand. They embraced to seal the bargain.

John's visit, a month or two after the Ben Davids' evening discussion of him, came as a complete surprise.

It was late afternoon. Jesus was sitting on the front step, idly whittling a piece of scrap wood from the carpenter shop. Out of the corner of his eye, he saw a figure approaching down the road.

As the figure got closer, it was clear that it was a large man. If one were to judge by his appearance, he was some sort of vagrant. His garments, torn and unkempt, were of coarse brown flax. His curly brown hair was disheveled, and his beard obviously hadn't been trimmed for months, if indeed it ever had been trimmed at all. His piercing brown eyes peered out of a face caked with road dust.

It wasn't until he spoke that Jesus knew it was John. "Jesus, my dear man, don't you know me?"

At that, Jesus jumped to his feet and ran to embrace his dear cousin. Now both men were laughing.

"John! John, old fellow, what has happened to you?"

"Nothing has happened to me except the Lord and the wilderness. I have little time to care for my appearance."

"But certainly you must be uncomfortable. Come into the house and bathe, and let my mother wash your clothes."

"Dear Jesus is always concerned for the welfare of others," John thought as he said, "If you insist. I didn't know I looked so bad."

"And if you'll forgive me, my dear friend, you don't smell like a spring garden."

"Then, by all means, I must bathe."

When they went into the house, Mary was astonished. At first, she thought Jesus had brought home another beggar for a bath and a meal, as he was wont to do.

"It's John, Mother. Back from the desert."

"John! John! It's you! What has happened to you, my boy? Are you all right? I'll bring something to eat."

"Time for that later," Jesus said. "I promised John a bath and some clean clothes."

"Of course," Mary said. "Go into Jesus' room and let me have your clothes to wash. While they're drying, Jesus will give you something of his to wear. It so happens, I have a kettle of soap and

fresh water boiling on the hearth this minute."
John obeyed, and Jesus accompanied him.

About 30 minutes later, Jesus and John reappeared. A bath and a hair trim had completely obliterated his "wild man of the wilderness" look. He was scrubbed clean. His beard was trimmed, and his hair combed. Although Jesus' clothes were a trifle short, John looked very presentable indeed.

Following the afternoon meal, which John had wolfed down as if he hadn't eaten in months, Jesus suggested that they take a walk around Nazareth. John was agreeable, saying, "An hour or two ago I would have declined. I knew I looked like a beggar, and I feared meeting old friends. But thanks to you and your dear mother, I'm presentable again."

They walked for about an hour, Jesus pointing out changes that had been made in the town since John's departure. As the golden sun turned to orange and then blooded the sky with red, Jesus suggested they had better turn back toward home.

"But Jesus, I have so much to tell you," John said.

"We'll talk more at home," Jesus said. And so the two spent several hours in animated conversation until long after dark. Joseph and Mary said little. They were fascinated by these two young men, and were content just to listen.

"So tell me of your experiences," Jesus began.

"Well, of course, living in the desert wilderness is not easy. I wanted this experience because I felt it would cleanse me spiritually. I thought if I could exist without any of the luxuries and comforts of civilization, I would get closer to God."

"And it happened?"

"Yes! Yes! In many ways great and small. Unbelievable things. For example, just when I thought I was going to starve to death, I came across a berry patch. It was clear that God was watching over me."

"I'm sure he was. How did he help you protect yourself from the elements and the wild animals?"

"First I built a shelter of branches. I made a bed of soft leaves. And at night I would rub sticks together until they would spark, so I could make a fire. On rainy days, I could make no fire, and had to exist on cold berries, locusts, and honey. But sometimes there was meat. On the second day I went hunting. After a time I was lucky to come upon a jackal. For a while it was uncertain who would win the battle, but I had made a spear of a stout stick and finally pierced him right behind and above one of his front legs. I must have pierced his heart, because he died instantly. After skinning and dressing him with my large knife, leaving his entrails for the big scavenger birds, I was able to preserve much of the meat with the large bag of salt I had brought along. Fortunately, there was a gushing spring of fresh, cool water nearby, and so I dined quite well from the start, supplementing my diet of jackal with wild boar, locusts, and honey.

It wasn't long before I became a proficient hunter. And soon I learned that I could make a palatable tea from the dried leaves of one of the bushes nearby."

"Didn't the animals bother you at night?"

"No, they soon learned that if they came near me, they would be in danger."

"Did you see any people at all?" Jesus asked.

"Oh yes. It wasn't long before the peasants in a village at the edge of the wilderness learned of my existence. Their curiosity got the better of them and they ventured closer and closer to my camp each day until they were close enough for me to call out to them and show them that I was friendly."

"Were these Jewish people?"

"Yes, but being pretty much cut off from the outside world, they had little understanding of the Torah, really no religion at all. I soon saw this as my opportunity to teach them my own version of the Law."

"One founded on brotherly love, I trust," Jesus said.

"Exactly. The ideas you and I exchanged before I left Nazareth were, in time, formulated into a primitive religion, without any rabbis or priests to charge me with heresy."

"God was at work in you, John."

"Yes, but unfortunately the people soon began to think of me as the Messiah. This was an idea I had to quickly purge from their minds."

"How did you accomplish that?"

"I quoted the words of Isaiah... 'Prepare the way of the Lord. Make straight in the wasteland a highway for our God.

Every valley shall be filled in, every mountain and hill made low. The rugged land shall be made plain, the rough country a broad valley. Then and only then the glory of the Lord shall be revealed. And all mankind shall see it together. For the mouth of the Lord has spoken!"[1]

---

[1] Isaiah 40:3—5

"Good choice of scripture." Jesus was pleased with his cousin. His smile and the twinkle in his eyes showed it.

"But there's more," said John. I told them they must repent their sins because the kingdom of heaven is at hand. I took them in groups to the banks of the River Jordan and cleansed their souls with the river water in a ritual I call baptizing. Again I had to put down the rumors that I was the Messiah."

"And this time?"

"I said to them, 'I am baptizing you with water, but one mightier than I is coming. I am not worthy to loosen the thongs of his sandals. I baptize you with water, but he will baptize you with the Holy Spirit.'"[1]

"Well said!" Jesus had a broad smile on his face now. John had obviously learned much and learned well from their many discussions. "I'm fascinated

---

[1] Matthew 3:11.

with your idea of spiritual cleansing with water. What did you call it? Baptizing?"

"Yes, it's from the Greek baptizein, meaning to dip."

"You are a learned man. I didn't know you knew Greek."

"Only a few words, but for some reason, baptizein was one word I learned."

"Amazing! It's perfect!" exclaimed Jesus. "Baptism!"

John was pleased that Jesus liked the idea. He had feared that perhaps he had gone too far on his own. "It's amazing," he said, "to see how happy people look after they've been baptized. They really believe their sins have been washed away."

"And indeed they have," Jesus said.

Realizing they were keeping Mary and Joseph up past their normal bedtime, Jesus finally said, "John, we have much to talk about, I know, but there are other days ahead."

"Yes," said Mary. "What you're telling us is so fascinating, John, we can hardly wait until tomorrow to hear more." Joseph nodded agreement.

Standing, John said, "Thank you. And thank you for your hospitality." Joseph and Mary smiled lovingly.

As they went into their bed chambers, John said, "Just one question, Jesus."

"All right."

"You know my faith is strong, but there's one thing that puzzles me. — How can God be everywhere at once? How can he know everyone's needs and fill these needs simultaneously?"

"Good question. — First you must understand that God is omnipotent. Some day it will be revealed that God is three persons in one ...the Father, the creator of heaven and earth; the Son, the Messiah here on earth; and the Holy Spirit, which is God everywhere at once, dwelling in every human. Some people call it conscience, but it is really the Holy Spirit of God."

"You certainly make things clear, Jesus."

Even in the dark, lying in their beds, tired as they were, the two talked on. Finally John got up the courage to ask Jesus the all—important question, "Jesus, you are the Messiah, are you not?"

There was a long silence before Jesus said, "You will know in time, John." John thought, if it were not true he would have said so, and he finally fell asleep contented with the answer Jesus had given him.

In the morning, John said, "Jesus I'll be going back to the wilderness in a few days. Won't you come with me? We could do so much together for the spirituality of those people, and we could do it without any interference from rabbis or priests."

Jesus didn't answer right away. John hoped he was considering the invitation, but finally Jesus said, "No John, not just yet. The time is not right. But one day I'll come to find you, I promise."

"When you do come, we could organize a new secret sect together," John said. "Our people would not fear God, they would love him. And God would not bring his wrath down upon our people. Instead he would shower them with love."

"Yes, John, you've got the right idea. But I'm afraid you'll have to start the work by yourself. I have much to do here and in Jerusalem before I can join you."

"Jerusalem?"

"Yes, I was called to Jerusalem for a hearing last year. Fortunately I was found not guilty on charges of blasphemy. What's more, Rabbi Hillel was present in the audience. He sent me a kind message after the trial. I have the feeling he may be summoning me back to Jerusalem to sit in on meetings with the Temple rabbis."

"Just don't let them divert you from your idea of a loving God." As soon as John said this, he knew it was a foolish thing to say to the Messiah.

Jesus could tell by the look on John's face what he was thinking, and so he smiled and said, "Don't worry about it, John," and he changed the subject. "I'm afraid it's time for me to help in the carpenter shop. Why don't you bring a stool in from the house, and we can talk more while I work." Joseph didn't mind, because their conversation didn't seem to interfere with Jesus' work. And he loved to listen to the two young men.

When Jesus left for the synagogue, he looked back three times as he walked down the road. He was glad he did because there was John, still standing in the doorway, waving and smiling.

John spent several more days in Nazareth before he returned to the wilderness. Except for Jesus' visits to the synagogue, the two young men were almost inseparable during that time. Truly, John

had become Jesus' first disciple.

## CHAPTER 6 — JAMES VISITS FOR ROSH HASHANAH

James, son of Salome, Mary's sister, was a big man like his cousin John. He loved to fish on the Sea of Galilee near Gennesareth, where he lived in a crude camp, selling his fish to the nearby townspeople, or bartering with other tradesmen for food, clothing, and other modest needs of a simple life. He also worked in the date and fig groves at picking time.

For the holidays, it was James' custom to visit his cousin Jesus. And so, near the end of Elul, after the annual date and fig harvest, he started out for Nazareth. He wanted to be sure to be there well before Rosh Hashanah, the first day of Tishri and the first day of the new year.

James, like John, was always welcome in the home of Mary and Joseph Ben David. And when he arrived on the last day of Elul, the family was delighted to see him.

How will I entertain him? Jesus wondered. He's not a spiritual man like John. He much prefers games to philosophizing. Jesus was not one to spend much time playing games, but he knew how James loved them; and so, after the mid—afternoon meal, Jesus asked, "How would you like to play stick—ball, James?"

The sparkle in James' eyes and the smile on his face gave Jesus his answer. His cousin hardly had time to speak before Jesus had fetched the ball and stick from his bed chamber.

When they were younger, Jesus, James, and John had played jumping games, and games using stones and a ball. But now that Jesus was 19 and James 21, they had outgrown these childish games in favor of stickball, which adults played as well as older children.

The game was a simple one, easily played by two. The defender would throw the ball of wound flax to the aggressor, who would try to hit it with a stick which had been specially selected from the firewood and stripped of its bark. If the aggressor could hit it beyond a predetermined line, drawn in the dust, he would score a point. If the defender caught the ball, he would score a point. If neither happened, there would be no score. Every time three points were scored by the defender, the players' roles would be exchanged.

James always outplayed Jesus, and this day was no exception. They both soon tired of the one-sidedness of the game, and so Jesus suggested they go for a walk.

It was a delightful day. As the two young cousins started down the road, they enjoyed the delicious smells of fresh bread baking. The flowers too blended into a heady fragrance, and their many colors formed tapestry—like borders for many of the houses.

They saw children playing games, women hanging laundry out to dry, and men picking the last of the dates from the palm trees.

Before long, they came upon a young boy walking toward them. As they got closer, Jesus realized it was David, an orphan who lived with foster parents on the other side of town. His surrogate mother and father took good care of him as far as food, clothing, and shelter were concerned; but, because they were not religious people, the boy was undernourished spiritually. He satisfied his hunger for religious knowledge by visiting Jesus from time to time, usually on holidays.

Jesus and David had met at the bazaar. Jesus was buying foods for his parents' seder table. The boy had expressed interest and curiosity, and so Jesus took him aside and they talked for over an hour. The boy and Jesus instinctively liked each other, and so it was a natural thing for Jesus to invite him to visit his home.

As they met on the road this fine early autumn day, David spoke first. "Jesus! I was just on my way to your house."

"Of course. You always come for Rosh Hashanah. This is my cousin James. Why don't you walk with us first?"

Shaking hands with James, David then turned to Jesus and asked, "Are you sure it's all right to come for the holiday? Are you sure I won't be too much of a burden on your parents, seeing you already have a guest?"

"Not at all. My mother loves to have a lot of people around on the holidays."

James asked, "Won't your parents want you at their table for the holiday, David?"

"They don't celebrate it. You see, they're not religious."

"Then you are wise to seek out religious people like Jesus and his parents," James said. "After all, you bear the name of our great ancestral King David, from whom Jesus and I are directly descended. You should be interested in religious things."

Jesus nodded, asking, "What does Rosh Hashanah mean to you, David?"

"The new year," the boy responded.

"True. But there's more," Jesus explained. "Rosh Hashanah is not just the first day of the new year, but a new beginning in each of our lives ...a fresh start in other words. Actually, God gives us a fresh start every day, forgiving our sins of the day before, provided we deserve that forgiveness."

"What do we need to do to earn God's forgiveness?" David asked.

"If we forgive those who have offended us in any way, God will, in turn, forgive our sins."

James spoke now. "Forgiving others is sometimes hard for me. There's another fisherman at the lake where I fish who once stole my entire day's catch. Since he deprived me of my day's earnings, I have never been able to forgive him."

"You must, James. You must forgive those who do you wrong if you expect to be forgiven for your own sins. When you get back to the lake, go to him and make peace."

James was not happy about the prospect of facing this man. "I never heard that in a synagogue," he said.

"And you won't," Jesus said. I have a lot of my own ideas about God." The boy David looked surprised.

"Usually I like your thoughts better than the rabbis," James said, "but I'm not so sure about this one."

"Try it. You'll find forgiving others makes you feel very good. That good feeling is God forgiving you."

"But," James protested, "we're taught to repent once a <u>year</u> ...at Yom Kippur, the day of atonement."

"I'm not suggesting there's no value in a thorough cleansing once a year. My mother cleans her house every day, but once a year she really pulls everything apart for a thorough annual cleaning. It's the same with us. Certainly it's good to fast and search our inner souls in the ten days following Rosh Hashanah in preparation for Yom Kippur. I'm simply saying that to ask God's forgiveness once a year is not enough. We should do so every day of our lives, because sin is present every day of our lives."

"I'll ponder your words when I'm back at camp. But I'm afraid I interrupted your explanation of Rosh Hashanah to David."

"So many of the holidays seem to be so solemn," David said.

"You're forgetting the feast of Succoth, the most joyous time of the year. And Hannukah too is joyous." Jesus was pleased to be able to correct the boy's erroneous impression.

Tell me more about Hannukah," David was smiling now.

"It'll be here before we know it. Two months go by very quickly. As you probably know, David, the eight days of Hannukah are celebrated beginning on the 25th day of Kislev. Hannukah commemorates the joyous occasion when the Temple in Jerusalem was rededicated by Judas Maccabeus. This occurred about 180 years ago, some time after the desecration of the Temple by Antiochus the Fourth."

David had a puzzled look on his face. "It's not really a holy day then?"

"Not in the strictest sense of the word. Hannukah is a bit like the feast of Succoth in the autumn season, and Purim, which comes in late winter. These are occasions of general merrymaking."

"Purim. I had forgotten that one."

"Perhaps it's not as important as some of the others, but Purim should be observed because it reminds us to remember the deliverance of our people from their enemies."

"What would you say is the greatest of our holidays?" David asked.

"James, you know the answer to that," Jesus said.

"I'd say Passover," James replied. "What would you like to know about it, David?"

"Well, I guess I don't really know why we have Passover."

"That's easy. It commemorates the deliverance of our people from the yoke of Egypt. God punished the Egyptians by striking down every first—born in the land, but he wanted to spare the Jewish people, and so he passed over their houses when he brought down his wrath on Egypt."

"True," Jesus interjected, "but there's more. Passover actually combines two ancient celebrations ...the deliverance from Egypt, as James said, and also an even more ancient tradition, probably associated with the spring migration of flocks."

"That's why Passover is in the spring, then? David asked.

"Yes, and that's where the tradition of serving dried fruits and cakes at the seder table comes from."

"Interesting. My religious education certainly has been neglected." David was frowning.

"It needn't be from now on. — Do you know where the Passover ritual comes from, David?"

"I'm afraid I don't."

"From Exodus Chapter 12."

"Do you know it, Jesus?"

"Let me see if I can remember it all...'The Lord said to Moses and Aaron in the land of Egypt: On the 10th of this month every one of your families must procure for itself a lamb ...a year—old male without blemish. You shall keep it to the 14th day, and then, with the whole assembly of Israel present, it shall be slaughtered during the evening twilight. They shall take some of its blood and apply it to the two doorposts and lintels. That same night they shall eat its roasted flesh with unleavened bread and bitter herbs ...(And the Lord said) This night I will go through Egypt, striking down every first—born of the land ...but the blood will mark the houses where you are. Seeing the blood, I will pass over you."'

James seemed disturbed. "Do you believe God could be so cruel as to strike down first—born children? Even children of the oppressing Egyptians?"

"No, I don't. My God is a <u>loving </u>God. He would never do such a thing."

"Are you saying scripture isn't always correct?" James was surprised to hear Jesus disagree with the Law.

"We have to make up our own minds about these things, James. And you too, David. But by all means, don't utter disbelief aloud in the synagogue, or you'll be charged with blasphemy as I was."

"Well, this certainly has been a helpful conversation for me," David said. "I now feel I know more about our holidays than I ever did before."

There's one holiday we haven't mentioned. Do you know what it is, David?"

"I'm afraid I don't."

"Shavout," said James.

"Yes, the festival of Shavout in the month of Sivan. Shavout celebrates the end of the grain harvest. It comes seven weeks, or 50 days, after the start of Passover.[1] Shavout also commemorates the revelation on Mount Sinai when God gave Moses the ten commandments."

Having exhausted the subject of Jewish holidays, the two cousins and the bright—eyed youngster walked on silently for a few minutes, arriving back home as the sun was beginning to sink in the west. They sat down on a bench in the courtyard. Now the boy listened as his two friends talked on.

And so, Jesus, we are told to pray for forgiveness as we start the new year. That's easy for me. My sins are numerous. But what does a holy

---

[1] Known to Christians as Pentecost.

man like you have to pray for?" James was truly curious.

"Because I am human, it's my nature to be sinful. Fortunately, God has spared me from sin up to now. But I've come close. For example, I've been on the verge of committing the sin of pride several times... on occasions when I was able to clarify a passage that the elders were struggling to interpret. At those times, I've been cautioned by God's voice within me reminding me that my abilities are God—given, that my accomplishments are also gifts from him."

"You have a wonderful, natural holiness within you, Jesus. I envy that."

"Envy itself is a sin, James. And don't forget anger. All men get angry from time to time."

"So true. And I'm lazy too. One of my major sins is sloth. I'd rather fish than work."

"But fishing is your work, James. Doesn't fishing provide a lot of your livelihood?"

"Yes, but..."

"Don't feel guilty about your fishing, James. God put the fish in the sea for men to eat, and he gave you the ability to catch them so others could share his bounty."

"You make everything so clear, Jesus."

Just then they heard the sound of the shofar, signifying the beginning of Rosh Hashanah. The two men and the boy embraced in a new year blessing. "We had better go in," Jesus said. "My parents will be ready for the new year ritual."

And so they were. Joseph and Mary were waiting. Joseph was standing at the head of the table. On the table was an apple dipped in honey, which Joseph blessed, asking God for a sweet year. Mary then served round, smooth loaves of bread, symbolizing her prayer for a smooth year ahead.

Finally, Joseph asked Jesus to intone the traditional New Year psalm.[1]

After the holiday meal, David said his thank-yous all around and departed for home. The family

---

[1] Psalm 69:29—37.

was glad he was leaving early enough to get home before dark.

Finally James said, "That was the best meal I've had in ages, Aunt Mary. I really appreciate it. And Uncle Joseph, you have been most kind. But now I must go.

"Where are you going?" Jesus asked.

"I must get back to my camp at Lake Gennesareth before dark."

"You'll never make it, James. You forget the days are getting shorter this time of year. Stay the night with us, and start out in the morning."

"By all means!" The four of them laughed at Joseph and Mary speaking in unison.

James was secretly pleased. He had been dreading the long walk. And he had not been as naive about the early nightfall as Jesus had thought. Indeed, James had been fearing what might happen to him on the dark road to the lake.

"Come. I'll prepare an extra bed in my room," said Jesus. Mary had already appeared with extra bedclothing, which she piled on Jesus' outstretched arms.

"You're all too good to me." James' heart was full of love and gratitude.

Mary regarded her nephew fondly. "You're a good man, James. You and John are like sons to us. You deserve everything we do for you."

And so the two young men went into Jesus' bed chamber, knelt down next to their beds, and silently asked God's help to make them better persons in the new year.

# CHAPTER 7 — JESUS ADDRESSES HUMAN SEXUALITY

As Jesus and James lay in their beds in Jesus' room, both of them were far too excited by the events of the holiday just past to fall asleep. And so, as Jesus and John had done not long ago, they talked on in the darkness, far into the night.

"Jesus, I'm glad you asked me to stay the night. To be honest, I was afraid of walking home alone in the dark. The roads are full of robbers and ruffians after dark. And they'd just as soon kill you for a shekel as look at you."

"I know. We're glad you agreed to stay, James. You're so right. You do indeed take your life in your hands on the road at night.

"I'm not ready to die yet. Not for a shekel coin anyway. Actually, Jesus, I'm afraid to die. Are you?

"No I'm not. In some ways I look forward to it."

"Do you believe there is life after death? Some of my friends believe in reincarnation. Do you?"

131

"I believe the only earthly reincarnation is through one's children. They have their parents' spirit within them. For each person, though, there is heavenly reincarnation after death."

"I don't understand."

"I believe that, when we die, all our sins are forgiven and our souls go to heaven, to be with God. And there our souls will be reincarnated into a heavenly body that will never know any sin or pain or suffering."

"This heaven you speak of, what is it like?"

"I can't tell you what it's like, but I can tell you in what ways it is not like earth. — Unlike earth, there is no disease, no pain, no sorrow, no grief, no sin, no guilt, no violence, and no money in heaven."

"No money?"

"As they say, 'The love of money is the root of all evil.' In heaven there can be no evil and therefore there can be no money. Anyway, there's no need for it. All our needs will be provided for in heaven."

As the two talked on, they soon exhausted the subject of life after death, but James was not about to let Jesus go to sleep.

"There's something else that's troubling me, Jesus."

"What is it, James?"

"My own disbelief. For example, burnt offerings. I find it hard to accept the practice of holocaust."

"If you read Genesis[1] you'll find it began with Noah when he built an altar to the Lord and chose a clean animal and a clean bird from every species and offered them up in a holocaust on the altar. Also, in Exodus[2] Moses tells us we must also offer sacrifices and holocausts to the Lord."

"I'm still not comfortable about it."

"James, we must always remember that hundreds of years passed before the Law was written down.

[1] Genesis 8:20
[2] Exodus 10:25

During those years, the stories were told and retold, handed down from one generation to the next. Certainly many errors were made before the stories became scripture. I believe that when God told Moses to offer up sacrifices he probably meant that man should return a portion of his goods to the Lord, but not necessarily in burnt offerings."

James was comforted. "That sounds sensible to me. But are we committing heresy by questioning scripture?"

"The rabbis would say so, but as long as we do it in secret, I'm sure God approves."

"There's one more thing in scripture that troubles me," James said.

"Just one thing? There are many things in scripture that trouble me," Jesus replied.

"This is in Leviticus[1] I can accept what the Lord said to Moses about incest, but when he tells Moses 'you shall not lie with a male as with a

---

[1] Leviticus 18 relations would be to a person like you. Their natural physical attraction is to members of their own sex."

woman', I can't help but wonder. Among the fishermen and date harvesters I know, there are a few men who are sexually attracted to each other. They are very good men otherwise. Are they destined for hell?"

"I can't believe that they are. I believe that there is a small percentage of men, and women too, who are born that way. They can't do anything about it. They may try, but sexual relations with the opposite sex are as distasteful to them [as same—sex relations are to a person like you].

"So you don't consider them sinners?"

"No. But of course, <u>any</u> sexual activity can become sinful if it becomes obsessive, blocking out one's ability to live life as God wants us to, doing good for others."

"What about sexual activity between a man and woman who are not married?"

"Not seriously sinful unless they bring a child into the world and they are not equipped or willing to care for it."

"Is self—gratification a sin?"

"You refer to nocturnal emission?"

"<u>And</u> masturbation."

"To decide whether any sexual activity is sinful, one should ask himself...'Is God in control of my sex life? or has sex become a god to me, controlling me?' If the answer is yes to the latter, you're committing serious sin.

James looked relieved. "Well, I'm certainly glad to know the friends I mentioned are not sinners. You see, I <u>like</u> these people."

"Of course you do. — You know, it's interesting we should be having this conversation. Tomorrow at the synagogue, we'll be discussing the story of Sodom and Gomorrah, and I plan to challenge the interpretation of that scripture passage that says sexual acts between people of the same gender are sinful."

"I thought you said we shouldn't question scripture in the presence of rabbis." James was puzzled.

"<u>You</u> shouldn't, James. But I feel compelled to do so. If I'm charged with heresy again, so be it."

"I think we'd better change the subject, James, or we'll never get to sleep. Tell me, have you ever met a fisherman named Simon?"

"Indeed I have. He's a very likeable person, but at the same time very rough—and—tumble. He angers easily, and he's often too ready to fight. At least that's my opinion of him."

"Yes, Simon is a diamond in the rough, but he has a heart that's larger than life. I met him briefly through his brother, Andrew, and was much impressed. I'm sure that God will, in time, bring out the goodness in this man."

James started to say something, but his voice drifted off into gibberish and then silence. Jesus was glad they could both finally get some sleep.

The next morning, as the red sun was rising, James, Jesus, and his parents said their goodbyes. Mary had packed an ample mid—morning meal for

James, as she did every day for Jesus; and Jesus had filled two goatskin bags with fresh cool water, one for James and one for himself to take with him to the synagogue. As James went down the dusty road, turning several times to wave, the family watched until he was out of sight. All were happy and grateful that the Lord had made this visit possible.

"Now I must go too," Jesus said. And kissing his parents on their cheeks, he waved and made his way in the other direction.

At the synagogue that day, after Manasseh had read the 19th chapter of Genesis, Jesus said, "Up to now, my questions relating to the veracity of the Law have been questions about omission. Today, I believe the passages Manasseh has just read to be full of error."

"More heresy!" Achim exploded. He had reached the end of his patience. obviously his quiet period was over.

"Let him finish," said Jacob.

"Let's look at verse 5," Jesus continued; and he read, "'All the townsmen of Sodom called to Lot and said, Where are the men who came to your house tonight? Bring them out to us that we may have intimacies with them.' Certainly the attempts of the men of Sodom to rape the two angels were indeed wrong. But through the years, we have interpreted this chapter and others to mean that all intimate relations between people of the same sex are sinful. I don't believe that. In fact, I was discussing this subject just last night with a cousin of mine. I don't believe God intended us to interpret this chapter of Genesis or the 18th chapter of Leviticus to mean that these activities per se are sinful."

"I won't listen to this!" exclaimed Achim, and he again gathered up his cloak and his scrolls and dashed out of the room.

Needless to say, the others were also a bit uneasy as a result of Jesus' boldness in expressing such a radical idea; but Jacob, always open—minded, said, "Continue, Jesus."

"It is my belief that all babies are born with latent biological urges, originating in the brain.

Most males, when they reach adolescence, begin to experience a sexual attraction to females. And likewise, young girls are attracted to boys.

"Sometimes, however, there is a genetic accident that occurs at birth, and the male is born to have a natural attraction to other males instead of females, or the female will grow to have a natural sexual attraction to other females."

The teachers had questioning looks on their faces, but at least they weren't hostile as Achim always was.

As it turned out, Jesus' conversation with James the night before had prepared him well for this meeting with the teachers. While a bit more sophisticated, their questions were very similar to James'.

"While we're on the subject of sexuality, Jesus, what about incest?" Josiah ventured. "Of course we're warned against it in Genesis 19 in the story of Lot's daughters."

"There's no question in my mind that incest is a sin ...a very serious sin." Jesus was emphatic.

"And what about oral sex?" Manasseh asked.

"Between married partners or consenting adults, oral sex is not sinful, in my judgment," Jesus said. "But when one partner forces it upon the other, then it is serious sin."

"What about self—abuse?" Achim had returned quietly a few minutes after he bolted from the room. Surprisingly it was Achim speaking now, although in a challenging way.

"First of all, I think the term self—abuse is a misnomer. Masturbation is a much more accurate term. And I see nothing wrong with it, provided it doesn't become obsessive and is not practiced to excess. Practiced in moderation, I believe masturbation is a perfectly natural and normal sex

141

act." Surprisingly, Jesus got little argument on this, not even from Achim. He suspected the reason was that there were few if any of the teachers who had not from time to time indulged in the practice themselves.

Achim was still speaking, now a bit subdued. "What about intercourse between unmarried partners? Surely you must believe that's a sin."

"When it's between two faithful partners, I see nothing wrong with it. Of course, when it's promiscuous that's another story, if only because there is the danger of contracting and spreading disease and conceiving unwanted children."

The teachers looked at each other in disbelief. To say the least, they were more than a bit shocked to hear Jesus' liberal views on human sexuality.

The problem was growing. Jesus' unusual beliefs, as expressed by Achim's hostility, were indeed becoming difficult to accept. Should they reprimand Jesus or not? Would it be necessary to send him to Jerusalem again for another hearing? Even Jacob felt this was something they'd have to think seriously about.

## CHAPTER 8 — THE SEBASTIAN WOMAN

When Jesus was a child he was slender, and not very strong. As he matured, however, his years of hard work, combined with frequent swimming and long walks, helped him grow into a handsome, broad-shouldered young man. By the time he was 21, Jesus was admired by women and envied by men everywhere he went. His soft dark brown hair was always clean, and fell gently around his shoulders. His mustache and short beard were kept carefully trimmed. His sun-tanned complexion was ruddy. When he smiled, he revealed teeth that were even and white, the result of daily scrubbing with salt and water. His brown eyes sparkled and twinkled when he smiled. His strong arms were muscular; and his hands, so often outstretched in greeting, were large and firm. His voice was mellow and rich, and his walk was quick and sure-footed. His clean, simple garments always hung loosely over his body. If it had not been an unseemly thing to do, many feminine heads would have turned to look at him. Indeed there were occasional women, usually the local harlots, who did shamelessly turn and watch him when he passed by.

Jesus always had a smile and a greeting for everyone he passed, from the wealthy merchants and synagogue elders to the beggars and harlots in the town square. He never refused to give alms to the poor, and often invited a beggar to walk with him to the Nazareth Inn, where he would buy the man a hot meal and be sure the beggar had money in his pocket when they parted.

It was a particularly hot day in the month of Sivan, about six months after his 21st birthday, when Jesus took a long walk to a dangerous place ...Sebaste, just inside the Samaritan border. It was dangerous because the Sebastian people were a mixture of Galileans and Samaritans who were often fighting among themselves. He had to be careful whom he talked to. On hearing his Galilean accent, the Samaritans would become openly hostile.

However, he wanted to see the temple in Sebaste. Herod had built this entire city. In addition to the palaces and fortresses in Jericho, Masada, Ascalan, Sepphoris, Jerusalem, and elsewhere, Herod commissioned numerous monuments and buildings in every corner of his realm. He built an entire city at the Mediterranean seaport Caesarea. And where the ancient city of Samaria had stood, he built Sebaste.

By the time Jesus reached Sebaste this hot summer day, he was tired, hungry, and terribly thirsty. He had brought a water bag, but by then it was empty. He needed to find a well or some other place where he could fill it.

When he came upon the well in the center of town, he noticed a large sign on it. As he got closer, he could see that it said, "For Samaritans Only". Turning away, he felt his thirst becoming almost overpowering. If he could find an inn, perhaps he could persuade the innkeeper to fill his water bag if he bought a meal and a goblet of wine.

Recognizing their accent, he overheard two Galileans talking in the town square; and he approached them to ask directions to an inn.

"There's one right down this street," said the first man, "but you'll be turned away if you go there. It's run by Samaritans."

"True," said the second man, "but there is an inn run by Galileans on the northward road to Nazareth." This was the road Jesus had come in on, and he vaguely remembered seeing a small inn on the outskirts of Sebaste.

"I'll be heading home that way in mid—afternoon," Jesus said. "But I wanted to see the Temple before I left, and I desperately need a drink of water.

"If it's only water you need, I can help you," the first man said. "Come with me to my home. It's only a few steps from here." And so the stranger and his friend shook hands, kissed on both cheeks, and parted. The first man, taking Jesus' arm, led him down one of the dusty streets that branched off the village square like spokes of a wheel.

What the man had described as "a few steps" turned out to be almost a mile, but finally he pointed to a hut of clay and stones, saying, "Here we are." The men touched the Mezuza with their fingertips, kissed their fingers, and entered the tiny home. Inside he introduced Jesus to his wife as "a stranger from Nazareth".

The woman barely greeted him. Apparently her husband was always bringing unwelcome strangers to the little one—room home.

Sensing this, Jesus smiled and said, "I won't be a minute. All I need is a drink of water."

"Good," the woman said rudely. "God knows we hardly have enough food for ourselves."

The man poured a large goblet of water from a huge clay pitcher. Jesus drank it thirstily, until it was all gone. "More?" asked the man. Smiling, Jesus nodded, and a second goblet of water was poured. When Jesus had his fill of cool water and the man had replenished his water bag, he thanked the strangers profusely and pressed a half—shekel coin into the man's hand.

"Please, no," the man said. "I'm always happy to help a fellow Galilean."

"Take it and be quiet," the woman said. "God knows we can use it."

Saying the ancient blessing, Jesus departed and, in so doing, he thought he detected a trace of a smile on the woman's lips. "God be with you," he said.

"And also with you," replied the pair.

Refreshed by the cool water, Jesus made his way back to the town square. The Temple was clearly visible down the widest street.

Jesus' first impression of the Temple was that there was little to distinguish it from an ordinary synagogue except its unusual stone steps. There were at least 10, which ran the full width of the Temple and led up to a pillared porch.

*Joseph Radder*

As Jesus entered, however, he could tell he was
in a genuine Temple, for there in front of the
massive curtains, which .sheltered the Holy of
Holies, was a high priest with two ordinary priests
in attendance. They were praying in a rhythmic
chant, so Jesus stayed quietly at the back of the
large room. Jesus was impressed with the elegance
of the high priest's vestments ...a glowing deep
rich red with bands embroidered in royal blue. He
wore a crown—shaped headgear; the long red robe
fell over a white ankle—length tunic; and a vest,
called an Ephod, was embroidered in blue, gold, and
scarlet. Each of the ordinary priests wore an
ankle—length white tunic, with a rope tied three
times around the waist and then trailing to the
floor. All three were barefoot.

As the priests continued their prayer ritual,
Jesus was wishing it was holiday time. In a few
months it would be Rosh Hashanah, followed quickly
by Yom Kippur, the day of atonement. On that solemn
fast day, the high priest himself would administer

all the Temple services and enter the Holy of Holies for the first time. In the Temple at Sebaste, the Holy Sanctuary was hidden by two beautifully embroidered curtains the full width of the temple and about as high as three or four tall men.

After passing through the two curtains, the high priest would, on Yom Kippur, heap incense on the coals he was carrying and enter the Holy of Holies. The night before the day of atonement service, he would bathe ten times and keep a vigil all night long. The high priest was then considered pure enough to enter this holy place. Jesus did not tarry long inside the Temple, because he was afraid he would disturb the priests. And so he said a short prayer and departed.

He had left Nazareth shortly after dawn, and he had skipped the usual mid—morning meal. Now that it was mid—afternoon, he was famished. And so he hurried along the Nazareth road until the inn came in sight. It was on a hill near the edge of town.

Unlike the large caravanseries where Jesus had stayed with his family on pilgrimages to Jerusalem, the Sebaste—Nazareth road inn was much more modest ...an ordinary place built to provide overnight shelter, a goblet of wine, and a simple meal to travellers who could not afford the bigger, more elaborate inns.

Ordinarily such an inn would not be located as close to another as this was to the inn at Sebaste. Normally they were a day's travel apart. This one had obviously been built here to provide a last opportunity to the Galilean traveller before he entered Samaria, where he would be unwelcome.

As Jesus approached the innkeeper's table, he noted that the scruffy man looked to be just a cut above a highway robber, ready and eager to squeeze every coin he could from his guests no matter how unscrupulous his actions might have to be.

Jesus inquired if the inn had a dining room; and the innkeeper, without saying a word, thrust a grubby thumb over his shoulder toward a dark entrance door marked "Wine and Food".

The room seemed unnecessarily dark. It had no windows and only a few long tables and benches. on two of these tables were flickering candles. Clearly this place was designed more for wine imbibing than for dining.

At first Jesus thought he was alone in the room, then he noticed a figure at another table in the corner. As his eyes became accustomed to the darkness, he noticed it was a woman. She must be a harlot, thought Jesus. No self—respecting woman would go to a wine room alone. Indeed in Galilee, even a harlot could not do that. There they were forced by the town council to ply their trade around the village well in the square.

After what seemed to be an unreasonable length of time, the innkeeper entered the room with a dirty cloth over his arm. "Wine?" he inquired.

"Yes," answered Jesus. "But I'm more interested in food."

"We have only soup, bread, and cheese," said the innkeeper.

The innkeeper went behind a curtain and reappeared promptly with a flagon of wine.

"I just want a goblet—full," Jesus said.

"You must buy a flagon," scowled the innkeeper. "She'll drink the rest," he said, again thrusting his grubby thumb over his shoulder toward the harlot.

Jesus did not reply, but poured himself a goblet of the wine and tasted. It was terribly sour, but he knew better than to ask for a different wine.

As Jesus sipped the wine, he noticed that the woman was smiling at him. He nodded to her, but took care not to give her the impression that he was a potential customer.

He had never seen a woman so immodestly dressed. Even the harlots in the Nazareth square kept to a certain standard of decorum, set by local law.

But this woman, actually she was not much more than a girl, wore a bright red garment with all the

154

upper buttons open so that the tops of her ample breasts were revealed. Her nipples were clearly visible through the thin cloth. Her shoulder—length hair was wheatcolored. Her lips had clearly been reddened by the juice of berries, and her eyes darkened with the rind of the pomegranate.

Jesus tried not to look at her, but she was indeed a very beautiful woman. And after all, he was a healthy young man.

This, however, was a new experience for him. He had admired many women, but had never been physically attracted to them.

He poured a second goblet of wine from the flagon, which he had not intended to do, and sat there wishing the innkeeper would hurry with the food so he would have something else to occupy his mind.

Just then, the woman spoke. "Could you spare some of that wine?"

Jesus knew his answer was dangerous, but he said, "Yes, of course." At that, the woman stood up

155

and sauntered over to his table. As she sat down, she deliberately let her gown fall apart to reveal something Jesus had never seen before ...a woman's naked knee.

"Thank you," she said as Jesus poured wine into her goblet.

"I'm afraid this is terrible wine," he said.

"After you've had several, it doesn't matter," she said, continuing, "What's your name?"

"Jesus. Jesus Ben David, from Nazareth."

"What do you do?" the woman asked.

"I'm a carpenter," Jesus answered.

Just then the innkeeper appeared with a bowl of soup, a basket of bread, and a plate of cheese. Jesus offered some to the woman, but she refused. As he ate hungrily, the woman chattered on about how terrible it was that the Samaritans and Galileans couldn't get along better. Jesus had already detected, by her accent, that she was a Samaritan.

"I'm a Sebastian," she said, "born and raised in Samaria. But I come to this inn because I like Galileans."

"You're a rarity in Sebaste," Jesus said.

When he had finished his meal, the woman boldly took the flagon and refilled the two goblets. This done, she reached over and put her soft white hand on his.

"Why don't you come with me to my room?" she murmured. I could make you very happy."

Jesus was experiencing something he had never experienced before. The combination of the wine, her soft touch, and her perfume, had given him a feeling every young man experiences, but one which he had escaped by the grace of God.

"No! I can't!" Jesus said. And getting up from the table, he left a half shekel coin for the innkeeper and walked out of the inn abruptly. He did not mean to be rude to the woman, but he knew he had to get out of there right away.

*Joseph Radder*

As Jesus hurried up the dusty road toward Nazareth, he prayed, "God help me!"

The walk home to Nazareth seemed much longer than the trip south that morning. Jesus was weary; one of his sandals was rubbing against his toes, but worst of all, he was feeling guilty about the woman at the inn. It was very difficult for Jesus to get to sleep that night. He couldn't forget the Sebastian woman, and he was experiencing guilt feelings unlike any he had ever known. He prayed fervently, as he lay on his cot, that God would forgive his evil thoughts.

Finally, God the Father came to him in a dream and said, "Fear not, my son. It was necessary for you to experience these feelings so you would know what ordinary men go through almost every day. The feeling is good when active within marriage, but outside marriage it often causes men to sin. I promise you that from this day forward I will shield you from sins of men so that you may go forth in the world to do my work. You will experience much pain in your life, my beloved son, but never again will you experience the pain caused by sin."

Jesus awoke with a start, thanking God from the bottom of his heart. It was at this moment he felt transformed. It was at this moment that he knew he was not an ordinary man, but was indeed the Son of God.

It was purely coincidental that the next subject discussed in the council room was that of lust. Jesus had read the scripture passages on this subject from Exodus, Deuteronomy, and Numbers to prepare for this session. Little did he know two days ago, when he had his firsthand experience with this deadly sin, that it was about to be discussed by the teachers.

After about an hour of discussion during which Jesus had little to say, Josiah read from the Haftorahl[1] "Lo, the woman comes to meet him robed like a harlot... she wins him over by her repeated

---

[1] Proverbs 7:10, 21—27

luring. With her smooth lips she leads him astray. He follows her stupidly, like an ox led to slaughter, like a stag that minces toward the net 'till an arrow pierces its liver. Like a bird that rushes into a snare unaware that its life is at stake. So now, O children, be attentive to my words. Let not your heart turn to her ways, go not astray in her paths, for many are those she has struck down dead, numerous those she has slain. Her house is made up of ways to the nether world, leading down into the chambers of death."

And so, that day's session was concluded. If the teachers noticed that Jesus was unusually quiet, they didn't say anything. In fact, old Achim seemed to have an uncharacteristically benevolent smile on his face. Perhaps he too had once been tempted by a Sebastian woman.

## CHAPTER 9 — JOSEPH OF ARIMATHEA

A year had passed since the trip to Sebaste, and Jesus was growing restless. The daily routine with the teachers at the synagogue had become tiresome. They had completed discussion of all five books of the Torah and were now starting over with Genesis.

Jesus couldn't see himself getting into the same old arguments with Achim. And while Jacob and the others were much more tolerant of Jesus' liberal views, they still were not entirely supportive.

Jesus was sitting on the front step trying to make himself want to go to the synagogue one more time, when a stranger in a donkey cart stopped in front of the house.

"Jesus? Jesus Ben David?" the man inquired.

"Yes. I am Jesus—"

I have a message for you from Joseph of Arimathea. And I have been instructed to wait for a reply." As he said this, he handed Jesus a small scroll of parchment. Jesus had heard of the wealthy

161

merchant ship owner, worldwide trader, and member of the Sanhedrin. What could such a man possibly want from a humble Nazarean carpenter? These were his thoughts as he unrolled the message and read:

"Jesus of Nazareth:

"Last Sabbath, I had a most interesting conversation with one of your teachers, a man named Jacob. He told me of your remarkable ability to interpret the scriptures in ways with which Jacob and I tend to agree.

I would be pleased if you would join me for dinner on the first day following the Sabbath in the week ahead. If you reply in the affirmative, I will send for you just past midday. Please reply in care of my messenger."

The message was signed, "Joseph, Merchant, Arimathea".

To have dinner with Joseph of Arimathea would be a new experience for Jesus. He had never met a man of Joseph's stature, let alone been asked to dine in a mansion. In fact, the word dinner was seldom heard in the Ben David home. Only the wealthy ate three meals a day. Poorer families dined only twice — at mid—morning and mid—afternoon.

"Why yes, please tell your master I'd be happy to dine with him. Here, let me write my reply." And he took the messenger's stylus in hand and wrote a grateful acceptance. With that, the messenger saluted Jesus and was off in a cloud of dust.

Jesus was very excited about the forthcoming meeting with Joseph of Arimathea. It seemed the appointed day would never come. When it finally did, he bathed and dressed early in his best white robe. He was ready at least two hours before the appointed time. And so he paced restlessly from room to room, then to the workshop and the little garden.

When mid—day finally arrived, Jesus started looking for the messenger's donkey cart. What finally came around the bend was not the donkey cart at all but a handsome carriage, not unlike the one Jesus had admired so long ago in the caravanserie on the way to Jerusalem. It brought to his mind the tragic death of the beautiful Maryamne, and he said a short prayer for her soul.

The carriage stopped and Jesus hardly recognized the driver. This time he was dressed in fine blue livery with gold piping and epaulets. He stepped smartly down from his seat to open the carriage door for Jesus.

The interior of the carriage was nothing like any Jesus had ever seen before. Even Maryamne's family carriage paled by comparison. These seats were upholstered in a powder blue velvet, and there were extra cushions to match. There were even cushions on the floor for the passengers' feet. And the carriage was not drawn by donkeys or even mules. Not at all! There were two fine white horses, wearing the same blue and gold as the footman's livery. As the horses trotted along, Jesus tried to sink down below the sideboard. He didn't want any of his Nazareth friends to see him enjoying such luxury. Above all, he hoped none of his teachers from the synagogue would see him. It wasn't long, however, before they were outside the town and speeding along the road to Arimathea, churning up a great cloud of dust in their wake.

Finally getting used to the luxurious ambience of the carriage, Jesus drank in the beauty of the countryside. It was early summer, the month of Tammuz, normally hot and dry. But this day was comfortably cool.

Along the way, although he had seen it many times before, Jesus was enthralled with the natural beauty ...date palms, almond trees, and olive trees with their magnificent gnarled trunks. Some of these trees, Jesus had been told, were over two thousand years old. Though the olive harvest would not come until autumn, the trees in the groves along the way were already heavy with fruit.

Arimathea was a very small village near the great sea, nestled between two mountain ranges. It was a ride of about a mile or two by fast horse from Caesarea, where Joseph docked his great merchant ships.

Within three hours after leaving Nazareth, the driver slowed the horses to a canter for the ride up the hillside on Joseph's private entrance road. When they reached the top of the hill Jesus saw two iron gates. Two sentries stood at attention when they saw the carriage, and promptly opened the gates. Within a minute or two, a marvelous mansion overlooking the great sea came into view. — Jesus literally gasped, for it was the most magnificent residence he had ever seen. Surely only Herod's palace at Jericho could be grander, he thought.

A wooden bridge with a criss—cross balustrade on each side spanned a moat—like canal across the front of the great house. The road was now paved with what looked like crushed marble. It led to a columned porch, in the center of which were two highly polished wooden doors carved with biblical figures. Most of the mansion was built of white marble, interrupted here and there with windows and dark marble mullions. The floor of the columned porch was of blue and white mosaic tile.

As Jesus stepped down from the carriage, the great doors swung open and a large man with a great brown beard appeared. He was wearing a rich dark green robe trimmed in gold. "That's the master," advised the carriage driver, who departed quickly leading the horses and carriage around to the rear. Jesus wanted to thank him for the comfortable and pleasant journey, but the man was gone before that was possible.

Joseph approached with arms outstretched. "Jesus, my boy, welcome to Arimathea. I've heard so much about you. At last I get to meet you. Come. Come into my home."

"Thank you, sir. I'm honored and awed to be a guest in such a splendid mansion."

"Indeed. Well, let me show you around a bit before we go in for dinner."

To the left of the great entrance hall was the bath complex. Joseph explained that the bather entered through a dressing room and then passed through a tepidarium, a shallow pool of warm water. Next came the caldarium, a room heated by fires kept burning continuously by slaves; and finally the frigidarium, a cold room with a large pool of deep cool water. All around this room were six—foot niches for reclining bathers.

Next, Joseph led Jesus into his private theater, a room which could seat 30 or 40 guests on stone steps before a small stage where musicians, performers, dancers, and magicians entertained Joseph and his family and friends.

As Joseph led him through rooms and corridors, Jesus noted artfully carved stone, forming columns, valances, door and window frames in unusual geometric designs, obviously the work of a fine artisan.

Occasionally there would be murals, some painted, some carved in relief. Most of these depicted merchant ships and seamen, others were of merchants in marketplaces, but all related to Joseph's profession as a worldwide trader.

Finally, Joseph led Jesus into a grand salon, or sitting room. Here the walls were of colorful panels in warm, soft pastels edged with gold scrolls. In the center of one wall were two marble columns framing a dramatic painting of a ship at sea. Brass oil lamps stood on pedestals around the room; and ceramic vases, some as tall as a small boy, stood in strategic places on the intricately patterned red rug. Two cabinets held more vases and jardinieres. In the center of the room were a large throne—like chair and three smaller chairs with crossed legs. Toga—clad servants moved about the room lighting lamps and filling jugs with wine. Joseph invited Jesus to sit in one of the smaller chairs as he himself took his place on the large chair and leaned back against the royal blue velvet cushion. On the table was a large bowl of grapes, three different varieties. "Try these, Jesus," said Joseph, passing the bowl. "I prefer the green grapes from the shores of your Sea of Galilee, but you might like the blue ones from Iezreel."

Jesus found them all succulent and delicious. Servants filled handsome goblets with ruby wine, and Joseph nodded at Jesus and toasted him, saying, "To a long and lasting friendship."

"Amen," replied Jesus, thinking, "But who am I to be the friend of such an important person?"

After the two drank their wine and made small talk about the trip from Nazareth to Arimathea, a servant announced that dinner was served.

Joseph led the way to the dining hall, a long and narrow room decorated to complement the salon. It too had marble columns, framing paintings of merchant ships and seamen. In the center was a long, highly polished table surrounded by 20 or more tall—backed chairs. Down the center of the table was a wide cloth of fine gold tapestry.

There was a place set for Jesus at Joseph's right. Apparently no one else was dining with them. Servants passed the abundance of Joseph's kitchen from the sideboard, serving each of the two men fresh fruit in crystal goblets, a delicious spicy game soup in pewter bowls, fish roasted in herbs, and two kinds of wine, light and dark. Jesus had never before tasted food this good. And now, two servants brought in a great silver platter. on it rested a crusty brown roast leg of lamb. Another servant held a large carving knife and fork which he presented ceremoniously to Joseph.

While Joseph was carving, the servants brought out dishes of rice, and a tray of green, yellow, and orange fresh vegetables. Another servant poured more wine, and still another passed a plate of meat to Jesus and set another before Joseph.

As the two men ate, Joseph talked, between mouthfuls, of the growing difficulties of being an international merchant. one had to deal not only with several governments, each extracting its own pound of flesh, but with bandits raiding one's caravans, and pirates raiding one's ships. Finally, he said, "Enough of all this. What is <u>your</u> goal in life, Jesus?"

"I guess to be a teacher, sir ...a <u>good</u> teacher ...one who teaches the <u>truth</u> and teaches it lovingly."

"Well, your experience at the synagogue has trained you well for that."

"Yes, but there's something missing."

"And what might that be, my son?"

"I feel I need to know more about other religions of the world if I am to be able to teach convincingly of <u>our</u> religion."

"A wise idea," said Joseph. "And how would you propose to do it?"

"Well, I would like to be able to travel—to places like Persia, India, and Tibet ...to talk to their priests and monks, and get a better understanding of <u>their</u> religion."

"You wouldn't let them convert you?"

"There's little chance of that."

Joseph ate on silently for a few minutes. As the servants poured an aromatic herb tea, he said, "You've given me an idea. See what you think of this..."

Jesus looked at him with interest.

"How would you like to travel with one of my trading expeditions, first by sea, then by land, as my people visit various lands to trade the products of Judea?"

"Sounds wonderful, sir. But I couldn't begin to be able to afford such a trip."

"You'd go as my guest. Your travel and food and lodging would be provided. All you would have to do is bring adequate clothing."

Jesus was excited. "I'd work for my passage," he exclaimed. "Do they need carpenters on your ships? I'm reasonably skilled at that trade."

"No. I have people for that. Your task would be to record all you see and hear. My reward would come from borrowing your diary after your trip for my scribes to record on scrolls."

Jesus was overwhelmed. Not only would he have the opportunity to travel to foreign lands, but a longfelt desire to write would be fulfilled. "I can't tell you how much I appreciate this, sir. But, of course, I'd need the permission of my teachers."

"I'll see to that. I'll send details of the trip by messenger. Now you must go, in order to get home before nightfall," Joseph said. And turning to one of his servants, he ordered, "Jamal, make sure our young guest has some fruit to take on the road with him." The servant bowed and disappeared into the kitchen, reappearing quickly with a basket overflowing with grapes, plums, pears, dates, and figs.

Joseph stood to signal the end of their meeting, and he escorted Jesus to the reception hall, where the carriage driver was waiting.

"You'll be hearing from me soon," Joseph said as the footman helped Jesus into the waiting carriage.

"I can't thank you enough, sir."

"Please call me Joseph. And a safe journey to you." With that, he disappeared into the great house.

As the carriage driver eased the two white horses across the bridge, down the hill, and then from Joseph's road onto the eastward road to Nazareth, Jesus looked over his shoulder for a final look at the sea. Then he realized it wouldn't be a final look at all. He'd soon be seeing a lot of that sea, from the deck of Joseph's ship.

Jesus had never been so excited. Where, he wondered, would the journey with Joseph's traders take him? To Egypt? To Athens? To Antioch? He couldn't wait for the day when the messenger arrived with instructions.

Perhaps he shouldn't have done so, but he had to share his good fortune. So, shouting above the noise of the horses' hooves and carriage wheels pounding the road, he told the carriage driver of Joseph's invitation.

"That's typical of the master," the driver shouted back. "He's a very kind and generous man."

"Do you have any idea where the mission might go?" Jesus was leaning way forward now.

"That's difficult to say," the driver yelled hoarsely. "Sometimes they go to Alexandria, sometimes west to Corinth, sometimes north to Cyprus. It all depends on the goods they are carrying and the kind of goods they are seeking to bring back to Judea on the return trip."

It was too difficult to carry on any more conversation over the noise. And so Jesus tried to occupy his mind with the scenic beauty, as he had done before. But it was of no use. He could think of nothing but his good fortune and the trip to come.

After what seemed like much more than three hours, the carriage finally arrived at the Ben Davids' door. Before Jesus could open the door, the driver was there to do it for him. And so Jesus thanked the young man, who removed his hat and bowed deeply, then climbed aboard his perch at the front of the carriage and was quickly on his way back west.

Taking the basket of fruit in to his mother, Jesus was bursting to tell her the news. Mary could tell that something wonderful had happened to her son, but she persuaded him to wait until Joseph came in from the carpenter shop. Finally they were all together, and Jesus excitedly but carefully told Mary and Joseph of his great fortune.

"What a wonderful opportunity for you, my boy!" Joseph exclaimed.

But Jesus could tell by the way Mary looked at him that she had mixed emotions. She didn't want him to be away so long, but certainly wouldn't do anything to prevent him from going.

The next day at the synagogue, Jesus waited until after the usual discussion of the scriptures to tell the teachers of Joseph's invitation. Jacob had already heard from his friend Joseph, and was smiling approval. indeed, all of them except Achim seemed pleased; and after some discussion, they voted three to one to release him, provided Jesus would supply a detailed written diary of his trip when he returned. Jesus happily acquiesced. Since he had already agreed to keep such a diary for Joseph, it would simply be a matter of making a second copy for the teachers.

Finally Joseph's driver arrived with details of the trip. Again he was in the donkey cart and wearing plain flax garb instead of his handsome livery. Jesus took the scroll with thanks and read it as he walked back into the house. He was to report to the caravan master who would be aboard the ship Cyprus Star in the Caesarea harbor. The time was set for daybreak on the first day of next month. The written instructions also advised him to bring bedding and plenty of clothing for both warm and cold weather. Wondering how he'd get to

Caesarea, he walked back outside where the driver was waiting and sent his grateful thank yous.

After the driver left, Jesus told his father of the instructions. Joseph was pleased and couldn't understand why Jesus looked so dejected. "What's wrong, my son?" he asked, putting his hand on Jesus' shoulder.

I have no way to get to Caesarea." Jesus was at the point of feeling that all was lost.

"Of course you do. I'll take you."

"Do you mean it? It's a very long trip, and over bumpy roads."

"Of course I mean it!"

Jesus threw his arms around his father and the tears rolled down his cheeks as he said a silent prayer of thanks to God.

On the day of departure, there were tearful goodbyes with Mary. And his parents gave him a bon voyage gift ...a set of small scrolls. It was the book of Isaiah, Jesus' favorite. Joseph said the scrolls had been made especially for him by the synagogue scribes through the generosity of the teachers.

"Even Achim?" Jesus asked.

"Even Achim."

And so the father and son got into the donkey cart and were on their way, turning around to wave at the weeping Mary for as long as they could see her.

The trip to Caesarea was uneventful. Joseph was a quiet man, and this day Jesus was unusually quiet. His mind was lost in thoughts of what might lie ahead.

Finally the great sea came into view, and then the magnificent city of Caesarea. They found the coastal road and followed it north until they came to the port. Among the ships docked there, the Cyprus Star was easy to find. It was much larger and had taller masts than any of the others. Jesus had never seen such a ship. It had two great masts, a prow taller than a house, and a large cabin amidships painted white. The hull had obviously been recently painted a deep green, with gold scrolled lettering on the bow identifying it as the Cyprus Star. Slaves were scurrying about the dock and the deck of the ship — loading baskets, boxes, large clay jars, and bales of wool. Soon several camels appeared on the dock with their drivers, and they were eased up the gangplank and back to the afterdeck. other men in colorful clothing were loading four-wheeled carts, horses, and mules.

Finally Jesus felt he could tarry no longer with his father, and they embraced lovingly. "God go with you, my boy," Joseph said.

Jesus was too choked up to answer, and he simply waved his hand slowly as Joseph directed the donkey cart back down the coastal road. Now, burdened with heavy sacks of bedding and clothing, Jesus climbed the gangplank.

"No visitors!" snapped the sentry on deck. Jesus wondered if he thought a visitor would be bringing bundles of bedding and clothing.

"I'm to report to a man named Ahaz, the caravan master," Jesus said, "and then to Amos, the captain."

"Who sent you?" the sentry asked.

"Joseph of Arimathea." Jesus presented the written instructions he had received.

As soon as he read them, the man's demeanor changed, and he stepped aside and bowed, politely directing Jesus to come aboard with a sweep of his right hand.

Just then a slender, clean—shaven man stepped forward and introduced himself as Ahaz, the caravan master. "Welcome aboard, Jesus. We've been expecting you. Put your things down on the deck over there and we'll go to meet Captain Amos."

Ahaz knocked on the door of the captain's cabin. "Amos, our passenger is here." The door opened to reveal a gigantic man with a red beard, huge teeth in a grinning mouth under a bushy red mustache, and the thickest of eyebrows.

"Welcome, Jesus," Amos growled. If he hadn't been grinning, Jesus would have thought him angry.

Amos summoned two servants. "This is Ram and this is Boaz. They'll attend to your needs throughout the journey. Ram! Boaz! Take your master's things to his cabin! Quickly now!" Amos' facial expression had changed to match his growling voice.

Jesus didn't know what to make of this. He'd never had servants before, and he didn't really like being called "master". But before Jesus could say anything, Amos disappeared back into his cabin and slammed the door.

"That's Amos," said Ahaz. "You'll get used to him. He has a heart of gold, but the manners of a mule. You'll get to know him better tonight when you join us for dinner."

Ahaz showed Jesus to his cabin, which was surprisingly spacious and comfortable. Ram and Boaz had already made up the bed and hung Jesus' clothing neatly on pegs. Jesus was displeased, however, to learn that it was the lot of Ram and Boaz to sleep on the deck outside his door. Later he would invite them to share his cabin, only to be refused by the shocked servants. No one had ever shown such kindness to them before. Later they chuckled as they shared the thought of what Amos might say and do if he found them sleeping in their master's cabin.

After a while Ram knocked on Jesus' cabin door and told him it was time to join the captain and the caravan master for dinner.

At dinner in the captain's cabin — a simple meal of soup, beef, and bread — the two men gave Jesus a preview of their journey.

First they would go by sea from Caesarea to Cyprus, then from Cyprus to Antioch. At Antioch, the camel caravan would disembark and the Cyprus Star would take on a homeward—bound caravan for the return trip to Caesarea. Cautioning Jesus of the dangers in the desert, Ahaz said the camel caravan would go from Antioch, across mountains and more desert en route to Palmyra. From Palmyra, they would follow Alexander's route along the Euphrates River to Babylon and the Persian Gulf. Here they would board another of Joseph's ships, the Persian Star, and sail south in the Gulf to Persia. From there they would go by caravan to India, across India to Indraprasthal, and finally through the Himalayan pass to Tibet. They would then spend three weeks in Tibet to unload the last of their goods, negotiate with Tibetan merchants, buy, and reload for the return journey.

Jesus was speechless. To say he was overwhelmed would be an understatement. He had no idea the journey would be of this magnitude. Finally he asked, "How long will we be away?"

"Maybe three months, maybe six," Ahaz said. "You never know. We're at the mercy of the tides and the winds, the pirates at sea, the bandits and the dust storms and mountain blizzards on land. If we're lucky, we'll be home in about four months. I hope you had no plans for the rest of the year."

"No, nothing at all. My life is dedicated to this journey for as long as it takes."

"Good!" growled Amos, and Ahaz nodded agreement.

For the rest of the evening, Jesus answered questions about his schooling, his carpentry apprenticeship, and his goals in life. The two men seemed disappointed to learn that sailing and trading had no place in Jesus' thoughts of his future.

When it was time to retire, Jesus found that the servants had turned down the covers on his bunk and put a carafe of fresh water on a table near his bedside. There was even a fresh bowl of grapes nearby. But the servants were nowhere to be seen.

Jesus tried to read himself to sleep by candlelight. He had unrolled the first scroll of the book of Isaiah, but he was too preoccupied with everything Ahaz and Amos had said, and found himself reading and re—reading the same words over and over again.

The ship was rolling like a cradle in the gentle waves of the harbor, and this made Jesus feel very sleepy. Finally he fell asleep, and the next thing he knew it was first light. The gulls were noisily calling everybody to get up, but when he looked out the window, there was no land in sight. He went out on deck and looked in all four directions, still no land. Apparently they had sailed from port during the night.

## CHAPTER 10 — JOURNEY BY SEA

And so at last they were at sea. The full sails of the Cyprus Star were catching the same gentle wind that was moving some fluffy clouds northward. Otherwise, the sky was a brilliant blue.

Jesus was getting his first look at the great ship. He admired the sailors as they went quickly about their work. Muscular, deeply tanned men, they wore no shirts and a garment that was unusual for Jewish men, tight-fitting black trousers. And they did not wear sandals; they wore something on their feet that was unique to sailors, something made of leather called shoes. The sailors moved about the deck quickly, clambering up the rope ladders to the tops of the masts to tie a rope here, remove one there, all at the command of Captain Amos, who stood at the great wheel, shouting orders in his deep, rasping voice.

Every nook and cranny of the ship was as clean as a whistle. Everything seemed to be freshly painted or polished... the hull was a deep green, the cabins gleaming white, the trim bright red and green. The masts and decks were highly polished cedar, but were not slippery.

As Jesus made his way to the starboard side of the deck, he came across Ram and Boaz. They were both mending clothing which Jesus recognized as his own.

"Good morning sir," they said, almost in unison, as they sprang to their feet.

"Good morning. Please continue your work. But ...are those my garments you are mending? I didn't know they were in need of repair."

"We just thought we'd tighten up the seams," Ram said.

Jesus smiled. He suspected they were making work for themselves so the captain wouldn't find something harder for them to do.

"Good. And thank you," Jesus said as he moved farther forward.

All around the forecastle which served as the crew's quarters, were the camels. Durinq the niqht all four of each camel's legs were securely tied to deck cleats. But now that the camel drivers were awake and able to care for them, their legs were free. only a slack rein was tied from each camel's harness to the gunwale.

"Good morning," Jesus said, introducing himself to the camel drivers. They were a bit taken aback. They knew Jesus was Joseph of Arimathea's guest aboard ship, and therefore a person to be honored. They were surprised when Jesus seemed to treat them as equals. "Tell me about your cargo," he said.

One of the drivers, a man named Perez, jumped to his feet. Pointing to the bales, and barrels, and stacks of wood amidship, he said, smiling, "We have barley and wheat from Galilee, cedar from Lebanon, olives and olive oil from Judea, plums and figs from Samaria, salted fish from the Sea of Galilee, perfumes and spices from Idumea, papyrus from Egypt, wool from Judea, dyes made in Tyre, vessels, goblets, bottles, and gold jewelry from the artisans of Jerusalem and Caesarea.

"How does the captain gather goods from so many places?" Jesus asked.

"It isn't the captain who does it," Perez said, "It's Joseph of Arimathea himself. He travels almost continuously in his fine carriage, stopping in many cities and rural places to buy goods. Then he dispatches camel caravans to fetch them and bring them to his ships in the port of Caesarea."

"And where will you trade these goods?"

Another camel driver spoke up. "In every city we visit, the captain or caravan master Ahaz, or the two together, will visit local merchants and sell or trade for local products they know Joseph can sell at a profit."

"What kinds of goods will you acquire?" Jesus asked.

"Ivory and cotton in India, silk in Tibet," the man answered. Smiling to reveal several teeth missing, another man said, "Tapestries in Persia, and crafted leather goods in Palmyra, fancy jardinieres in Babylon."

"Very interesting," said Jesus, thanking the men and moving on around the bow of the ship and back along the port side deck toward his cabin.

When he arrived there, he found Ram and Boaz folding the garments they had finished "mending". It was obvious they were doing their work slowly and laboriously.

Jesus smiled and thanked them.

"Tell me," Jesus said, "you two seem to be intelligent men. How did you happen to become slaves.?"

Ram spoke first. "I was a successful dye merchant in the bazaar at Tyre. But I was easily tempted by strong drink and loose women. It wasn't long before I was deeply in debt and thrown into debtors' prison. When I was finally brought to trial by the Romans, I was sentenced to a lifetime of slavery. Fortunately, I was purchased at the slave market by one of Joseph of Arimathea's clerks. Joseph is very kind to his slaves and insists that his ship captains and caravan masters follow his example."

"Ram is right," said Boaz. "I too was purchased by one of Joseph's clerks at the Jerusalem slave market. And I have always been grateful. The word gets around quickly in the slave markets about the kindness of masters like Joseph and the cruelty of others."

Jesus didn't approve of slavery, but he was pleased to hear this about Joseph, although he was not surprised. "Were you sentenced to slavery also, Boaz?"

"No. We were very poor, and my wife and children were on the verge of starving. So, in spite of the protests and tears of my family, I sold myself into slavery to give them a better life than I could have given them. Unfortunately, I heard later that thieves robbed the money from my beloved before she could get home with it."

Jesus said a silent prayer for the slaves and their families.

By the time Ram and Boaz had finished their stories, it was time for the mid—morning meal. And so the two slaves departed for the crew's mess, and Jesus found his way to the captain's cabin.

Amos and Ahaz were already seated at the wooden table, which had been scrubbed for so many years that the tabletop edges were rounded. The white—clad ship's cook stood at the head of the table, but jumped to pull Jesus' chair back for him.

"Sorry I'm late," Jesus said.

"You're not," said Ahaz. "We just arrived ourselves."

The cook disappeared into the galley, and quickly reappeared with plates of hot barley cakes, fresh from the oven, steaming cups of hot wine sweetened with honey, and a plate of cold meat. The two older men ate hungrily, leaving little time for conversation. And so Jesus, between bites of food and sips of wine, told them of his morning tour of the deck.

"Don't get too friendly with the slaves," growled Captain Amos. "They'll take advantage of you."

"I'd say the same for the camel drivers," Ahaz warned. "If they think you're their equal, they'll be expecting too much of you on the journey across the desert."

Jesus took both of these pieces of advice with a grain of salt. If it cost him some advantage to be friendly with the slaves and servants, so be it. He was not about to treat these people in an unfriendly way.

"You'll need the protection of these men at times of trouble," Ahaz continued. "There are often pirate raids at sea and bandit raids in the desert. The camel drivers and the ship's crew have the weapons and the skills to fight them off. You don't want them to think you should be fighting alongside them."

"Fighting is very distasteful to me," Jesus said.

"Take heed then. The crew will be your protectors at sea, and the camel drivers on land."

Changing the subject, Ahaz said, "I hope you brought plenty of warm clothing. The cold and snow and wind in the mountains can be very severe."

"I brought several woolen garments," Jesus said.

"They may not be enough. We'll try to find some sheepskin for you in Antioch." Unfortunately Ahaz forgot his promise, and Jesus was not bold enough tǫ remind him.

The rest of this first day at sea was spent enjoying the pleasant weather and the invigorating sea air. Passing Jesus on deck, Captain Amos growled, "Don't get too used to this good weather; I feel a storm in my bones."

Jesus took the seat on deck that Ram and Boaz had prepared for him. He found it was a wonderful place to read the scrolls of his beloved book of Isaiah.

In the morning, Jesus awoke to find that they were docked in a large port. This must be the port of Salamis on the island of Cyprus, he thought.

When he had bathed and dressed, Ram and Boaz confirmed this, telling him the captain had sent a message saying Jesus was free to explore the city since they would not be sailing for another 24 hours. The captain had also suggested that Jesus take his meals on shore until the mid-morning meal the next day, since the ship's cook had been given the day off. Their next stop was Antioch, and they would be setting sail for that Syrian mainland port the next morning.

Jesus was glad to have this opportunity to explore a new place, and so, taking a few belongings with him in a small sack, he walked along the dock until he came to a seaside road. Should he go north or south? There seemed to be more habitation northward, but more natural beauty southward. And so Jesus headed south.

Soon the road deteriorated into a trail along the beach, an expanse of white sand bordering the azure blue sea that was gently lapping against the shore.

A man lounging on the beach greeted Jesus in Greek. But he could only respond in Aramaic, saying, "Sorry, but I do not speak Greek."

Kicking up a lot of sand, the man jumped to his feet saying, "But I speak Aramaic!"

The two then engaged in a conversation about Cyprus that lasted the rest of the morning.

The man told Jesus that Cyprus had been inhabited for over 6,000 years, that the Greeks had come about 1,200 years ago, establishing city—states like those on their mainland. Salamis was one of these city states—

At an hour much later than Jesus' usual mealtime the man asked Jesus if he was hungry. Eagerly answering "Yes!" he asked the man where he might find a meal.

"Come with me," he said, leading Jesus back toward the city.

Soon they came upon a seaside hut in which a man and his wife were boiling fish in a pot over a coal fire.

"Have you ever tasted fish like this?" his new friend asked.

"Never."

"Then you're in for a treat."

As the woman served piping hot fish in pottery bowls with ramekins of olive oil, chunks of bread, and goblets of cool wine alongside, Jesus watched as his new friend removed the bones from the flesh.

"Dip your fish in the olive oil," the man said.

Jesus obeyed, and was thrilled with the unique taste. "Delicious!" he exclaimed. "I've never tasted anything like it." And the two consumed three large bowls of the delicacy.

That night Jesus returned to the ship, not wanting to spend any of his limited funds on lodging ashore.

The ship was almost deserted. The lone crewman on watch was surprised to see Jesus, telling him most of the men would stay on shore, drinking and wenching the night away.

"Even the slaves?" Jesus asked.

"Even the slaves. Joseph gives his slaves a lot of freedom, and they never try to run away."

After a good night's sleep on the gently rocking ship, Jesus was tempted to go back to the Cypriot beach to try to find his friend again, but he thought better of it.

Instead, he wandered around the narrow streets of Salamis, taking in the sounds and the sights, and the smells of a strange city. Soon he came upon a synagogue. He went in, knelt down, and meditated. After a really long conversation with his heavenly Father, Jesus finally fell asleep. He was embarrassed to be awakened by a rabbi. But after telling the holy man that he too was a synagogue teacher from Nazareth, the older man invited Jesus to stay for the mid—afternoon meal.

After sharing the rabbi's meal of flat bread, goat's milk cheese, and tea, and much conversation about the religions of the world, Jesus made his way back to the ship.

Unlike the sailing ships that would ply the seas centuries later, the ships of Jesus' time, like the Cyprus Star, were heavy and slow—moving. While as large as some of the later ships, these ships of Joseph's utilized only four sails ...a mainsail and two triangular top sails from the main mast amidships, and a fourth square sail from a short stern mast.

When Jesus woke up in the morning it was as dark as night. The wind was howling, and the rain was lashing against the little window of his cabin. The great ship was pitching from side to side, and

Jesus could see the spray coming over the sides at least a man's height above the gunwales.

Ram and Boaz were nowhere to be seen, so Jesus decided to stay in the shelter of his cabin until, hopefully, the storm would die down.

The shouts of the captain, echoed by the sailors, were clearly audible through the walls of the little cabin.

"All hands make haste!" the captain shouted. "Loose the top sails! Man the main sheet and be prepared to haul her in."

The rain soon soaked the crewmen to the skin, and the wind tried its best to pull them from their positions on the deck or on the mast.

Within minutes the captain was shouting, "Double reef the top sails! Likewise the trysail!" Soon the ship was under only the loosened mainsail, and the captain would soon give the order to double reef that one too, lie under easy sail, and wait for the storm to blow itself out.

The storm lasted the full day, and there was no relief for the small crew ...no food, no rest, no comfort for their bleeding hands. Jesus prayed for them, and wished he had the skills to relieve them, one at a time.

Finally it was over. The wind eased off. The rain stopped, and the sun peeked through from between two black clouds.

The crew fell exhausted to the deck, and the captain slumped over his wheel.

Summoning the slaves and the camel drivers to help, Jesus rushed to minister to the men, wiping their brows, binding up their wounds, helping them eat a cup of the soup from the huge kettle the cook had brought up on deck.

By nightfall, all was peaceful again, the few crew members who were able, got the ship under sail again, and the journey continued eastward.

In the morning, soon after Jesus ventured out on deck, the city of Antioch came into view ...hundreds of gleaming white buildings arranged

*Joseph Radder*

like steps on the green hillsides. occasionally a
red or blue roof punctuated the scene.

    "Syria! Antioch! At last!" Jesus thought.

    "Thanks be to God!"

## CHAPTER 11 — ANTIOCH AND ARABIA

Antioch[1] was the ancient capital of the Greek kings of Syria. It had long been one of the most important cities in Asia. Actually 14 miles from the sea, Antioch's seaport was a coastal suburb called Seleucia. There the Greeks had built a port to accommodate the great merchant ships like Joseph's, as well as the Syrian warships which were kept in readiness there.

When Jesus went ashore at Seleucia he quickly noticed that the buildings, which had appeared from the sea to be gleaming white, were actually many different shades of white, ivory, and beige. And the hills, which appeared to be solid green grass, were, in fact, abundant with flowers. In the distance, the larger buildings of Antioch could be

---

[1]Antioch was destined, some years later, to be the place that followers of Jesus would first be called Christians. It was also to be the first place Judaism and Christianity would separate, and the Christian mission to gentiles would begin in earnest.

seen, also on green hillsides. In Seleucia, each house had flowers of every color around it, from borders of sweet alyssum to tall lilies. Jesus particularly noticed one flower, very delicate in shape. All of its petals were white except one which had an intricate pink and red design on it. What an imaginative creator my heavenly father is, Jesus thought.

There were hedges and shrubs too, many with blossoms or berries. Flowering trees were everywhere. Jesus had never seen a more beautiful place.

With a small sack of belongings over his shoulder, a leather sack of coins tied to his cincture, Jesus hired a donkey cart to take him into the city. Once there, he dismissed the cart and driver and set out to explore its winding, hilly streets.

In time, he came upon a wine shop, went in, and found it not unlike similar establishments in Galilee. Dark and cool inside, the shop featured a huge wine press in one corner. Wine of various vintages and origins was kept in earthenware jars sealed with bees—wax. Piled three or four high on shelves, some were open to provide wine to the customer, who would either purchase a goatskin bagful to take home, or a goblet full to consume on the premises.

Jesus was reminded of a similar place in the hotel at Sebaste, where he had met the temptress. He wondered if similar women frequented this place as well. Jesus was confident, however, that this would not be a problem, since God had promised him he would never again be tempted by lust.

Unlike the surly tavern keeper in Sebaste, the proprietor here was a talkative, jovial man. While most Syrians spoke Greek, this man also knew Aramaic. He seemed pleased that Jesus wanted only a goblet of wine to drink at one of the crude tables. He hoped his lone customer would stay for a while and they could talk.

A pesky fly kept buzzing around the two men, first lighting on the wine merchant's nose, then on Jesus' arm. Try as they might, they could not shoo him away. First the man would swat the fly with his big hand, then Jesus would wave him away, but to no avail.

"Why do you suppose God made flies? or are they the work of the devil?" the wine merchant asked.

Perhaps they are the work of the devil," Jesus said. "But the evil one did not make all insects. Some were made by God and serve good purposes."

"Why, then, does God allow evil works to exist on earth?" the man asked.

"I learned long ago," Jesus said, "that God reigns supreme in heaven, and the devil reigns supreme in hell. But here on earth, both God's power for good and the devil's power for evil are at work, and constantly in conflict."

"That makes sense," the man said.

"But if, as you suggest, the fly is the work of the devil, it is merely a small and unimportant manifestation of the devil's mischief. He works more dangerously through men, causing them to be murderers, adulterers, warmongers, liars, thieves, all kinds of evildoers."

"You seem to have an unusual knowledge of such things," the wine merchant noted.

"I am a teacher ...in the synagogue at Nazareth. I'm presently on leave, traveling with a trading mission."

"That sounds interesting." The man noticed that Jesus had finished his wine, and offered to refill his goblet without charge.

"It's a good vintage. And you're very kind," Jesus said, "but I must be on my way."

The man was clearly disappointed to see him leave.

The sun was blinding after the dark wine shop, but Jesus soon became accustomed to it again, as he continued to follow the curving, narrow street up the hill.

Before long, he came upon a bazaar. Remembering the star of David pin he had purchased for his mother, he thought, now I can look for something for my father.

Going from table to table, he saw nothing suitable, until he came to a table full of knives. The man there had expensive artfully—carved ivory—handled knives, some reasonably priced knives with bone handles, and others with wooden handles. These were the least expensive. Jesus couldn't afford the ivory; and the wood was not, in his judgment, adequate for a gift. But there was just one knife with a handle of lightcolored bone that caught his fancy. This one would be perfect for Joseph to use to whittle shapes of wood in his shop, Jesus thought.

He knew enough not to pay the first price the man asked; and so, after some haggling, the two agreed on what Jesus felt was a reasonable price.

"I'll take it if you'll put it in one of those blue velvet bags with the gold string," Jesus said.

Slapping the side of his head with his hand, the man exclaimed, "How can I feed my family when my customers steal from me?" As he said this, he was inserting the knife in the velvet bag Jesus had selected.

Smiling, Jesus accepted the knife in the bag, paid the man, and went on his way.

After leaving the bazaar, Jesus sensed that someone was following him. Turning quickly, he saw a large dark figure in dirty rough flax garments. The man had unkempt hair and an tangled black beard. His eyes were piercing, even though barely visible under bushy black brows. He quickly looked away when he realized Jesus had seen him.

Several minutes later, Jesus again turned around quickly. The man was still following him.

Luckily a Temple came into view. Jesus hurried to it and went in, waiting in a dark corner just inside to see if the man would come in also. He didn't. And so Jesus went into the Temple and knelt to pray.

After some time, he went out into the street again. And there was the man waiting for him. The street seemed to be deserted except for the two.

"What do you want from me?" Jesus called.

Quickly, the man ran to Jesus' side, pushed him into a narrow alley between the Temple and the building next door, and pressed his foul—smelling body against Jesus'. Jesus resisted, and the man struck him in the face, encircling his waist with his other strong arm, applying so much pressure that Jesus cried out in pain, "Please stop! What do you want from me?"

Clamping his dirty hand over Jesus' mouth, the man whispered, "That knife you bought at the bazaar. And your money." His breath smelled of a mingling of stale wine, onions, and garlic.

The man was so much bigger and stronger than Jesus there was no point in resisting further, and so he handed over his small leather pouch of coins and the knife. The man made off with it quickly as Jesus tried to rearrange his clothing. Jesus could feel his cheek swelling, and the blood running down from the side of his face where the man had struck him.

The building next to the Temple seemed to be the rabbi's residence, and so Jesus went to the door and knocked.

A rabbi opened the door just a crack, but when he saw Jesus' appearance, he tried to close it again.

Pressing on the door, Jesus begged, "Please! I am a teacher from Nazareth, and I have been assaulted in your alley by a thief."

Noting Jesus' educated manner of speaking, the rabbi opened the door for him to enter.

The rabbi turned out to be a kindly man, and both he and his wife ministered to Jesus' wounds, gave him cool water to drink and to wash with, and asked him to stay and rest a while.

After a time, Jesus thanked the two and made his way down the hill toward the port, hoping he would not see the thief again.

He had intended to find a meal in town, but now that his money was gone, he was forced to go back to the ship to share whatever food the man on watch could provide. There was no way to hire a donkey cart now, and so Jesus had to walk the 14 miles back to Seleucia. Fortunately, it was all downhill.

Thank God I brought only a small portion of my money with me, Jesus thought. The rest of his small stake was safe in his cabin on the Cyprus Star.

After getting over the shock of seeing Jesus' bruised face and soiled garments, the watchman welcomed him aboard. Surprisingly, he was able to come up with a much better meal than Jesus expected. Bread and cheese, with water to drink, would have been enough; but the watchman took advantage of this excuse to go into the cook's pantry and help himself to a large portion of cold meat, some fresh fruit, olives, bread, cheese, and wine.

As the two ate together on the deck, Jesus told the watchman about his experiences in town.

"Someone should have warned you against going to that bazaar alone!" the watchman said. "That's right on the edge of the very worst part of Antioch. It's a haven for thieves and all sorts of bad people."

Jesus knew from experience that the man spoke the truth.

Now, their holiday in Antioch over, it was time for the caravan to leave the ship and make room for a homebound caravan to board.

Jesus said farewell to Captain Amos and with Ram and Boaz in the high drivers' seat up front, he boarded the carriage that had been provided for him.

The covered carriage was not as luxurious as the one he had admired on the way to Jerusalem, but it was certainly comfortable enough ...well—furnished with cushions, rugs, and heavy removable curtains. The waterproof camel—hide roof could be rolled back when it was cool enough to do so on sunny days.

It was not practical to take a camel caravan through the city's narrow, winding, hilly streets. And so, leading the little band from his carriage at the head of the line of camels and mule—drawn wagons, Ahaz took the caravan around Seleucia and then Antioch. Jesus' carriage had a preferred safe position about halfway back.

Their route, Jesus had been told, would take them across the low mountains and into the Arabian desert. Jesus had expected it to be a long journey from the lush greenery of suburban Antioch to the parched, cactus—pocked desert, but in less than an hour he could see nothing but sand, purple rocky hills, an occasional cactus, and now and then a gray—green bush. From time to time a scorpion appeared on a rock, or a coral snake slithered across the sand. otherwise, the desert seemed totally lifeless. Jesus marveled that there was a trail, apparently well—traveled, through such a desolate place.

Just after sunset, they reached a caravanserie, very unlike those where he had stayed with his parents on the road to Jerusalem. This caravanserie was much more austere, obviously designed to accommodate trader caravans. Each stable had a bunk—room alongside for camel drivers and slaves. There were only three rooms at one end, for the caravan master and privileged travelers. Jesus was assigned to one of these rooms, which Ram and Boaz prepared for him, making up the cot with bedding, and bringing a pitcher of water and a basin. Again Jesus felt guilty about enjoying relatively comfortable accommodations, while Ram and Boaz and the camel drivers were, in fact, sharing their sleeping quarters with the smelly camels.

Ram, always the more talkative of the two, took it upon himself to warn Jesus not to go outside the walls of the caravanserie. "It's dangerous out there at night," he said. "The hills are full of predators, and there are deadly snakes and scorpions all over the desert floor."

"But the gate seems to be wide open. Won't they come in here?" Jesus asked.

"That's why there's always a camel driver on watch, two hours on, four hours off. If a predatory animal enters the gate, the watchman will sound the alarm, and the others will come running with slingshots, rods, and clubs."

"I'll stay right here in my room then," Jesus said. Both Ram and Boaz nodded approval.

In the morning, they started out again, heading eastward toward Tadmor[1]. When mid-morning came, they stopped for a meal; and Ram told Jesus that

---

[1] Palmyra.

CaravanMaster Ahaz would like him to join him at his wagon.

It was already hot, and so the slaves had quickly erected a lean—to alongside the caravan—master's wagon, to provide shelter from the sun. Ahaz was sitting in a chair under this lean—to when Jesus arrived. "Come, my boy," he said, "share a cup of wine and take your meal with me, and I'll try to scare you to death about what lies ahead."

And so, for an hour, as they shared the meal of soup, bread, cheese, and wine, Ahaz warned Jesus of the dangers of desert travel. "There are not only wild animals and reptiles out there," he said, "there are bands of robbers as well. We were fortunate not to be raided by pirates at sea, but that means we're due for some trouble. Just keep one eye open when you sleep."

Jesus smiled and promised he would.

The trip to Tadmor the next day was as uneventful as Ahaz said it would be exciting. After dreary hours of bumping over rocks and sand, they heard Ahaz' loud voice shouting, "Stop! We'll make camp here!"

Jesus could see the silhouettes of buildings in the distance. That must be Tadmor, he thought. I wonder why we're stopping here. Why didn't we go into the city?

Ahaz told him later that he always camped far enough from a city to make it difficult for the men to wander in there at night. "If you get too close," he said, "they'll all go into town, get drunk, and half of them won't ever come back."

When night fell, the temperature dropped dramatically. Ram and Boaz built a campfire outside Jesus' tent. When he went outside to warm himself by the fire, he could see other fires all over the camp.

After a while, he decided to go for a walk around the camp. Soon he came upon a group of camel drivers shooting dice. They invited Jesus to join them; but he declined, electing to watch instead.

Later that evening, while Jesus was still watching the dice game, they heard a sudden noise.

The camel drivers all jumped to their feet and picked up their rods, slingshots, and clubs, whispering, "Arab robbers!"

One of the drivers advised Jesus to go to his tent, but he preferred to try to help. And so, even though he found all violence to be distasteful, he picked up one of the extra clubs and followed the men in the direction of the noise.

By the time they arrived at the scene of the robbery, the bandits were already driving their horses at a fast gallop out of camp. They carried their loot on the back of one of the horses.

Two of Ahaz' drivers, obviously in pain, lay bleeding on the ground. A third was not moving. Jesus ran to him.

"He's dead," Jesus said.

"It's Perez! Those bastards!" one of the drivers shouted.

By that time Ahaz had arrived on the scene, and said, "Abed, you'll have to take over. Pick up all of Perez' things and add them to your pack. The rest of you, take care of the injured men first, bury Perez in the sand here, and mark the spot by writing his name in his blood on a stone."

Jesus went to the injured men and helped bind up their wounds, saying a prayer for them and for Perez' soul as he worked. Two of the drivers made a stretcher with two rods and a large camel skin, and carried the men, one by one, back to their tents.

After all the men had left, Jesus saw Ahaz sitting in the sand with his head in his hands. He was crying. Jesus went to comfort him.

"He was only a camel driver; but when I too was only a driver, we were best friends," Ahaz said in a shaky voice. "Because of the difference in our positions, we could no longer be friends; but when we saw each other, we'd always look at each other knowingly. I think he knew I still loved him, even though I couldn't speak to him except to give him a command."

"I'm sure he did," Jesus said. "And you can be assured he is with his God."

"Do you really believe that?" Ahaz asked.

"By all means," Jesus said. "We're on this earth only to prepare for a better life ahead. Don't mourn for Perez. Rejoice for him."

"I really mourn for myself," Ahaz said.

"I know. I know," Jesus took Ahaz' hand in his and squeezed it.

The next day, Ahaz delayed the usual early morning start because of the injured men. But they appeared for the mid-morning meal looking much better, and wellrested. Ahaz and some of the drivers had counted the losses and repaired the damaged saddle bags.

"Much jewelry and gold were lost," one of the drivers told Jesus. "And half that loss will come out of our pay. Why is God so cruel?"

"God isn't cruel. Long ago he gave men free will. Using that will, some men decided to become thieves and murderers, others chose to be less generous than they should be. We all suffer from man's inhumanity to man, not from God's cruelty."

"I wish I could believe that," one of the drivers said.

"One day you will," Jesus replied.

When they arrived at Tadmor, they stopped at a trading center on the edge of the city. Here buyers and sellers of all kinds of goods gathered to meet both eastbound and westbound caravans.

Ahaz told Jesus that he would have a half day to explore the city, whispering because he didn't want the slaves and camel drivers to hear him. He needed their help in unloading and loading of goods.

Even so, Ram heard, or suspected, what Ahaz had said. "I could go with you, Master," he said. "I know the local language and the way around the city. I can keep you away from the bad areas."

Remembering his experience in Antioch, Jesus thought this would be a good idea, and so he ran after Ahaz and asked his permission to take Ram with him. "Then you'd better take Boaz too," Ahaz said. "These slaves can be troublesome when they get jealous of each other."

Ram was obviously not pleased when he heard Jesus invite Boaz to accompany them. He had been hoping to have something to boast about and lord over his fellow slave.

Jesus found Tadmor to be smaller, less interesting, and not as beautiful as Antioch. The three visited a bazaar, and Jesus looked for a knife like the one the thief had stolen from him in Antioch, but nothing like it was to be found.

After a time they stopped in a wine shop. The proprietor would not serve the slaves, who wore large identifying tattoos on their foreheads. And so Jesus refused to buy any wine. Jesus then asked for water for the two slaves and himself. Scowling, the wine shopkeeper filled three goblets with water, placed them on the counter, and then promptly took two of them and smashed them on the stone floor. Jesus, horrified, took the remaining glass, smashed it too, and then left hurriedly with his two friends.

Jesus asked Ram where there was a Temple, but the slave knew of none. Jesus concluded then and there that he didn't like this apparently pagan city, and decided they should go back to camp. Ram and Boaz were disappointed. They had hoped Jesus would give them some time alone to find some slave girls. But even though Jesus had been told the slaves were loyal to Joseph and would never run away, he didn't want to take that chance. After all, these men were, under Roman law, Joseph of Arimathea's property. And they had been entrusted to Jesus' care.

By late afternoon all the goods Ahaz had sold had been unloaded and delivered to the buyers, and the newly purchased goods had been bundled and strapped to the camels' backs or placed in the cargo wagons.

As they departed, Ahaz announced, "Next stop — the Euphrates River."

Jesus wondered how they could make all that distance before nightfall. He soon had the answer, however, as the caravan turned onto a paved road heading east. Ram told him this road went all the way to the river, and then to Babylon. "Tomorrow we'll begin following Alexander's route," he said.

Jesus took a turn riding up top with Ram as Boaz walked alongside. He would not ride in the carriage as Jesus invited him to do. "It'll be bad enough if the master sees you up there and me walking alongside."

Jesus found the view of the desert much better from his new position. And the conversation with Ram was interesting. Later Boaz would come up to drive the horses while Ram walked. Boaz was a man of few words, responding, "Yes" and "No" to Jesus' questions and comments, but not saying much more.

Jesus found it difficult to try to carry on a conversation with him, and soon they rode along in silence.

At the next rest stop, Jesus motioned to Ram to resume his place up top while Jesus climbed back into the carriage. As he sat among the cushions, enjoying the fact that the road was finally smooth enough to enable him to read, Jesus reflected on what Ram had told him about the roads. Apparently they had been built by the Assyrians and Persians, but were not paved until the Romans came. The main purpose of the Romans' great network of paved roads, of course, was to move their armies quickly to wherever they were needed.

They reached the banks of the Euphrates well before nightfall and made camp there. It was much cooler now. Jesus surmised that the air was cooled by the water of the river flowing from the north.

Before retiring, Jesus took a walk along the riverbank, enjoying the cool night air and the moon's reflection on the water. He thanked God again for all that was beautiful, and stood by the river meditating for a long time, finally returning, reluctantly, to his tent.

Ram and Boaz each took a turn standing guard outside Jesus' tent, and so he slept well through the peaceful moonlit night.

In the morning, the caravan started out for Babylon, following the route of Alexander the Great. This day, being unusually cool, Jesus decided to open up the carriage and take full advantage of the invigorating fresh air. First he removed the side curtains and then rolled back the top. Suddenly he found himself able to converse with Ram and Boaz as well.

At the last overnight stop, Ahaz had given Jesus a scroll telling the story of Alexander the Great. And so, he decided to share it with Ram and Boaz.

Standing in the front of the carriage with his head just below their seat, he said, "Ram, Boaz, listen to this."

229

Reading aloud from the scroll, he read, "When in his early twenties, King Alexander III of Macedonia built an army of Macedonian and Greek troops, stormed into Persia at the head of that army, and defeated the last Persian ruler. In less than twelve years, he assembled the largest empire Asia Minor had ever seen."

"When did this happen, sir?" Ram asked.

"About 300 years ago," Jesus responded. Continuing, Jesus read, "Alexander then marched through Palestine and Egypt, where he founded the city of Alexandria on the Nile."

Breaking a long silence, Boaz said, "Nobody ever read to us before. Thank you, sir. We really appreciate the way you treat us as equals." Ram nodded in agreement.

"All men are equal," Jesus said. "But let me continue: Alexander then led his army back through Palestine to Persia and toward India, executing his captured enemies by a method he invented called crucifixion."

"What is crucifixion?" Ram asked.

"Apparently it's a very slow and painful method of execution whereby the prisoner is nailed to two crossed tree limbs. The cross, as it is called, is then raised to a vertical position, and the man is left there to die. The Romans use it occasionally to this day."

"Sounds horrible," said Ram.

"I daresay it is," said Jesus, and then finished the story of Alexander, telling how he came down with a severe fever while sojourning in Babylon, and died.

"How old was he?" asked Ram.

"We don't know exactly. It's believed he was still in his early thirties."

"I say he deserved to die," Ram said. "Any man who would kill other men by crucifying them doesn't deserve to live." Jesus didn't comment. He had a strange feeling that one day he would hear the word "crucify" again.

Shortly after Jesus returned to his cushioned seat, they passed another paved road branching off to the west. "Where does that road go?" Jesus asked.

"To Antioch," Boaz said. Just then Jesus saw a large rock on which the word Antioch had been inscribed with an arrow pointing west.

"Why didn't we take that route here instead of the rough trail through Tadmore?" Jesus asked.

"This paved road from Antioch misses Tadmor by many miles, and it was important for Master Ahaz to stop at the trading center there," Ram explained.

Satisfied, Jesus settled back to read the scrolls of his favorite book of Isaiah. Soon he dozed off.

About two hours later, he heard Ram's voice, "Wake up, sir, you can see the city of Babylon from here."

Wiping his eyes and shading them from the blinding sun with his hand, Jesus looked south.

Yes! There it was ...a hazy but unmistakable group of buildings silhouetted against the blue sky.

In his studies to prepare for this trip, Jesus had read that Babylon was one of the oldest cities of antiquity. Now, in Jesus' 23rd year, Babylon was almost 2,000 years old. On both sides of the Euphrates River, halfway between Baghdad and the Persian Gulf, Babylon was Ahaz' next major destination.

Before long they could see that the city was surrounded by a wall. Jesus guessed it was about 15 miles long on each side. Unlike Antioch's white and green look, Babylon was much more colorful, with many spired buildings, some with onion—shaped tops.

Jesus remembered that his mother Mary had told him of three Magi from Babylon named Gaspar, Melchior, and Balthazar, who had stopped at his birthplace in Bethlehem and had left gifts of gold, frankincense, and myrrh. They would be very old men now, if indeed they were still alive. Jesus wondered if they might still be living in Babylon.

Joseph Radder

Wouldn't it be wonderful if he could meet them, he thought.

Again Ahaz made camp far enough outside the city to prevent the wanderings of his slaves and camel drivers. However, he told Jesus he would be taking a wagon—load of goods into the city in the morning and Jesus was welcome to join him.

When they arrived in the great city, Jesus was impressed by its orderly design. Unlike the narrow, winding streets of Antioch, Babylon's streets formed a geometric pattern, mostly squares and triangles. Ahaz left Jesus at the corner formed by two of these streets, telling him he'd meet him at this corner to go back to camp, in about six hours. Jesus suspected Ahaz had a woman friend somewhere in Babylon. He had looked forward to Ahaz' company, but smiled at the thought of Ahaz' illicit escape.

Jesus spent his first three hours in the city asking everyone who would listen if they knew any men named Gaspar, Melchior, or Balthazar. But he had no luck.

234

Finally, he accidentally came upon the tomb of Alexander the Great, a magnificent structure decorated with sculpture and clay tablets depicting Alexander in battle.

Next he visited a temple, not of the Jewish religion, but dedicated to Babylonian gods, the chief of which was named Marduk. The temple[1] was a staged tower of molded bricks, lavishly decorated with statues, tablets, and paintings. Jesus became so fascinated with it that he almost lost track of time and, glancing at a sundial in the temple, he noted it was time to meet Ahaz. And so he ran back to the appointed corner to find Ahaz just arriving also.

Ahaz' face was flushed, and he was smiling in a contented way. His breath revealed that he had enjoyed more than one goblet of wine. Jesus smiled too, recognizing that his friend had indeed enjoyed a pleasant afternoon.

---

[1] On the site of the structure known in the Bible as the Tower of Babel.

235

During the walk back to camp, Jesus talked enthusiastically about what he had seen in Babylon. Ahaz just smiled. He had seen it all many times.

Early the next morning the caravan left the camp and passed through the streets of Babylon. At a city square, the caravan was halted to allow a person of royalty to pass. Carried on a litter by six brightly dressed attendants, this man, a very old man, was bearded and wore a deep blue turban on his head, fastened by a gold medallion signifying his royal birth. He too was dressed in colorful garments, but unlike those of the attendants, his were trimmed with gold. The litter bearers chose a route through the square that brought the royal personage very close to Jesus' carriage. And as they passed, there was a momentary spark of recognition between the two. Could it be Gaspar, Melchior, or Balthazar? Jesus would never know.

As the caravan moved on and turned a corner, Jesus could see the river through an open gate in the city's wall. As they passed through the gate,

Ram told him the Euphrates widened here and, not much farther south, it flowed into the Persian Gulf. A huge ship stood at anchor just offshore. Jesus could see its name inscribed on the bow ...Persian Star ...with Joseph of Arimathea's seal, just as it had appeared on the Cyprus Star. The ship was too large to come up to the river's edge, so the caravan boarded via smaller ferry tenders. After a time, all the men, animals, and goods were aboard, and the captain gave the signal to haul anchor, beginning the last leg of their trip through Persia to India.

## CHAPTER 12 — THE PERSIAN GULF,

## INDIA, AND TIBET

Captain Isaac of the Persian Star did not seem as friendly as Captain Amos of the Cyprus Star had been. However, he did assemble all the non—sailors on deck after the ship had been under way for an hour or two for the little orientation speech he always made at this point in the journey. Most of the caravan people had heard it so many times it bored them, but Jesus found it interesting.

"Welcome aboard the Persian Star," the captain began in a tiresome monotone. "We will be sailing straight south in the Persian Gulf[1] for three days until we reach the port of Maceta, the Gateway to Gedrosia in Southern Persia. The Persian Gulf is 29 miles wide at this point and 250 miles wide where

---

[1]The Persian Gulf, actually an arm of the Arabian Sea, which is itself a large gulf in the Indian Ocean, is, of course, not as large or as deep as the great sea to the west, now called the Mediterranean, but it is indeed a significant body of water.

we reach our approximate halfway point. It is 420 miles long; however, because we must turn east into a deep bay before reaching Maceta, our trip will be about 500 miles. Almost all of the Gulf is navigable, having an average depth of 25 fathoms. It is shallower, of course, near the shores of its several islands. That's why we pass them at a safe distance.

This ship, as you can see, is smaller than the Cyprus Star, which brought you to Antioch from Caesarea. However, it is very sturdy and most seaworthy. Joseph of Arimathea had her built by the same Greek shipwrights who built the Cyprus Star. Her sails are fitted for reefing... that is reducing their size, with a system that's much more efficient and safe than the system used on older square—riggers. The hull is built of heavy cedar planks, secured by dowels to assure they will not come apart. The outside of the hull is covered with pitch to preserve the wood and make it watertight. Then, over the pitch, the shipwrights covered the

239

hull exterior up to the water line with a layer of tar-impregnated fabric, and then covered this with a thin sheathing of lead. Any questions?"

There never were any, and so the captain concluded his speech with some routine announcements about mealtimes and a frightening precaution about pirate raids. "Don't be surprised if we're boarded in the night by pirates wielding large knives," he began. "But if you do not resist them, they will not hurt you. They want only one thing, and that is whatever gold and precious stones we may be carrying. They're not interested in the heavier things like the papyrus, wheat, and olive oil."

Jesus remembered that most of the gold and jewels had been stolen by the Arabian thieves in the desert. He wondered if, finding none of these valuables, the pirates might turn hostile; but he decided not to ask. What Jesus didn't know was that a few of the better pieces of gold, intended to trade in India for diamonds, had been safely hidden away in the sheaves of wheat by Ahaz and had survived the Arab raid.

As it turned out, the trip south in the Gulf was uneventful. The sea was relatively calm, and there were no pirate raids. Perhaps the desert robbers and the sea pirates were all in league, and had some way of communicating with each other. Jesus would not have been surprised to learn that they communicated by way of some of the less loyal camel drivers and seamen. Some of them looked very sinister.

Later the next day, the Persian Star sailed into the Port of Maceta in a southeastern bay of the Gulf. A westbound caravan was waiting to board, and as soon as Ahaz' caravan had disembarked, the caravan masters and camel drivers animatedly exchanged accounts of their experiences and information about the routes.

The men from both caravans made camp together along the shore, and they were joined for an evening of merrymaking by some of the members of

241

the ship's crew. The town of Maceta was too small to offer much in the way of entertainment or debauchery, and so the men contented themselves with staying in camp, shooting dice, drinking wine, and exchanging gossip about people along the route.

Jesus elected to take a walk alone along the Gulf shore to think and to pray. Soon it would be Hanukkah. Little did he know a year ago that he would be spending his 24th birthday in this part of the world.

At Maceta, Joseph of Arimathea maintained a series of buildings for the storage of goods. Here the caravan workers stored everything, such as the fine rugs and embroideries acquired in Babylon, and other goods acquired along the way which would fetch better prices in the west than in the east. Only the merchandise to be traded farther east was loaded in the packs on the camels' backs for the long and difficult trip to India. The first westward caravan that was traveling light would pick up the stored goods and take them to Caesarea.

242

Jesus marveled at the efficient system Joseph had worked out, and the fact that his control and influence were felt so far from Caesarea.

Among the stored materials was a good supply of frankincense and myrrh. The raiding thieves in Arabia had not bothered with these bulky items, but had concentrated on gold and jewels. Had it not been for this, Ahaz might have considered turning back at Babylon. But the frankincense, burned on the altars the length and breadth of the great sea, and the myrrh, a key ingredient in ointments and salves, were intact, and made it well worth continuing the journey. In addition, they had many other items to sell and to acquire in India and China.

Jesus noted that, before goods were warehoused, they were marked with a large letter "A". Apparently this meant they had been acquired by Ahaz' crew and Ahaz would get the credit back at Joseph's headquarters.

243

On the 25th day of Kislev (Hanukkah), Ahaz asked Jesus to have the mid—afternoon meal with him. When Jesus arrived at Ahaz' tent, he found the entire group assembled there... slaves as well as camel drivers. Brightly—colored candles were burning everywhere. And colored cloth from the cargo had been draped in a festive way from every available tree and tent pole.

Jesus immediately assumed it was a Hanukkah feast, but wondered why he had not been told. As he approached the tent, he knew. The men began clapping and chanting a traditional birthday song. It was not only a Hanukkah feast, but a birthday celebration for Jesus as well.

All the men were smiling, and shook Jesus' hand or slapped him on the back as he entered the circle of celebrants. A colorful spread of food adorned a side table. Apparently Ahaz had asked the cook to prepare special foods and breads for the occasion. And, of course, wine flowed abundantly from several jardinieres. Jesus was indeed surprised, and happy to share celebration of his birthday as part of the caravan's Hanukkah feast.

Ahaz intoned the traditional ritual which would begin the eight—day observance of Hanukkah. Commemorating the rededication[1] of the Temple to God by Judas Maccabeus after it had been profaned by the King of Syria some 189 years past. When Ahaz finished, he asked Jesus to step forward.

"The men want you to have this as a token of their affection," Ahaz said, handing Jesus a small camel, beautifully carved from ivory. The camel carried a pack much like those used in Ahaz' caravan. "We hope it will help you to remember us and this trip," Ahaz said.

Jesus had difficulty holding back tears as he took the tiny camel and said, "Thank you all, so much. You will always be in my heart."

The cheers could have been heard back to the gulf shore, and the feasting and merrymaking went

---

[1] In 165 B.C.

*Joseph Radder*

on well into the night. Finally, Jesus fell exhausted on his cot in his tent.

"Goodnight, master. I hope you enjoyed your party." It was Ram, the true and faithful servant.

"Goodnight, Ram. I did indeed. Thank you." Jesus was very pleased that Ahaz had included the slaves in the party.

It took six days to cross Persia to the Indian border, and then three more days to reach Indraprastha.[1] Jesus wondered why they hadn't stayed aboard the Persian Star to take the easier, faster route by sea. The answer soon became clear. The caravan stopped every day to buy and sell goods. This, of course, would not have been possible at sea. The diamonds Ahaz obtained in northern India en route to Indraprastha were, alone, worth the trip.

Indraprastha was dominated by ornate Hindu temples. There were Buddhist sanctuaries too, and Jesus learned that, like these, the Hindu temples

---

[1] Delhi.

carried a symbolic meaning in almost every element of their design. Each had an inner sanctum, built in the form of a square and housing a replica of the temple's deity. Hinduism has an untold number of gods, many represented by animals. There is the elephant, usually depicted with a mouse at his feet, the sacred cow, and of course the monkey, to name but a few. One of the more prominent of these gods is Brahma, one of the few thought to be a human figure.

The first temple Jesus visited was dedicated to Brahma, and was served by Brahman priests. Because of their high prestige and tradition of education, the Brahmans influenced secular as well as religious affairs. The temple, therefore, was a place of utmost importance.

The Brahman temple Jesus visited in Indraprastha was a very ornate building ...a series of spaces beginning with a pagoda—roofed entrance—way through a series of sanctuaries increasing in size and height until the tallest, which housed the inner sanctum and featured an elaborate spire.

All of the Brahmans in the temple passed by Jesus without acknowledging him. He assumed they were meditating and he didn't want to disturb them. Actually, they were simply preoccupied. Jesus learned later that when Hindus meditate, they sit quietly and focus on one thought or idea for hours.

Finally, one of the priests smiled at him, and Jesus risked a greeting. The man spoke no language Jesus understood, but he beckoned Jesus to follow him and led him into a room where a scholarly—looking old man sat at a table.

"I speak only Aramaic," Jesus said, not expecting the old man to understand him.

Surprisingly, the old scholar replied in Aramaic, "What brings you to our temple?"

"I was curious, and I admired its great beauty from afar and wanted to get a closer look. I am a teacher in a place called Galilee, and I'm interested in writing about the world's religions. What can you tell me about Hinduism?"

No question Jesus could have asked would have been welcomed more by the old priest. He proceeded to talk for over an hour about the rise of sectarian worship in the late Vedic period of Indian history. "Brahmans believe," he said, "that the God Brahma was born from a golden egg and then created the earth and everything in it. Brahma is believed to have four faces, symbolic of the four sacred scriptures or Vedas, the four ages, and the four social classes. In art and sculpture he is shown with four arms, sacrificial instruments, prayer beads and book.

After Jesus thanked the old priest and left him, he explored the temple and saw relief sculpture and statues everywhere depicting Brahma just as the old man had described him.

Thinking about it, Jesus found little in common with his own religion except that Hindus believed their god created earth and everything on it.

Moving through the streets of Indraprastha, Jesus came upon a great statue of Buddha. He remembered then that he had been told Buddhism began in India about 600 years past as a protest against the religioussocial monopoly of the Brahmanic caste of priests.

The road Jesus was on suddenly began to ascend a steep hill. Without a good reason, he would not have attempted to climb it, but something seemed to draw him up there. At the top of the hill, seeming to jut out of a cliff, was, he learned later, one of India's oldest surviving examples of religious architecture, a Buddhist sanctuary, carved from the rock of the cliff. As he got closer, he could see that it was a man—made cavern, hollowed out of the mountainside.

On the hill, he met a young student—guide who carried a sign on his shoulders: "7 LANGUAGES SPOKEN".

Jesus was pleased to see that Aramaic was one of the seven languages listed. He happily paid the young man the designated number of coins to take him up and into the Buddhist temple.

Inside was an ornate corridor flanked by intricately—carved pillars and an arched ceiling. At the end of this corridor was a replica of the earliest Buddhist monuments, whose hemispherical top, the guide explained, symbolized the dome of the heavens.

Continuing, the guide said, "The Buddha's enlightenment by God is periodically celebrated by a procession of monks who walk around the stupia[1] chanting Buddhist scriptures." Jesus had to ask him to repeat this three times before he fully understood him. Unfortunately his Aramaic was not as fluent as Jesus had hoped it would be.

On the way back to the entrance, the guide pointed out the temple's features as well as he could by repeating himself and using sign language. About the only thing Jesus got out of all this was the fact that not all of the temple's features were

---

[1]Altar

strictly Buddhist, and that the sumptuously carved pillars and the arched ribs of the vaulted ceiling were stone approximations of the wooden columns and beams of India's earliest jungle shrines, the timbers of which were believed to contain the spirits of the gods.

At several points along the way they passed meditating monks saying their mantra ...repeating one word over and over again. Jesus thought this was not unlike the Hindu priests' idea of focusing on one thought or idea during meditation. Jesus had hoped to find a monk who spoke Aramaic; but the guide assured him there would be none, and offered to sell him a scroll, written in Aramaic, containing information on Buddha and Buddhism. Jesus gladly purchased it even though he felt it was terribly over-priced.

Later, Jesus did meet a Buddhist monk outside the temple who spoke Aramaic fluently. The two talked for almost an hour over tea from a roadside vendor. The monk was obviously a disciple of the philosopher Confucius. He told of Confucius' rule, that man should do unto others as he would have them do unto him. And he told Jesus that Confucius' strongest ethic was love. He told the following story to illustrate this:

"It seems a wealthy Chinese man had two sons. one was loyal and worked hard on the man's land. The other left home and went into the city to live a life of debauchery. After a long absence, the bad son returned home and the man put on a great feast for him, angering the loyal son.

The moral," the monk pointed out, "was the idea that one who sins and then repents is even more worthy of love than one who lives a good life."

Jesus thought, I can use that story in my teaching and, of course, some years later he did, calling it the story of the prodigal son.

Back in camp that night, Jesus read the scroll he had purchased from the guide, and learned that Buddha means "the enlightened one". Buddha was reared in a royal family of the ruling warrior caste. Distressed by the idea of sickness, old age, and death, Buddha renounced his family to wander as an ascetic, in search of religious understanding. Becoming enlightened through meditation, Buddha developed a following, and instructed his followers in the truth as he saw it ...the middle way ...a path between a worldly life and the extremes of self—denial.

An egalitarian, Buddha preached four "Truths":

1. Life is filled with disappointment and suffering.
2. Suffering results from the pursuit of pleasure, power, and trying to avoid death.
3. To stop disappointment and suffering, one must stop desiring.
4. The way to stop desiring is via the doctrine of selflessness.

Some 500 years before the day Jesus studied this scroll, Buddha died in northeast India. By that time he had developed a huge following, which had spread from India to the Orient.

Jesus saw a great deal of truth in Buddhism, especially the concept that all men are equals, and that one must live a life in service of others if he expects to be rewarded with happiness.

The next morning Jesus learned that Ahaz had found Indraprastha to be a ready market for goods he had brought from the west, and a treasure chest of goods for the return trip ...not only diamonds, but spices, especially pepper, which Galileans and Judeans loved for spicing food, but which was not available locally.

As the camel drivers prepared for departure to the north, Jesus noted that they were dressed in clothing which seemed especially warm for Indraprastha's mild climate. So he took a cue from this, and also the advice of Ram and Boaz, and made sure all of his woolen garments and blankets were within easy reach in the carriage.

By nightfall, they made camp at the foot of the Himalayas. Seeing such high mountains was a new experience for Jesus. He couldn't wait to see them in daylight.

When morning broke, the Himalayan Mountains stood before them in all their splendor ...bearing vegetation in the foothills, then craggy rock, and finally, in the upper portions, snow—capped peaks. As the sun shone on these mountains, Jesus wished that he were an artist. He would love to be able to capture their magnificent beauty on canvas.

Soon the caravan was under way, but not until Ram and Boaz had fastened side curtains all around the carriage. Jesus noted they had hooded sheepskin garb handy on the seat beside them.

It wasn't long before the party began its ascent and, almost immediately, Jesus could feel a chill in the air. He put on his woolen garments and a hat his mother had knitted for him.

The caravan climbed on until there was snow—covered rock on both sides of them. Now Jesus really felt the cold; he pulled on the woolen gloves that matched his hat and covered himself with a heavy woolen blanket.

After no more than an hour had passed, it started to snow, and a cold wind began howling around the carriage. Jesus pulled up his second blanket. He was now using everything he had to keep warm.

He couldn't see Ram and Boaz because the carriage roof was closed, but he could hear them shouting at the reluctant horses, and he could imagine them in their sheepskin garb with the snow blinding them, driving the unwilling horses on.

It seemed the temperature was dropping far below anything Jesus believed was possible and, in spite of all the woolen clothing and blankets which he had thought would be adequate, he started to shiver. He could see through the small openings in the side curtains that they were now in the middle

257

of a blizzard. Even though the rocky walls of the pass were just a few feet away, they couldn't be seen, and Jesus wondered how Ram and Boaz were able to keep from hitting them.

It seemed to take forever to reach the peak of the pass, but finally Jesus could feel that they were starting downhill. By then his shivering was out of control, and his teeth were chattering. He couldn't remember ever feeling such misery. It must be way past time for the mid—afternoon meal, he thought, but he would have gladly traded food for a warm fire if he had the opportunity.

At long last they reached a plateau, and they heard Ahaz shout, "Halt! We'll make camp here."

"Make camp? How can they think of staying overnight in such a place?" Jesus thought. Just then, Ram opened the roof of the carriage and asked Jesus to stand and look out. He was stunned to see the sun shining on a sparkling plain of snow and, following Ram's pointing finger, he saw a large cave. "That's where we'll spend the night," Ram said.

The cave was not warm, but it provided shelter from the wind. Soon the slaves had built a huge fire at the mouth of the cave and the wind out of the west was pushing the warmth of the fire into the cave.

The cooks had already set up a makeshift kitchen near the fire and were stirring a huge cauldron of soup. They had been saving some lamb for a special occasion, and they put two legs and a breast on a spit and turned it slowly over the fire.

The warmth of the fire, the aroma of the soup and roasting lamb were very comforting after their ordeal in the blizzard, but Jesus was still shivering. When Ahaz noticed this, he asked, "Where are your winter clothes?"

Jesus replied, "These are all I have."

"Well, they may be winter clothes in Galilee, but not in the Himalayas. — Abed! Where are Perez' sheepskins?" Ahaz' voice was loud and commanding.

259

"In my saddle bags, master."

"Go out and get them, and give them to Jesus."

Soon Jesus was wearing the dead man Perez' sheepskin clothing. At last he was warm and comfortable.

After the men had eaten hungrily they shared legends of other blizzards they had experienced in these very mountains. The worst story was told by Ahaz himself, who recounted the time two camels, a horse, and three men froze to death before they could reach the cave.

Ahaz had insisted Jesus take a place near the fire, and soon he nodded off to sleep in a sitting position.

Back in Nazareth, Joseph was snoring gently by the time Mary got to bed She was bone—tired, having gone early in the morning to the home of a neighbor who was about to give birth to a baby. Mary's intention was to be with the new mother, comfort her, and attend to her as a midwife. But when she

260

got there, she found the house in such disarray, the food supply so low, that she spent the entire day doing "back—breaking" chores ...cleaning, baking, and mending, as well as spending time at the new mother's bedside. The woman's husband was apparently helpless when it came to simple household tasks.

After the baby was born and Mary had left the woman in the care of other neighbors, rest, at last, was close at hand.

All day long Mary had been thinking about Jesus and saying little prayers for him. It had been almost a year since he had left with the trade mission, and only two letters had reached her via Joseph of Arimathea's couriers. And these had arrived months after they were written.

When Mary arrived home she noted that her house was as neat and clean as she had left it. Fresh loaves of bread were on the sideboard, and a kettle of soup on the hearth gave off a hearty aroma. Clearly, Joseph had intended she have some soup and

261

bread when she came in. Mary was too tired to eat, but she thanked God that her husband was more resourceful than the head of the house she had visited that day. After washing and changing into her nightclothes, Mary knelt down next to her bed and prayed... "Dear God, thank you for this day of service to my neighbor. Please watch over your son, Jesus. Keep him safe when he is in danger, healthy when exposed to sickness, strong when the burden is heavy. Bless Joseph too, dear Lord, and thank you for your many gifts, especially the gift of love and this happy home. Amen." Mary took care not to wake Joseph as she got into bed. She was so tired she expected she would fall off to sleep immediately, but she couldn't stop thinking about Jesus.

Finally, in sort of a half sleep, Mary dreamed she saw him. He was in the midst of a blizzard. His teeth were chattering, and he was shivering violently. Obviously, he was close to freezing to death. How can this be? We were told the journey would take him through lands where the climate is warm. "Oh please, dear God, save Jesus from this bitter cold."

Just then, an angel appeared to Mary in her dream. "Fear not, Mary, the angel said. "Your son will soon be warm again." And the angel disappeared as quickly as he had appeared.

Suddenly, Mary was at peace, and she fell into a deep and dreamless sleep. It was at that very moment that Jesus, warmed by the fire and Perez' sheepskin clothing, had fallen off to sleep as well.

Rested and warm at last, Jesus and the caravan people awoke to a bright blue sky. The sun reflected on the snow into the cave entrance. Ahaz quickly ordered everyone to wash, dress, and prepare for departure.

The camels and horses had been sheltered in a nearby gap in the rock, where the camel drivers rotated watch shifts, keeping a second fire going.

*Joseph Radder*

Soon the cargo packs had been strapped on the camels, the horses were hitched to the carriages and wagons, and everything was in readiness.

It was such a nice day, Jesus was tempted to ask Ram and Boaz to remove the side curtains, but remembering the blizzard of the night before, he thought better of it.

They hadn't traveled along the pass very long before it got wider and began a gradual, then steeper, descent.

Just before they reached the Tibetan border, Ahaz ordered the caravan to halt for the mid—morning meal. It was now quite warm and the slaves did indeed remove the side curtains from the carriages.

After the meal, they mounted again to continue the journey, but before long they stopped. This time they had been halted by Tibetan soldiers.

"They usually have to be bribed to let us through," Boaz said. "Ahaz carries some trinkets and strong wine in his carriage for just such

264

purposes. The wine sometimes softens them up when gifts will not."

After what seemed like hours they were moving again. As Jesus' carriage passed the soldiers, there was no doubt which method Ahaz had used. The soldiers were staggering around, singing and laughing, and they waved to Jesus with silly grins on their faces. Jesus returned their greetings with a smile.

Tibet, a province of China, is bounded on the north and east by other Chinese provinces, on the south by India and on the west by Kashmir.

In the foothills of the Himalayas, Tibet is very high above sea level. The rarefied air was quite a change for the travelers. Jesus was told to expect sharp drops in the temperature after sundown because of this high elevation.

Just behind the caravan were some of the highest summits known to man. To the north was another Himalayan chain of mountains, but here in the valley, between the two mountain ranges, was a plateau with sparse vegetation, but some trees ...conifers, oak, and cypress.

Jesus was thrilled to see so many wild animals frolicking nearby ...deer, wild sheep, goats, antelopes, leopards, bears, wild dogs, and monkeys. Ahaz forbade his men to hunt any of these animals, but once in a while a party of two or three camel drivers would sneak away from the camp and return with a deer or an antelope. Ahaz would be aware of this when he detected the aroma of roasting animal flesh. By then, however, it was too late to do much about it, so he didn't reprimand the men too strongly. At this point in the journey, he needed them more than they needed him. on the other hand, Ahaz knew, the men were all very far from home and had only one way to get there ...with his caravan.

The next day they entered the city of Lhasa. Ahaz soon called everyone together and announced that all but the four of his assistants who were skilled traders would be free for three weeks

266

before starting the return journey. He and these four would stay in camp to trade for musk, hides, furs, herbs, and salt. With that, the men formed a single—file line and Ahaz gave them each a small pouch of coins as he shook each man's hand and wished them all a safe, enjoyable vacation.

Jesus thought about inviting Ram and Boaz to accompany him on a tour of the city, but then decided against it, thinking they would be happier on their own. As was Joseph of Arimathea's tradition, the slaves were just as free as freemen on these vacations. Their forehead tattoos were Joseph's guarantee of their voluntary return to camp at the appointed time. They too had shared in Joseph's largesse when the bags of coins were passed out. Few slave—owners were that generous.

As Jesus entered the city, he was impressed with the colorful dress of the Tibetan people, who seemed to be predominantly of the Mongolian race, the product of inter—marriage between Indian and Chinese people.

In touring the city he was disappointed when he could not find temples of any kind. When he finally found an Indian man who spoke Aramaic and asked him about it, he was told there were none, that Tibet was a pagan country; but he had heard there was a settlement of Buddhist monks ...missionaries from India ...just outside the northern edge of the city.

The walk was long, but worth it, when Jesus found the settlement. Indeed, here was a group of Buddhist monks living in tents. Two or three of them spoke Aramaic. They greeted Jesus in a very friendly manner. They told him they were there to try to establish the Buddhist religion in Tibet. As it would turn out later, they would soon give up and return to India, and it was to be 700 years before Buddhism was successfully established in Tibet.

The monks insisted that Jesus share a meal with them and, when they learned he had not yet found a place to stay in Lhasa, they urged him to stay with them until it was time to return to his caravan.

Jesus was especially taken with one of the monks who spoke Aramaic. He liked him instinctively, and was very pleased upon being assigned to his tent. The man was a Mongolian named Chen Tu.

When they went to the dining tent, Jesus was intrigued by a mother cat and her litter of kittens curled up in a corner of the tent. She was a beautiful apple—face Siamese, beige with very dark brown markings, and sapphire blue eyes. "What's her name?" Jesus asked.

"Harm," Chen Tu responded.

"Harm? That's a strange name for a cat."

"We named her that because, when she was a kitten, we had to keep everything out of Harm's way."

Jesus laughed as he picked up one of the kittens, a male with a little brown face and feet, marked very much like his mother.

"Would you like to take him with you when you go?" Chen Tu asked.

"I'm not sure the caravan—master would allow it," Jesus replied, sadly adding, "Then I'd have to abandon him in Lhasa."

"I'll accompany you to your camp when you go," Chen Tu said, smiling. "If he won't allow it, I'll bring him back to his mother."

Jesus was overjoyed. He had missed the love of his mother and father, cousins, and friends, since he had left Nazareth. At last he would have something to love.

During the next three weeks, Jesus became particularly fond of the monk Chen Tu and the little kitten who had taken up residence in their tent.

During this time he and Chen Tu shared their knowledge of their religions. Jesus found much similarity in Judaism and Buddhism, particularly the doctrines of selflessness.

Jesus recited the ten commandments God had given to the Jewish people in Moses' care..."You shall not have other gods besides me. You shall not worship idols. You shall not take the name of God in vain.

You should keep holy the Sabbath day and honor your father and mother. You shall not kill. You shall not commit adultery, you shall not steal, you shall not bear false witness, you shall not covet." The Buddhist nodded agreement with every one of them.

The three weeks passed quickly. Jesus was fascinated by his conversations with Chen Tu about Buddhism and Judaism. But soon it was time to pack up his belongings and return to camp.

"Don't forget your cat," Chen Tu said.

"Not on your life," Jesus replied. "I'll treasure him as long as he lives, and I'll think of you and your brother monks every time I look at him."

Throwing his pack on his back and cradling the kitten in his arms, Jesus headed back into the city with his new friend, Chen Tu, at his side.

When they arrived at camp, Jesus introduced Chen Tu to Ahaz. "And who's your other friend?" Ahaz asked.

"He's my kitten, if you'll permit me to keep him." Jesus was pleading with his eyes.

"Why not?" Ahaz said. "He won't eat much, and he certainly won't take up much room. Jesus was happy to find Ahaz in such a good mood. Obviously trading with the Tibetans had gone well.

After thanking Chen Tu and bidding him goodbye, Jesus took his kitten to his tent. Ram and Boaz smiled when they saw him. "What's his name?" Ram asked.

"I think I'll call him Achim."

"Achim?"

"After a particularly cantankerous teacher back in Nazareth," Jesus replied. And so, Achim it was until he grew to old age in Jesus' home in Nazareth.

The return journey to Caesarea is another story for telling at another time. Suffice it to say that Jesus and Achim became fast friends, and the cat grew noticeably on the journey, thriving on scraps from the kitchen provided daily by the cook, who also took a fancy to the little kitten.

When they arrived at Caesarea some months later, Joseph of Arimathea was on the pier to greet them. When Jesus went down the gangplank, he extended his arms and embraced Joseph to show his great gratitude.

"Don't forget the diary you promised me," Joseph said.

"I won't. I'll finish it as soon as I get home, and send it to you the first chance I get."

Ram and Boaz then came down the gangplank. Ram was carrying Achim, and Boaz was carrying Jesus' bags. He embraced both men and took the bags and his purring kitten from them. He had become very close to these slaves on the long trip.

Ahaz then instructed Ram to take Jesus and his bags to Nazareth in the wagon Jesus had learned to call home.

Waving goodbye to everybody on the pier, tears welled up in Jesus' eyes. He was so grateful to God and to Joseph of Arimathea for making this trip possible.

Finally they were in Nazareth. When Mary and Joseph heard the wagon, they ran out to greet their beloved son. All three were in tears as they embraced. They were so full of happiness to be together again, and their gratitude to God for Jesus' safe return was a prayer on all their lips.

Meanwhile, Ram brought Achim and Jesus' belongings into the little house, and Jesus introduced his parents. "Thank you, Ram. You've been a good and faithful servant."

As Ram directed the carriage back down the road, Mary asked, looking at the kitten, "And who, pray tell, is this?"

"Achim," Jesus answered.

"Achim??!!" And they all laughed.

## CHAPTER 13 — A SENSE OF HUMOR

Jesus was a happy man as he returned to the Nazareth synagogue. The young students greeted him with big smiles and slaps on the back. Many embraced him, and all were happy to see him after his long journey.

The students were eager to hear about the trip. And when Jesus was alone with a group of them in the courtyard he told them about the cat he had named Achim... the gift from the Tibetan monks. They all laughed heartily when they heard this.

Just then, Achim the teacher passed through the courtyard on his way to the council room. He was scowling, as usual, and he glared at Jesus instead of greeting him as the others had.

The group fell silent quickly at the sight of Achim. Jesus spoke to him anyway, smiling warmly, hoping the grouchy teacher hadn't overheard them when they were talking about the cat. At best, Achim was just being his usual grouchy self. He

276

*Young Jesus*
*The Missing Years*

hated any sign of joy. Hopefully his anger this day arose simply from hearing the boys' laughter.

After Achim was out of earshot, Jesus told the students some of the jokes he had heard on the trip, and they told him the new jokes that had been circulating in the school in recent months. Suddenly, the laughter was interrupted again.

"Jesus! Come here!" It was Achim.

Jesus walked to the door of the council room, where Achim stood with his hands on his hips.

"Sir?"

"You shouldn't be encouraging the frivolous nature of these boys, Jesus. Their minds should be on serious studies. You should know better. After all, you're older than they are, and you should be more mature."

Jesus was angry, but he tried not to show it. "I meant no harm sir," he said. Jesus was always respectful and courteous.

"Don't let it happen again," Achim grunted as he turned quickly away and disappeared into the council chamber.

"Not within your hearing anyway," Jesus thought, as he followed Achim into the chamber.

When Jesus entered the council room, the greetings were more than enthusiastic.

Jacob was the first to embrace Jesus. He said, "Welcome home, my boy. We have missed you."

Josiah's and Manasseh's greetings were also warm and clearly genuine. only Achim failed to acknowledge Jesus' presence, pretending to go through some scrolls instead.

A good part of the day was spent listening to Jesus' account of his journey. Achim tried to feign disinterest, but at several points in Jesus' narrative, especially the account of the Himalayan blizzard, Achim was obviously just as interested as the others.

Finally, Jacob said, "Well, my boy, you certainly had a great adventure. Don't forget your promise to write it down for us."

"I won't forget," promised Jesus, remembering he had also agreed to copy his diary for Joseph of Arimathea.

"Well, we have a little time left, gentlemen, what would you like to discuss?" Jacob looked around the table for a suggestion.

Before the others had a chance to suggest a topic, Jesus said, "I'd like to hear your opinions on humor and laughter and singing, and other expressions of joy. Do you think God has a sense of humor? Or is it wrong to make light of things?"

Jacob welcomed the chance to respond. He was the one who almost always had a pleasant smile on his face. "I once read something that I think will answer at least part of your question, Jesus. In fact, I liked it so much I committed it to memory. Would you all like to hear it?"

"By all means."

"Indeed."

"Of course."

Jesus, Josiah, and Manasseh answered simultaneously. Again Achim was silent.

Jacob was pleased. "I don't know who wrote this, but it seems to fit...

God laughs in the sunshine, And sings through the throat of birds. They who neither laugh nor sing, Are out of tune with God."[1]

"Are you trying to imply that I'm out of tune with God?" Achim exploded.

"You said it, I didn't," answered Jacob with a twinkle in his eye. The others smiled.

"This whole subject is a waste of time," Achim growled. "I'll be back when you have something of importance to discuss." Storming out of the room was getting to be a habit with the old teacher.

"I know the royal households and many of the rich have jesters and comedians in their courts," Manasseh said, "but I can understand what Achim is

[1]Author unknown. Quoted in "A Man Nobody Knows" by Bruce Barton.

saying. Maybe as religion teachers we're different. Perhaps laughter is a luxury we shouldn't enjoy."

"Nonsense!" said Jacob. "I'm just as sure as I am that day will break tomorrow that God wants us to laugh. Goodness knows there's enough in this world to be sad about. And sadness can be like poison, destroying the soul. Laughter is the antidote."

"What about singing?" Now it was the usually quiet Josiah speaking. "I'm not a singer, but I love to hear a good song. And I believe there are no more beautiful songs than the psalms."

"Which psalm is your favorite?" Jesus asked.

"I think the 96th ...the Glories of the Lord, the King of the universe. Will you sing it for us, Jesus?"

He didn't have to be asked twice. The voice of Jesus was clear, his tones beautifully rounded, his pitch perfect as he sang out...

"Sing to the Lord a new song. Sing to the Lord, all you lands.

*Joseph Radder*

Sing to the Lord, bless his name;

announce his salvation, day after day.

Tell his glory among the nations;

among all the peoples his wondrous deeds.


For great is the Lord; and highly to be praised;

awesome is he beyond all gods.

For all the gods of the nations are things of

nought, but the Lord made the heavens.

Splendor and majesty go before him; praise and

grandeur are his sanctuary.


Give to the Lord you families of nations,

give to the Lord glory and praise,

give to the Lord the glory due his name.


Bring gifts and enter his courts worship the

Lord in holy attire.

Tremble before him all the earth; say among the

nations, the Lord is king.

He has made the world firm, not to be moved; He governs the people with equity."

And so Jesus sang on to the last line...

"He shall rule the world with justice and the people with his constancy."

The applause, while only that of three men, was as enthusiastic as if they were part of a large crowd. The three were amazed that Jesus knew this long psalm. Not once had he referred to the scroll.

"Jesus surely has taught us that singing can be divine," Manasseh said. "But what about dancing?"

Jacob was quick to answer. "Dancing is one more human expression of joy that I'm sure God loves to see. — Music, dancing, singing, laughter, they all go together, and they are all gifts from God."

And so the discussion continued until it was time to go back to their homes.

Just before the end of the session, Achim quietly came back into the room and took his place at the table.

"You missed a beautiful rendition of the 96th psalm, Achim," Jacob said.

"I heard. I was out in the courtyard."

"Let's have one more to conclude the day," Jacob suggested. "Who has a favorite they would like to hear?"

Surprisingly, it was Achim who answered, "I always liked the 23rd best."

"A Psalm of David, Jesus' ancestor," Jacob said, waving his upturned palm in Jesus' direction, as Achim winced at the reference to Jesus' royal ancestry.

And again Jesus sang in his beautiful voice:

"The Lord is my shepherd, I shall not want.

He leads me to rest in green pastures, beside the still waters.

He restores my soul.

He guides me in right paths for his name's sake. Even though I walk through the valley of the shadow of death, I will fear no evil, for you are with me. Your rod and your staff, they comfort me. You spread a table before me in the presence of my enemies. You anoint my head with oil, my cup runs over. Surely goodness and mercy will follow me, All the days of my life. And I shall dwell in the house of the Lord, forever."

Jesus watched Achim as he sang. He was delighted that the old man was silently mouthing the words, as a tear ran down his cheek.

The afternoon meal on Jesus' first day home provided the first opportunity to give Mary and Joseph a full account of his journey. And so they spent several hours listening to Jesus' beautifully—told tale, asking him questions, and taking great interest in his answers.

Finally Jesus said, "Wait! I've been doing all the talking. What have you two been doing since I went away?"

Mary answered, "My activity has been quite routine ...washing, cleaning, cooking, baking, weaving ...but your father had a very interesting experience."

"Tell us about it, father," Jesus said.

"Well, apparently my reputation as a craftsman somehow reached the royal ear, and I was summoned to the palace to build a balustrade across the front of a new balcony fronting the king's private quarters. He also wanted a banister built for a new marble staircase he had just had constructed."

Remembering Mary and Joseph's story of his birth at Bethlehem, the star, the three Magi, and how Herod had sent them to find him, he asked, "Didn't he know who you were?"

"Fortunately not," Joseph replied. "In fact he treated me quite well, even though he was very demanding about my work. For example, it was no ordinary balustrade and banister that he wanted. He insisted that it be very ornate. In fact, he had his royal architect draw a design for it, including the detail for the supporting posts."

"It must have taken you months to fashion them with your knife," Jesus said.

"No. I think I amazed the old king and everybody in his court with the speed with which I was able to make those posts. You see, I made them here at home in my shop on a device I'll show you later. I was able to turn each piece on this device[1] as I cut it, speeding up the process tremendously."

"Very clever." Jesus was proud of his father. "Did you see Herod often?"

"Oh yes. In fact, he checked my progress daily. He's not such a bad old sort."

"Oh no! He only wanted to massacre all the male Jewish infants in Bethlehem." Jesus was surprised Joseph could be so forgiving.

"Well, I once hated him for that; you're right. But God wants us to forgive even the worst of offenses against us."

"You're a good man to forgive, father."

"Forgive, yes. But I can never forget."

---

[1] A primitive lathe.

287

"Did you get to see much of the palace?"

"Yes, after a while they gave me free access to all but the king's private chambers. And, of course, I was not permitted to enter the royal reception room while he was on the throne."

"Tell us about the palace." Jesus was most curious.

"Well, at the risk of boring your mother, who has heard all this many times..."

Mary interrupted to suggest that she leave the two alone while she cleaned up after the meal.

"You see, Jesus, the palace is not only Herod's headquarters and residence, it is a fortress as well. There are sentries stationed in turrets at the top of every corner of the building. The palace is virtually impregnable. It has only one entry, a steep staircase ...200 steps of hewn stone. My leg muscles really grew strong climbing those steps every day."

"Weren't you stopped by the sentries?"

"Oh yes ...at the bottom of the steps and again at the top. But after a while, they got to know me."

"Did you have to carry your tools up that staircase every day?"

"Only the first day. Herod let me leave them in a palace closet. That's what I mean when I say he wasn't such a bad old sort."

"You would have thought worse of him if we hadn't been able to flee to Egypt when he ordered that massacre of children," Jesus said.

"I suppose so," Joseph allowed. "But let me continue ...As I said, the palace is also a fortress; but for all its strength, it was built to be livable for Herod and his court in a very luxurious style. Inside the walls is a sunken colonnaded courtyard with niches for beautifully—carved statues. All over this courtyard are beds of flowering plants of many colors, and carefully—tended ornamental shrubs. Herod has several gardeners in full—time service."

"Tell me more. This is very interesting." Jesus sat on the edge of his chair.

"There is a large reception hall with the throne at its center, a Roman bath, and of course, the private quarters, in front of which I worked daily. I assume they are very lavish. Of course, I never got to see them."

"How long were you in Jerusalem?" Jesus asked.

"Over a month. But I was not really in Jerusalem. The palace is in the hills south of the city. The king's secretary provided living quarters for me with a peasant family. Their home was very near a second part of the royal complex, a minor palace with a huge pool of water fed by an aqueduct from Solomon's pools."

"That's a spring near Bethlehem, is it not?"

"Correct." Joseph continued, "In the center of this deep pool is an elegant colonnaded pavilion of white marble, reachable only by one of the brightly colored boats on the pool. Altogether, Herod's various buildings and their beautifully landscaped grounds cover some 45 acres ...truly a sight to behold."

"I must see it some day. Are visitors permitted?" Jesus asked.

"Only to the outer grounds. Anyone who gets near the staircase of the main palace is ordered to halt. If he does not do so, he is stoned and, unless he can escape, he is forcibly detained and tried for disobeying the order of a soldier. Even if he does escape, the chances of avoiding such a trial are slim, because Herod's soldiers on horseback patrol the entire area."

"Are the trials as fair as those at the Sanhedrin?"

"You must be joking. There's nothing fair about them. You're considered guilty the instant you walk in the door."

"Who is the judge?"

"Herod himself. Oh, he has a few courtiers at the table with him, but he makes the decision. Seldom does he set a prisoner free."

"What's the punishment?"

"Often death. But if Herod is in a generous mood, he'll sentence the prisoner to a lifetime of slavery."

"Not such a bad sort," Jesus mocked, with a twinkle in his eye.

"Yes, I guess you're right. I shouldn't have said that."

"How did you prove you had a right to climb the staircase the first time you visited the palace?"

"I suspect the guards had been alerted to look for a man carrying a set of carpenter's tools. Furthermore, I had a letter from Herod himself."

"Do you expect to be called to do more work at the palace? And if so, don't you think it's risky? Suppose he should find out you're the father of the child he sent the three Magi to find."

"I think Herod has forgotten all about that. After all, that was 23 years ago. But to answer your question, yes I do expect to be called back; but I think my next assignment will be at the king's winter quarters in Jericho."

"A nice place to spend the winter."

"Yes, it's usually hot and sun—drenched. Herod has three palaces at Jericho. The country retreat, where I expect to be working, is just 15 miles from his main place south of Jerusalem. It was planned as a place of relaxation for Herod, his family, and his retinue. He even has a facility there for processing balm and dates. The date palms grow in profusion all around the winter complex."

"Carpenter by appointment to the king," Jesus said.

"I'm very proud, father."

"Not as proud as I am of you, my son," Joseph said, putting his hand on Jesus'. "Your mother and I couldn't have asked for a finer son."

*Joseph Radder*

And so the conversation went, far into the night.

Later Joseph took Jesus into his shop to show him his wood-turning device.

Before retiring, they each had a cup of wine.

This evening had been one of those rare and memorable moments when father and son shared their experiences, their love, and their admiration for each other.

## CHAPTER 14 — JUSTICE FOR WOMEN/

## JUSTICE FOR MEN

By the time Jesus was 24 years old, he had developed quite a following of young students. He loved these young people and thoroughly enjoyed his discussions with them. It was his custom to meet with these young men each day for about an hour before the council meeting. They met informally, sitting around the courtyard of the synagogue, some on benches, some on parapets, some on the ground, some standing.

A young man named Abraham was a particular favorite of Jesus', because he was so bright and asked such good questions. One day after the session concluded, Abraham stayed behind to speak privately with Jesus. The look on the young man's not—yet—bearded face betrayed the fact that he was troubled about something.

"What's bothering you, Abraham?"

"You see, sir, I have a sister. She's a year or two older than I am, and she is a very intelligent girl. She has the same curiosity about the scriptures that I have. She asked me to ask you the impossible."

"The impossible? Nothing is impossible with God's help."

"I doubt that God will help us in this matter," Abraham said. "You see she wants to come along with me and participate in our discussions. Before you say anything, sir, I know what your answer must be. The elders certainly wouldn't permit a female to meet with us. I must tell Rebekkah the answer is 'no.' But I wanted to ask if you would mind if I took extensive notes at our meetings to share with her when I get home each day."

"Of course I wouldn't mind," Jesus said. "But there's a better way. You're right about the elders' rules, but there are ways to get around those rules. For example, we could meet in a secret place instead of here at the synagogue. I happen to believe that women should have the same opportunities as men, not only to participate in religious dialog, but to take a role equal to males in all of life's roles. Talk to me tomorrow. Meanwhile I'll try to find a place for us to meet where your sister's presence won't be detected."

"But what about the other students?" Abraham asked. "I'm quite sure some of them have the same strong anti—female feelings as the elders. After all, that's the way we've been raised."

"You're probably right. But let me take care of that."

"Rebekkah and I will be in your debt forever, sir."

"It'll be my pleasure to welcome her into our group."

The next day, before the young people gathered, Abraham was the first on the scene. When Jesus arrived, it was apparent that he had good news.

"I found a place," Jesus said. "It's an olive grove on a hill about a mile south of here. I spoke to the farmer who owns it, and he agreed to let us start meeting there tomorrow."

"Did you tell him there would be a woman with us?"

"I knew better than that."

"Oh thank you, sir. Rebekkah will be thrilled."

When the group gathered, Jesus wasted no time forewarning the other young men they would have a woman in their midst from this day forward, and would be meeting in the olive grove he had found.

"Anyone who objects to this need not join us." Jesus was firm. There was no question that he was very serious about this.

Some of the boys frowned, but others nodded approval, and so they proceeded with the discussion of the day.

The subject they had selected was idolatry; and the text, Deuteronomy, 13:7. Jesus opened the discussion saying, "we know Deuteronomy, the last book of the Pentateuch, as the second law ...or, in other words, a completion and expansion of the law proclaimed on Mt. Sinai." With this brief introduction, he asked young Elishar to read the scripture...

"If your own full brother, or your son or daughter, or your beloved wife, or your intimate friend entices you secretly to serve other gods ...do not yield or listen."

"What other gods do you think Moses was referring to?" Jesus asked the group.

Ishar, a usually reticent young man, surprised Jesus by naming the golden calf of Aaron and some of the pagan gods he had heard about.

"True," said Jesus, "but we, as believers in the Torah, are more inclined to be tempted by gods such as power, money, lust, material possessions, and the like."

"But we don't worship these things," Abraham said.

"Perhaps not as you understand the word 'worship'. But when our pursuit of money, for example, gets in the way of worshipping the one

*Joseph Radder*

true God, it takes on the power of a god and competes with the one God to whom we should give all our devotion."

Isaac was next to speak. He was another of Jesus' favorites. His questions almost always involved healing. It was no secret that he hoped some day to be a medical man... if not a physician, at least a purveyor of medicines who could help sick people get well with his potions and his counsel.

Today was no exception. He asked Jesus, "Were there fewer diseases in earlier times? Or was the practice of medicine more effective then?"

"What makes you ask that, Isaac?"

"Well, men lived so much longer then. In Genesis, we're told that Methuselah, the son of Enoch, lived 969 years; and his grandson, Noah, was 601 years old when the great flood began to subside. There were others too. Like Eber, who lived 420 years. Yet today, a person is lucky to

300

live to see his 50th birthday. How do you explain that, other than the way I've suggested?"

"You've learned your scripture well, Isaac. But you have forgotten perhaps that in the days recorded in Genesis, the word 'year' meant something entirely different than it does today. A year then was probably about 30 days long, or a length of time similar to our month. In other words, if Methuselah lived 960 years, he probably lived about 79 years as we understand them. True, there may have been fewer diseases, but certainly the practice of medicine was not as advanced as it is today."

Just as he finished answering Isaac's question, Jesus caught sight of his cousin James approaching from the corner of the courtyard. "Come in, James. Join our discussion. We were just talking about life expectancy in Moses' time as opposed to the present."

"Thank you, Jesus," James said, "but I must speak to you alone." James was obviously worried about something.

Excusing himself from the group, Jesus took James outside the courtyard. "What is it, James? What's troubling you?"

"I've been accused of blasphemy, dear cousin."

Sitting down on some steps, Jesus said, "Following in my footsteps, are you? Tell me the whole story."

It seemed that James, in a religion class at school, had questioned the need for holocausts, sacrificing lambs on the altar. James' teacher had immediately accused him of blasphemy, and ordered him to stand before the local magistrate, who, in turn, ordered James to stand trial at the Sanhedrin.

"When will this trial begin?" Jesus asked.

"The first day of Tammuz."

"Just in time for the summer heat, usually unbearable inside the Sanhedrin, but have no fear, dear cousin. I'll be there, and I'll speak on your behalf."

"Oh thank you, Jesus. I knew I could count on you." James looked much relieved. "You stood trial for blasphemy once as well, did you not?"

"Yes, but in a much lower court. My trial was before rabbis. The Sanhedrin is a much higher court, and probably does not have a lenient voice, with one possible exception, Joseph of Arimathea, a friend of mine, who sits on the council. I don't understand why they're making so much of the charge against you."

James didn't speak. He was thinking something better not said out loud...that perhaps Jesus had enemies who were trying to get to him through James. He had heard that his elder cousin's reputation was already spreading through Galilee, and that many of Jesus' views irked the more conservative elders.

*Joseph Radder*

On the appointed day, Jesus again borrowed Joseph's donkey cart, picked up James at his home, and the two headed south to Jerusalem.

On the way, Jesus told James what he knew about the high court.

"Don't be too concerned about what I said about the Sanhedrin, James. Its 71 priests, scribes, and prominent laymen are known for their fairness. They dispense justice on a daily basis. The Sanhedrin is a much more just court than Herod's; but, of course, they have authority only on religious matters, and in these their decision is final. Civil cases, however, must be tried by the king's court.

On the other hand, the Sanhedrin has its own police force and can order arrests and mete out numerous punishments ranging from reprimand to 39 lashes. Only the death penalty is outside its authority. Putting men to death is the exclusive prerogative of Rome."

When they arrived at the Sanhedrin, James noted it was in a large stone building, not unlike a temple.

They passed through two sets of great doors, and once inside the courtroom they could see the 71 members assembled in a semicircle, all robed in blue, with white turbans ...except the high priest Annas, president of the Sanhedrin, who sat in the center and was robed in gold, with a red turban. Jesus recognized his friend, Joseph of Arimathea, halfway down the right side of the table. Jesus would have liked to exchange smiles with him, but knew that would not be proper.

At each end of the semicircle sat a clerk of the court, robed in black. Ahead of them were a number of benches. The front benches were reserved for defendants and their spokesmen. Behind these was a second bench for those awaiting trial, and then several rows of benches for students of the law.

After James and Jesus took their place on the second bench to wait for another man to be tried,

*Joseph Radder*

Jesus explained in whispers that even though the Pharisees now outnumbered the Sadducees, the Sanhedrin was still dominated by the latter. The Sadducees' beliefs, Jesus continued, were consolidated into a relatively strict legal and religious philosophy. However, they did believe that any Jew was free to follow God's instructions as set down in the Torah, and to conduct his affairs with honor and prudence as he saw fit. The Pharisees, on the other hand, those in the minority on the court, were separatists. This did not mean that they were liberals, but that they separated themselves from those who did not believe in the purity of the law. In other words, of the two groups, the Sadducees could be expected to interpret the law more liberally, the Pharisees more rigidly. A good way to remember the difference, Jesus said, was that Pharisee rhymed with heresy. These were the people who believed that anything not stated in the letter of the law was heresy.

After the high priest, Annas, had sentenced and dismissed the first defendant of the day, he called James to stand before him as he read the charges.

"James of Galilee," Annas boomed, "you are charged with a most serious offense ...that of blasphemy. Your teachers and the local magistrate at Nazareth report that you have questioned the tradition of holocaust. Indeed you were heard to say that the custom is cruel and pagan. How do you plead?"

"I meant no harm, sir." James was trembling. "I was simply expressing an opinion which I had no right to express."

"Guilty or not guilty of blasphemy?" Annas was angry.

Jesus stood and asked to speak on James' behalf.

"Proceed," thundered Annas.

"To those who interpret the law rigidly," Jesus said, "James is guilty. But those with an open mind will find that, as he said, he meant no harm. This young man is an outstanding student of the synagogue. He observes the law strictly, in all of his thoughts, words, deeds, and actions, even those parts of the law which he may secretly question. In this case his mistake was thinking out loud. I daresay many in this room have had similar thoughts. And one day, I predict, the time will come when we will be allowed to express our views. I submit, honored sirs, that James' only crime was being somewhat ahead of his time."

Most of the members of the tribunal looked at each other in amazement as Jesus sat down. Joseph of Arimathea, on the other hand, was smiling. But the majority were asking themselves who was this brash young man who had the audacity to suggest that even they might question parts of the law.

After much more questioning and much whispering among the members of the tribunal, a man who had been seated next to the high priest Annas, stood up and said, "The defendant and his spokesman will wait in the south anteroom while the tribunal considers his case." It was Ab—Beth—Din, the so—

called father of the tribunal. He too wore the blue robes of the judges. The only item of dress that distinguished him from the others was a white sash worn from his left shoulder to his right hip.

And so they waited, for what seemed like hours. Finally, the call came to return to the council chamber.

"All stand," said the clerk as the members of the tribunal filed in from their deliberation room, led by the high priest, Annas.

"The clerk will read the verdict," Annas intoned.

The clerk at the left of the chamber got to his feet and ceremoniously unrolled a scroll. He read: "The high court of the Sanhedrin, having convened this first day of Tammuz to consider the case of James of Nazareth, finds the defendant guilty as charged of blasphemy against the holy word of God."

Jesus' and James' faces were crestfallen.

"The defendant will stand for sentencing," Annas thundered.

"In light of your good record as reported by your spokesman, Jesus of Nazareth and the support of a minority of the Sanhedrin, this court reprimands you for the offense of blasphemy, and orders you to the custody of this man Jesus, who will send us written reports of your behavior at the end of each month. This supervision is to continue until such time as this court may terminate it. Dismissed."

Jesus and James looked at each other with grateful smiles, then all stood as the judges filed out of the room.

"I couldn't ask for a better sentence!" James exclaimed.

"I think our prayers were answered, James. Obviously Joseph, and perhaps a few of his friends, were on your side. Come, let us go home."

Back in Nazareth, Jesus sent word to the young students that their informal meetings would be resumed the next day, but this time in the olive grove about a mile south.

When the group began to assemble, Jesus was pleased to see that James had accepted his invitation to join the discussions. Abraham's sister, Rebekkah, was also there. She was a pretty, dark—haired girl with brown eyes, and wearing a simple coat of flax.

As Jesus waited for the last few people to arrive, he looked out from the edge of the olive grove across the valley. The hill on the other side of the valley was like a tapestry of reds, greens, and browns ...plowed fields, green olive groves, bright patches of flowers catching the morning sun. When Jesus saw beauty like this, he never failed to say a prayer of thanks for all the beauty of the world, just as he prayed daily to ask God to rid the world of ugliness.

When it was time to start the session, Jesus asked, "Rebekkah, do you have a topic you'd like to discuss?"

311

The girl blushed. She did not expect to be asked to participate so soon; but she quickly got over her embarrassment and after a minute of thought, she accepted Jesus' challenge. "Yes," she said, "I've often heard that there are two kinds of devout Jews, liberal and conservative. Can you explain the difference?"

"I'll try," said Jesus. "The Sadducees and Pharisees once represented two schools of religious thought, but that has pretty much gone by the boards as the Pharisees have grown in strength. Their version of Judaism has come to be the most respected by most of the Jewish people. Meanwhile, however, two opposing schools of thought have developed within Pharisaic thinking. We've come to know these schools of thought as liberal and conservative. But you asked me to explain the difference. Actually, most of the disagreement between liberals and conservatives centers on minor applications of Jewish law. They love to argue about these relatively unimportant rules and customs. For example ...how should one say prayers? What is the best way to observe the Sabbath ...and so forth."

"Rabbis Shammai and Hillel represent the two different factions, do they not?" It was Isaac asking the question.

"That's correct. These two rabbis have had many debates on relatively unimportant points of law. On the important points they agree, but on lesser points they disagree vociferously. Each has his own followers. Hillel's followers are called liberal; Shammai's, conservative."

"Can you give us an example of how they differ?" Rebekkah asked. Jesus was pleased that she was already an active participant in the group. "It is essentially a difference in their approach. Perhaps this legend will illustrate the difference...

A Gentile once approached both men with a strange request. He offered to become a Jew if, during the brief time he was able to stand on one leg, the rabbis could summarize the Torah.

Shammai got angry and sent him on his way, but Hillel said, 'Do unto others as you would have them do unto you. That is the whole of the Torah. Everything else is commentary.'" Just as Jesus was about to introduce another subject, a young messenger appeared at the edge of the olive grove. "Come quickly," he said. "Your father is very ill."

## CHAPTER 15 — TWO JOSEPHS

The young students in the olive grove had never seen Jesus react so quickly. It was not like him to leave them abruptly without a word. But he did ...running down the road toward his little house in Nazareth.

Sweat was pouring from him, and he was completely out of breath when he burst through the door. Going immediately to the bedroom of Joseph and Mary, he saw his mother at the bedside, holding Joseph's hand. When Jesus started to speak, she held a finger to her lips to silence him.

Joseph's complexion was as white as the bleached flax covering which he clutched around his neck. And despite the heat of the day, there were two heavy sheepskin blankets covering him.

"He's been having chills," Mary whispered. "I think you had better go for the doctor."

Without a word, Jesus wiped the sweat from his brow and again started down the road on the run.

315

Joseph was fully conscious. Mary had brought Achim the cat into the room to try to cheer him. Joseph tried to smile, but instead broke into a fit of coughing.

The little cat knew Joseph loved him; but he sensed something was wrong, so he scooted under the bed and hid there.

Joseph tried to speak, but the coughing started again. Mary held a cloth for him as he spat up blood. In her other hand she took a second cloth which she had dipped in a basin of cool water, and wiped his burning brow.

It seemed like hours to Mary, but was actually only minutes before Jesus returned with old Doctor Esau. A young apprentice physician from Antioch was with him. "This is my student, Luke," Esau explained as he parted Joseph's eyelids. He then took some mustard oil and dried brown leaves from his pack, asking Mary to brew a tea with the leaves. He pulled back the covers and lifted Joseph's night robe to rub oil on the aging man's chest. Next, he removed a knife and a speculum from his kit and took some blood from Joseph's arm, explaining to Luke that the color of the blood, at least, indicated Joseph was not suffering from the dread disease leprosy. "However, I fear his lungs are failing," Esau said. Then he turned to Joseph and asked, "Are you in much pain?" Joseph nodded.

Mary returned with the steaming medicinal tea; but when the old doctor tried to pour some of it into Joseph's mouth, it started another fit of coughing; and the tea spilled all over the coverlet.

Mary jumped to wipe up the spilled tea, saying, "I'll make some more."

"Never mind," Esau said. "I'll try something else."

Esau then took some powder from his kit that young Luke recognized to be an extract of poppies.[1]

"Please, sir, not the poppy," Luke pleaded. "It will give him horrible delirium."

---

[1] Opium.

"You're telling me how to practice medicine?" Esau scowled. Then, ignoring the young apprentice's advice, he held a handful of the powerful powder under Joseph's nostrils, holding his mouth shut to force him to breathe in the powder through his nose.

Jesus shuddered as he watched his father quickly slip into a fitful sleep. He remembered a time, not too many years ago, when Esau had given him the poppy powder to relieve severe headache pain. Jesus had had wild dreams while under its influence, and strangely, when he awoke, he had a craving for more of the drug. Fortunately, none was available. He certainly didn't want to become addicted to it, like those three helpless men who begged in the town square for money to buy poppy powder. He realized how easily one could become addicted.

After Esau and Luke left, promising to return in the morning, and giving Mary instructions for hourly oil massages, Jesus and his mother began a long vigil at Joseph's bedside.

During the night both Mary and Jesus prayed almost continuously for Joseph's recovery, but never failed to add, "not our will but thy will be done."

Joseph was delirious from the time the doctors left until just before first light in the morning. It was painful for Mary and Jesus to see him drooling, mouthing gibberish, and thrashing around in his bed.

Between prayers, Jesus spoke to Mary about the evils of drugs and his near brush with addiction, something he had kept from her until this very moment.

Finally Joseph lay still; and mother and son, exhausted, fell asleep in their chairs.

While Jesus was sleeping, God came to him in a dream and told him Joseph's time had come. "Be not afraid," God said, "Joseph will be in my care and will enjoy a special place with me among the saints. Soon you will see Joseph again and, eventually, your little family will be reunited to share your love once more. You will all enjoy eternal life ...without pain, without grief, without troubles, without illness, without any discomfort."

A rattling noise woke both Jesus and Mary. It was the sound of death, as Joseph gasped for his last breath and life passed from his body.

Mary and Jesus wept as they held each other's hands. Taking Mary in his arms, Jesus told her of his dream and what God had said to him. "Yes," Mary said, "he talked to me too."

Taking a scroll at random from Joseph's shelf, Jesus found it was the book of Ezekiel. Remembering the 37th chapter about the bones of the dead, Jesus read...

"See. I will bring spirit into you that you may come to life. I will put sinews upon you, make flesh grow over you, cover you with skin, and put spirit in you so that you may come to life and know that I am the Lord. Thus says the Lord God: From the four winds come, oh spirit, and breathe into these that they may come to life. Therefore, prophesy, and say unto them, thus says the Lord God, oh my people, I will open your graves and have you rise from them, and bring you back.

I will put my spirit in you that you may live and I will settle you upon your (heavenly) land. Thus you shall know that I am the Lord. I have promised, and I will do it says the Lord."

As he rolled up the scroll, Jesus and Mary looked at each other with knowing smiles. They knew Joseph was not ending, but beginning a wonderful life, and they would soon share it with him.

The faith in the little family was so strong, and so sure were they that they would both see Joseph again in God's good time, there was little grief.

Jesus hoped Joseph's funeral could be a celebration of his life instead of the usual weeping and mourning.

It was time now to make preparations for the funeral. Jesus had no taste for the great solemnity and ceremony of Jewish funerals. On the other hand, he had no desire to upset his mother by going against the teachings of the rabbis. And so Mary and Jesus set in motion a carefully—prescribed set of activities. These began with the preparation of the body. First, Mary washed Joseph and sprinkled his body with perfume. Then Jesus helped her wrap the body in long strips of linen. They packed fragrant aloes, myrrh, and other aromatic spices between the strips of cloth and the body. Finally, they bound Joseph's head with a linen napkin.

Already the word of Joseph's death had spread through Nazareth; and many family members, friends, customers of Joseph's carpenter shop, even his suppliers of wood and nails ...all arrived and gathered noisily outside the little house. Their lamentations and loud cries of sorrow attracted even more mourners.

Many of these people didn't even know Joseph. These were the mourners who took a certain morbid pleasure in funerals.

This loud grieving was not without precedent. Indeed, it had been prescribed in the book of Micah, where it was written, "I will make lamentations like the jackals and mourn like the ostriches."

There were other customs too that were distasteful to Jesus. The mourners wore coarse qoat hair qarments to the home of the deceased, and they tore these clothes to show their intentional sacrificial discomfort. Many took dust from the road or ashes from their fireplaces to disfiqure their faces.

At a time like this, many Jewish families hired professional mourners to weep and wail in sackcloth and ashes. Jesus and Mary had no trouble aqreeinq they would have no part of this custom. What's more, there were so many voluntary mourners, that there was no need to supplement their number.

Joseph's burial would follow the mandate to bury the deceased within 24 hours of death. This was a qood rule because, in this climate, there would

Joseph Radder

have been a sickeninq odor had the family kept the body at home much longer. It was against Jewish law to embalm or cremate the dead.

Jesus and Mary slept little that night, for the weeping and wailing outside their windows continued all night long. Furthermore, it was the custom to maintain a vigil with the body. Jesus and Mary took turns with cousins Elizabeth and Zechariah, John, and James, who had come over especially to share that burden.

There was no rabbi in the town; but several elders from the synagogue, led by Jacob, arrived in the morning with several flute players to lead the funeral procession. They also brought a bier with them, fashioned from two sturdy poles and draped with dark purple cloth.

The elders placed Joseph's body on this primitive catafalque and carried it out of the house. Jesus and Mary followed, then the flute players, then the close family members, then the

324

mourninq crowd, proceeding down the road slowly to the grave site.

About halfway to the grave, they stopped at the village square. Here Jacob called on Josiah to read from Ezekiel, the same passage Jesus had read to Mary the night before. Then Eleazar, cantor of the synagogue, chanted the eulogy. In monotonous tones, half speaking, half singing, he began...

"Many of us knew him only as the village carpenter." Eleazar's voice was clear and not unpleasant. The expression on his face was solemn. "Joseph was a very skilled carpenter who could fashion beautiful furniture and cabinets as well as build houses. He loved wood and was the master of it. Indeed, Joseph served Herod, the king, as palace carpenter. But Joseph was more than a carpenter. Above all, he was a man of God. He held the Mosaic law close to his heart, and never did he transgress from its commandments. Joseph was an ideal husband to his beloved Mary and a loving father for his son, Jesus, who will now carry on as head of the Ben David household. We mourn the loss of our brother, but we bid him farewell in the confident knowledge that God has already received him into his presence to live forever in heaven and be joined in God's good time, by his beloved family."

When Eleazar finished the eulogy chant, the procession continued to the grave site, a cave outside the village where other Nazarenes had been buried over many years. When uncovered, the stench from these graves was almost unbearable. That's why it was on the leeward side of town. The mourners ignored the odor, accepting it as a necessary part of the burial of the dead.

Joseph's grave, like the others in the cave, was in a simple rectangular opening in the rock which contained ledges and niches where the bodies were laid.

Jacob and the other elders took Joseph's body from the bier and placed it in its niche. Jesus was pleased to see that the termagant Achim was one of the elders who had volunteered for this task.

After a short prayer, offered by Jacob, the men rolled a huge rock in front of the cave to keep in the odor and keep animals out. The stone was then whitewashed anew to signify that there was a decaying body inside.

The people then stopped their noisy mourning and went their separate ways—the elders to the synagogue for a purification ceremony, for they had touched the dead body and would have been considered unclean without this ceremony ...Mary and Jesus to the home of Zechariah and Elizabeth, because a dead person's house was considered unclean for a week after the body was removed. No food could be prepared there during that time.

First, however, Mary and Jesus paused outside the tomb to pray, asking their cousins, friends, and neighbors to join them.

During the time at the home of Elizabeth and Zechariah, there was much talk about Joseph and about death.

In one of the evening conversations, Mary told a little—known fact about Joseph ...that he was intrigued that he was the namesake of Joseph, the eleventh son of Jacob. Joseph was fascinated by his ancestor and loved to read the story of the first Joseph and his coat of many colors.

"That's one of my favorite stories too," Jesus said.

"Tell it to us!" James said.

And so Jesus told the fascinating scripture story of Joseph, the handsome dreamer, the second youngest of Jacob's twelve sons. He told of how the coat of many colors, a gift from his father, enraged his jealous brothers. The fact that Joseph was clever, had a superior air about him, was handsome, and enjoyed a favored position in the family which excused him from farm tasks ...all these things fed the brothers' envy. "The coat of many colors was the straw that broke the camel's back," Jesus said. And so the brothers plotted to kill Joseph. Only Reuben disagreed, suggesting they show a little mercy and throw Joseph into a deep pit to let the wild animals devour him. And so, one day, when the brothers were working in the fields, Jacob sent Joseph out to observe his brothers' work and bring back a report. This was another practice that irked them. But Joseph cared little about that. The hostile brothers agreed that Joseph's time had come; and so, when he arrived in the fields on his inspection trip, they attacked him, bound him, and threw him into the deep, dark pit they had prepared for the purpose.

Judah, one of the older brothers, suggested it wasn't really being merciful to leave Joseph to be eaten by animals. Instead, he suggested, they could sell him into slavery. However, by the time they could act on this, some Midianites had rescued Joseph from the pit and sold him for twenty pieces of silver[1] to some Ishmaelite traders, who were passing through. In the confusion, one of the traders left the coat of many colors in the dust, and Joseph was able to retrieve it without their notice and take it with him into slavery. This was very important to Joseph because he not only loved the coat but he believed it was what gave him the power to dream such vivid dreams and then interpret those dreams as messages from God.

The Ishmaelites put Joseph up for sale in the slave market, where he was purchased by Potipahr, a minister of the Pharaoh of Egypt.

Reconciled to his fate, Joseph became the exact opposite of his former arrogant self. Now he was quiet, docile, and obedient.

As time went by, Joseph's intelligence made him a very valuable member of Pharaoh's palace. Eventually, Potipahr made him overseer of his house. Potipahr had a beautiful wife, who was not above flirting with the servants, and the curly—

---

[1]About 28 American dollars by 1997 standards.

black—haired Joseph with the big brown eyes caught her attention immediately. It wasn't long before she selected Joseph to be one of her illicit lovers. When Potipahr learned of this, he blamed Joseph and sent him immediately to prison.

Again Joseph's alert mind and clever wit were of great value to him. Soon he was put in charge of all the prisoners, and, in time, he was released and sent back into Pharaoh's service.

It seems Pharaoh had been troubled by nightmares. Hearing of Joseph's reputation as an interpreter of dreams, he summoned him to the court to become interpreter of his dreams.

In his new position, Joseph predicted seven years of plenty would be followed by seven years of famine. Trustinq in this prophecy, Pharaoh ordered his soldiers to store up a fifth of all the fruits of the years of plenty against the expected years of famine.

When Joseph's prophecy came true, Pharaoh was so impressed he made Joseph governor of Egypt and gave him the daughter of a priest as his bride.

The famine experienced in Egypt had also spread to Canaan. Hearing of the stored-up grain in Egypt, Jacob sent ten of his remaining eleven sons to deal with the governor of Egypt for corn. Keeping his youngest son Benjamin at home, Jacob sent the ten on their way with bags heavy with silver and diamonds.

When Jacob's sons met with the governor, Joseph immediately recognized them, but they did not recognize him. There were two reasons. First, they kept their heads bowed as was the custom, not really looking at Joseph. Second, Joseph's appearance had changed considerably and, of course, he wore the lavish robes of the governor and spoke in the Egyptian tongue through an interpreter. He was not ready to reveal his identity as their brother.

Finally, Joseph agreed to give them corn for silver if they would bring back their youngest brother for payment, leaving one brother as a hostage until they returned. They gave the silver to Joseph's attendants and were on their way.

On the way home, the sons of Jacob were surprised to find all the silver they had paid the governor, hidden away in the bags of corn. This baffled them, but they decided the governor must be an unusually generous man.

At home they spent hours arguing with their father, finally convincing him he must part with his youngest son, Benjamin. Sorrowfully and reluctantly, he did so, bidding them farewell with tears streaming down his face.

This time they took even more silver and diamonds with them, hoping to convince the governor to release their hostage brother and let them take Benjamin back to his father.

Agreeing to this, Joseph sent his brothers back to Canaan with still more grain, only to have his soldiers intercept them on the road and accuse them of stealing. As proof of their charges, the solders ripped open the bags of corn and found all the silver the brothers had paid the governor hidden in the corn as before. Taken back before the governor, Joseph said he would release the ten only if they would leave Benjamin behind.

Finally he revealed his identity, saying in his native tongue, "I am your brother, Joseph ...the one you left in a pit to die." Immediately the brothers fell to their knees and begged for mercy.

Joseph took his youngest brother, Benjamin, to his bosom and wept. "I want to see my father," he said. "Bring him to me." And so the ten sons of Jacob, leaving Benjamin behind, went home to tell the incredible tale to their father. It was not difficult to convince him to go back to Egypt with them. And so, at Goshen, the twelve brothers were reunited; and the old man and his long—lost son were reunited at last.

"Scripture doesn't tell us what happened then," Jesus said. "But I like to think Joseph forgave his brothers and they all lived in harmony from that day forward, the eleven brothers finally respecting Joseph for the man that he was."

Mary marveled at her son's ability to remember this long scripture story and to be able to tell it in such an interesting way. But she felt the story was unfinished. "What finally happened to Jacob and his sons?" she asked.

"Well ...on Jacob's deathbed several years later, it was revealed to him that his sons had been chosen to lead the twelve tribes of Israel. And when Joseph died many years later, the Egyptian people grieved for him as if he had been one of their own. They loved this handsome man... this outlander ...who had come from slavery to be their governor."

And so the evenings passed, with Jesus telling more scripture stories in his own colorful and descriptive way, until it was finally time to go home.

Jesus had sent word to the students that he would not be with them for a while. Not only was there the prescribed period of mourning to observe, but he wanted to stay close to his mother. Moreover, there was a backlog of orders in the carpenter shop.

One day, after Mary called Jesus to wash for the mid-morning meal, he returned to the table to find it empty. Then he saw Mary, standing with her back to him, in the doorway to the carpenter shop. When he went to her, he saw she was weeping quietly.

"Please, mother, don't cry," he said, putting his hands gently on her shoulders. "Joseph is with his Heavenly Father, and we'll soon be seeing him again."

"It's not that, dear Jesus. I know what you say is true. It's just that I miss him terribly. Soon you will be called to Jerusalem to continue your work, and I will be alone."

"You will never be alone, dear mother," Jesus whispered. "God will always be with you. Indeed he'll be with you more than any other woman." This was the first time Jesus had ever revealed to her that he knew of her special role in God's plan.

Mary said nothing; but wiping her tears away, she put her hand in Jesus' hand. Looking into his eyes, Mary's smile told him of her deep love for him and for God. He was confident she would be strong from that moment forward.

## CHAPTER 16 — JERUSALEM AND SIMON BAR JONAH

Mary was grateful that Jesus stayed close to home for several months after Joseph's burial. She enjoyed his companionship and appreciated his ability to earn enough in the carpenter shop to provide for their basic needs. She didn't worry about the day she knew would come ...when Jesus would be called to teach full time. She knew that somehow God would provide for her.

One day she said to him, "Jesus, you should look for somebody to take over the carpentry work. You can't stay here forever. You have more important work to do."

Jesus knew she was right, and so he didn't protest. "I know just the man," he said. "Father spoke of him often. His name is Benjamin, and he lives in Cana."

"Benjamin? The youngest son of Jacob?" Mary's beautiful blue eyes always twinkled when she made a little joke like this.

"No," Jesus laughed. "Benjamin the carpenter. He was father's apprentice at King Herod's palace, and a man of surprising skill for his young age."

"Is he trustworthy?"

"Scrupulously so. Father once told me of the time he sent Benjamin into town for nails. When he returned, he found he had one nail more than he had paid for. That evening, on his own time, Benjamin walked all the way back to the iron merchant's stall in the bazaar to return the nail to him."

"Was the iron merchant grateful?"

"On the contrary. He just laughed at Benjamin. But that experience didn't change him. He continues to be honest to a fault."

"He sounds like a good choice, if you think he'd be interested and can do the work."

"He's a better carpenter than I am. And I'm sure he'll be delighted to inherit Joseph's fine clientele. I'll arrange to have him pay you something weekly toward purchase of the business."

*Joseph Radder*

"That would be fine. Why don't you plan to go to Cana tomorrow to see him?"

Young Benjamin was so excited about working in the Ben David carpenter shop, he accompanied Jesus to Nazareth to start work the very next day. He would be happy, he said, to walk the five miles each way every day for such an opportunity.

Benjamin adjusted to the work of Joseph's shop quickly and worked so fast and so skillfully that there was little left for Jesus to do. And so, one day Mary said, "You should be about more important business, dear son. Why don't you go back to the synagogue with the elders or to the olive grove with the students?"

It was true. He had missed the learning and teaching experiences there, and was getting ready to leave for the synagogue one day when he heard somebody tapping at the door. It was Jacob, the leading elder from the synagogue.

"Come in, come in," Jesus said, noticing that Jacob had a scroll in his hand.

"I'll get some wine," Mary said.

"Thank you, Mary; but I must hurry back to the synagogue. However, I have good news that couldn't wait." And with that, he unrolled the scroll. "It's a message for you, Jesus, an invitation from Rabbi Hillel in Jerusalem to come there to teach and learn, to share his philosophy, and live at the Temple school."

Mary and Jesus were both overjoyed. Mary knew this was what her son wanted more than anything. Jesus was excited and eager to go, confident that Mary was now strong enough to live alone. He would visit her often, he thought.

And so one day soon, after a tearful parting with Mary, Jesus was on his way to Jerusalem in the donkey cart that had been Joseph's.

Jacob accompanied him, and on the trip he explained how all of the elders in Nazareth, even Achim, had agreed that Jesus had outgrown their little group. And while he was valuable in Nazareth as a teacher of the young people, they could not expect to keep him there forever. And so they wrote to Rabbi Hillel, telling him about Jesus, and suggesting they call him to serve at the Temple.

"Did all the elders sign the recommendation?" Jesus asked.

"If you're asking whether Achim signed it too, I'm pleased to say he did."

"He was probably glad to get rid of me."

"No. He really admires you, even though he would never show it."

"I guess he's basically a pretty good man," Jesus said.

"Better than any of us knows," Jacob replied.

When they arrived in Jerusalem, the two went immediately to Rabbi Hillel's study. The famous man was not in his office; but his assistant suggested Jesus and Jacob take seats at Hillel's desk, and he would be in to meet with them soon.

Covering all four walls were shelves containing more scrolls than one would expect to see in one place. on the wall behind Hillel's desk, and above the shelves, was an inscription in stone..."An ignorant man cannot be pious." Jesus was pondering the meaning of that inscription when Hillel walked in, his white tunic flowing behind him. He extended his hand in greeting.

"Thank you, Jacob, for bringing Jesus to us," Hillel said. "And thank you, Jesus, for coming. I'm sure you'll enjoy participating in our debates and studying at the school. Our debates are sometimes spirited, because not all of our elders believe as I do... that salvation lies in the here and now, and one can best be saved by leading a humane life and observing the Law to the best of his ability. He who has acquired for himself the words, and more importantly, the spirit of the Law, has acquired life in the coming world. That, in a few words, is the basis of my philosophy. Others, however, tend to think the little details of the Law are more important."

"I certainly agree with your view," Jesus said. "I'm not always one to observe the letter of the Law. To me the spirit of the Law is more important."

"We're going to get along just fine," Hillel said, smiling.

And so their conversation continued along philosophic lines until it was time for Jacob to leave. Hillel found much to agree with in Jesus' views, particularly his emphasis on love of one's fellow man as implied in the summary of the Law. Jesus knew at once that he would be in tune with this learned man, and he was very excited about his future in Jerusalem. He loved the elders in Nazareth, even Achim, but it was clear within minutes that Hillel had a much more profound understanding of the meaning of the Law than all of the Nazarean teachers put together.

After Jacob left, Hillel summoned his assistant to show Jesus to his room above the Temple school.

The room in the dormitory was much more austere than his room at home, and was barely large enough for the cot that filled one wall. There was also a table, a small basin for water, and a pole to hold his garments. As soon as Jesus had unpacked his small sack of belongings, however, the room was brightened by the tiny icons and small treasures he had brought with him... a beautifully painted clay jar, a going—away gift from his friend Jacob, and a painting of his mother by his Nazarean friend Saul. This became the centerpiece on the little table. The only decoration in the room provided by the school was a star of David, fashioned in brass, and hanging above the cot.

The dining hall was also sparsely furnished. It was there that Jesus found a camaraderie he had never known. Being an only child and one who had no neighbors his own age, and who lived some distance from his cousins, Jesus had little companionship while he was growing up other than his parents. Now, he made friends quickly at the Temple school, and he was delighted to renew his friendship with his cousin John, who was also a student there. The last Jesus had heard, John was living as a hermit in the desert, and that was indeed true. However, John had experienced growing doubts about the Law and the teachings of the prophets. To renew his faith, he had decided to spend a year in Jerusalem studying at the Temple. Unfortunately, his life as a student had exactly the opposite effect, and he was frequently very argumentative with the teachers and the other students.

In time, Jesus proved to be a good balancing influence on John. On one occasion, he followed John out of the room. When he caught up with him he was already angrily packing his things to go back to the wilderness. Only through Jesus' gentle persuasion was John convinced to stay and agree to try the Temple classes just a little longer.

"I'm a misfit here," John said. "Back in the wilderness, I'm among friends. Here, I feel that the teachers, and even some of the students, are my adversaries. — The only problem I have in the desert is that the people there not only listen to my preaching, they tend to worship me. That makes me feel guilty, because I know I am a sinful person. I keep promising them that the Messiah is coming soon, one whose sandal strap I am not worthy to untie. But they're tired of waiting."

Jesus listened carefully as John continued, "Jesus, I've had a feeling for some time that <u>you</u> are the Messiah we're all waiting for. Please tell me. Am I right? Is it true?"

However, Jesus knew it was not yet time, and so he simply said, "Be patient, John. Your Messiah will come."

By the time they parted, it was clear that John would stay; and in time Jesus and John became very close, much closer than they had been while growing up in Nazareth.

Jesus had not yet been told where or when to attend classes. So, when he heard the bell for the mid—morning meal, he decided to go to the dining hall to see if he could find someone who might tell him when and where he could start.

Noticing Jesus, a friendly young man asked, "You're new here, aren't you? Come sit with us."

Jesus was pleased, and they introduced themselves. Jesus learned that the young man's name was Abraham and he came from Bethany. The others at the table were friendly too.

Before the meal was served, Jesus told them of his dilemma about classes.

"Don't worry. They'll find you soon enough," Abraham laughed.

The meal, served on wooden plates, was a simple one of bread and a soft barley gruel. The only drink was cool water. However, the bread was fresh and still warm from the oven, and the gruel was flavored with some unidentifiable but tasty spice. And so Jesus ate hungrily.

When the meal was finished, Jesus saw John waving to him from a table across the room. Before Jesus could get up, John was on his feet and hurrying to meet him. He had a big smile on his face as he said, "I've been assigned to be your mentor. You'll attend classes with me. So come. We don't want to be late."

And so, bidding goodbye to Abraham and his friends, Jesus accompanied John to a classroom. It was not unlike the dining hall in appearance, but it was smaller. There were window openings in the whitewashed stone walls. The floor was of flagstone in various shades of gray. The room was indeed colorless ...that is it was until the students in their many-colored garments filled the benches. There were fig trees visible through the windows, and their green leaves, blending with the students' clothing, gave the place a cheery appearance indeed.

The rabbi was a gentle man in a long brown tunic. His beard matched his garment almost perfectly. "Our course of study today," he said, "will be based on the book of Numbers." Following his discourse, he opened the class for discussion.

*Joseph Radder*

He was obviously pleased with Jesus' knowledge of the census, the count of the twelve tribes, and Balaam's oracle.

At the end of the class, the rabbi asked Jesus to read the priestly blessing from Numbers...

"The Lord bless you and keep you.

The Lord make his face to shine upon you and be gracious unto you.

The Lord look upon you kindly and give you peace." That was a good start to a good day.

On the way back to their living quarters, John again told Jesus he felt like a misfit at the Temple School. "Take today's class, for example. All that talk about censuses hundreds of years ago. Who cares? We ought to be talking about how we can live a good life and love our fellow man."

"I agree," Jesus said. "But the Law and the legends that followed are all a good foundation for what we believe in and eventually will teach. You may not like the book of Numbers, John, but as time goes by you will find much of value in the

350

Scriptures. For example, my life would not be the same without the psalms of David. I start every day with a prayer taken from one of his psalms: 'Let the words of my mouth, and the meditation of my heart, be acceptable in your sight, O Lord my strength and my redeemer.' Again, dear John, I beg you to be patient. You must learn before you can teach."

"Perhaps you're right. I really meant to leave until our talk the other day," John said.

"Please forget about leaving, John." And taking both of John's hands into his, he looked into his eyes and said, "I need you."

"I need you more, dear Jesus. I only wish I had your even disposition."


Every single day was interesting and fulfilling as Jesus learned with his fellow students, shared his philosophy with the elders.

After classes each day, it was determined that Jesus should meet with the elders for an hour before mealtime. And after a time, they became more and more in awe of this remarkable young man. Soon it was as if he were the elder and they were his pupils.

When Jesus had first visited the Temple, he had come to listen and ask questions. Now the elders asked him questions and listened respectfully to his answers. Even the highly-respected Rabbis Hillel and Shammai would drop in on occasion when Jesus was in the council room, for word had spread of this young man's marvelous insight and wonderful interpretation of the Law.

While the conservative Rabbi Shammai had reservations about Jesus' theories, he was not as hostile as Achim had been. Hillel, on the other hand, was enthusiastic and supportive.

When Jesus got up in the morning, he couldn't wait for his day to start, and he was almost sorry when the weekly free day or the monthly three-day period of freedom came around.

The day after the Sabbath was always a free day and, following the first Sabbath of each month, students and teachers alike had three days free of classes.

It had been some time since Jesus had been able to explore the city, and so, on one of these free days, he decided to take a walk to the city square.

As he approached this central point in Jerusalem, he heard loud shouting and saw people standing around in a circle, some shaking their fists in the air. Then he saw what all the commotion was about. Two men were fighting in the dusty street.

"What started it?" Jesus asked a man on the edge of the circle.

"A Samaritan and a Galilean," he answered. They started calling each other names; and when the Samaritan told the Galilean he smelled like fish, that was all he could take and he struck the Samaritan in the head."

353

*Joseph Radder*

By then the big Galilean had thrown the smaller Samaritan down into the dust and was kicking him in the ribs. He was about to kick the poor man in the head when Jesus burst from the circle, ran up to the Galilean, and put his amazingly strong arms around the big man, pinning his arms to his side. As he did so, Jesus shouted, "Stop, man! Stop in the name of God!"

When the Galilean heard this he went limp. A Samaritan woman rushed to kneel beside the man on the ground and wiped the blood from his forehead with her apron.

Another rushed in with a cup of water, as Jesus took the Galilean's arm and led him to safety outside the circle of bloodthirsty people.

"What were you thinking of," Jesus asked quietly, "to beat a man so unmercifully?"

"He said I smell like fish."

Just then, Jesus recognized the man. He was Simon, a fisherman from the Sea of Galilee. He had met him once or twice while fishing there with his father, Joseph. "What would one expect a fisherman to smell like?" Jesus laughed.

"And that's not all. He made fun of the fact that I had just been in the Temple."

"You could spend every hour of every day in the Temple, and it wouldn't save you if you treat your fellow man so brutally," said Jesus.

"He's not my fellow man. He's a Samaritan!" Simon said the word as if it were a curse.

"He is your fellow man, Simon. All people are."

"How do you know my name? And how did you know I'm a fisherman?" the big man asked. "And how dare you tell me Samaritans are my fellow men?"

"You and I met some time ago on the Sea of Galilee," Jesus said. "I was just a young boy then, fishing with my father. And as far as my right to tell you that Samaritans are your fellows, I am a teacher at the Temple. There we believe all people of all races, colors, and creeds are children of God, and therefore we are all brothers and sisters." Actually this was not believed by everyone at the Temple. Only the followers of Hillel believed this; the followers of Shammai did not.

"Go now," Jesus said. "Go to the priests in the Temple. Confess your sins of anger and brutality, and you will be saved."

Ordinarily, Simon would have resented a stranger interfering like this, even a teacher from the Temple, but there was something about this stranger. Was it his gentle eyes? His soft voice? He didn't know, but something about this man made the big Galilean feel he had found a new friend.

"I don't remember you, really," Simon said. "Who are you anyway?"

"I am Jesus of Nazareth. And you are Simon Bar Jonah, the fisherman," Jesus repeated.

"Yes," the man answered.

Jesus and Simon walked together to the Temple on the other side of the city, stopping at the well in the square to clean up.

Instinctively Jesus knew this man would one day become one of his closest friends.

## CHAPTER 17 — THE TWELVE

The next time Jesus met Simon Bar Jonah[1] it was again in the city square, early one summer evening. Jesus was sitting on a bench, enjoying the cooling breezes when he heard a deep voice calling, "Jesus! Jesus of Nazareth!" It was the big, burly Simon he had rescued from the angry mob after his merciless beating of the Samaritan.

"Simon!" Jesus responded. "Come sit with me a while."

"I've been hoping I'd meet you again," Simon said. "Remember that day you pulled me away from that hostile crowd? I went to the Temple, as you suggested, and confessed my sin to the priest. He gave me absolution, and then some work to do around

---

[1] Some years later, Jesus would call him Simon Peter (see Matthew 16:17–18). "Jesus said to him in reply, 'Blessed are you, Simon, son of Jonah. For flesh and blood has not revealed this to you, but my heavenly Father. And so I say to you, you are Peter, and upon this rock I will build my church and the gates of the nether–world shall not prevail against it.

the Temple for penance. I've felt so much better ever since. I wanted to thank you."

"You will always find comfort in the house of God," Jesus said. "And what are you doing to stay out of trouble?"

"I'm going back to my job as a fisherman on the Sea of Galilee. I leave tomorrow morning. But I have been anxious to have you meet my friends first. Are you busy this evening?"

Jesus did have studying to do, but there was something about this man Simon that he liked a great deal, and he was intrigued by the idea of meeting his friends. And so he said, "I could spare an hour or two."

"Then let's go now," Simon said. "You can find them any evening in the tavern near Herod's palace."

On the walk to the tavern Simon was full of questions. What, he wanted to know, were Jesus' thoughts about the sinfulness of man.

Jesus' answer was quite lengthy.

As it turned out, Simon became a listener, not natural for him ...until he met this man. Usually it was Simon who dominated conversations, if only by reason of his loud, gruff voice.

"Sinfulness covers a lot of ground," Jesus said, "but in my judgment there are eight major sins common to man, sins which displease God the most. These are pride, envy, lust, anger, gluttony, greed, sloth, and dishonesty."

"Which of these is the worst?" Simon asked.

"They're almost equally deadly," Jesus answered; "however if I had to choose, I would have to say pride is the worst."

"Why?"

"Because pride is a self—righteous denial of the need for forgiveness. Anger, however, is almost as deadly. You see, anger manifests itself in so many ugly ways. It is usually the root of man's inhumanity to man. You experienced it yourself recently when that Samaritan angered you with his name—calling, and you reacted by brutally beating him."

"Ah, yes, I see what you mean. And now I am truly sorry to have let that happen." Simon was humble.

"I know you are. And God, through the priests, has forgiven you. But fighting isn't the worst expression of anger. Killing another person is the worst."

"And I could have killed that Samaritan," Simon observed.

"Indeed. And the worst of all, when nations become angry with one another, or covet their land, we have war ...mass killing. When this happens it surely distresses God."

"Covet. Is that the same as envy?" Simon wanted to know.

"Essentially, yes. When one man or one nation covets what another has, it often leads to anger and then to violence. In other words, one sin often leads to another."

"Can covetousness involve something other than land or worldly goods?" Simon had never before been so enlightened about sin.

"Of course. For example, a man can covet another man's wife, and lust manifests itself. If he is also married and succumbs to that lust, he will probably lie to his wife about it. You see how, again, one sin has led to another?"

Simon was fascinated. "What about greed?" he asked.

"Oh yes," Jesus nodded in agreement. "Greed is indeed a grave sin. For example, a rich merchant charges a poor man more than he can afford for a warm winter cloak he needs desperately. In essence the merchant has stolen money from a man who has much less than he."

"I can understand everything you've said so far, Jesus. But earlier you said pride is a sin. I am proud to call you my friend. Is that a sin?"

"Of course not. I'm a carpenter. And when I do a good job on something, I'm proud of it. That's not what I mean when I say pride is one of the major sins. In addition to what I said before about pride being the self—righteous denial of the need for forgiveness, sinful pride is also inordinate self—esteem. A person who gives himself credit for all of his abilities and achievements without thanking God for his talents is a person who is sinfully proud. We should all be humble before God and thank him daily for all that we have, including our talents and skills. Some people, in their excessive pride, forget God altogether. And this may surprise you, but I believe sloth is related to pride. A slothful or lazy person doesn't understand that God has given him abilities and talents to be used for the good of his fellow man."

"What about lust and gluttony?" Simon wanted to know.

"You're right to link them together," Jesus answered. "Both are sins of the flesh ...lust for the flesh of another person, gluttony for animal flesh to fill one's belly. See how these sins can

363

lead to others...envy, anger, and greed, for example."

˙Simon was beginning to see the light. "In other words, if a person commits one sin, he's likely to be guilty of others. But why, if God is all—powerful, does he let man commit sin?"

"When God created man, both male and female, as you have heard it read from Genesis, he gave them free will. As you go through life, my dear friend, you will find that good people do bad things, and by the same token, bad people can do good things. Likewise, bad things happen to good people, and good things happen to bad people. That's just the way life is."

"How can a bad person like me become a good person, Jesus? How can I avoid sin?" Simon was truly sincere.

"As a human being, you'll never be entirely sin-free, but if you <u>try</u>, you will please God. I think we dwell too much on the negative. We should try to be positive in our lives, try to live according to these nine <u>virtues</u>...humility, kindness, unselfishness, moderation, love, purity, industriousness, honesty, and truthfulness. Of all these, the most important is <u>love</u>. You can't love your fellow man and treat him badly."

When they reached the tavern, both men were ready for refreshment. As they passed through the tavern door, they could hear loud voices and laughter. As their eyes became accustomed to the darkness, they could see ten or eleven men sitting around a long table. They were all dressed in the rough, drab garb of peasants and laborers. Most of them had long unkempt hair and scruffy beards. A few looked as though they hadn't washed in weeks.

"Simon!" shouted the man at the end of the table. "Come and join us. And who is your friend?"

"This is Jesus of Nazareth."

Jesus smiled and nodded. Just then he noticed that his cousin James was one of the group, and he waved to him. James seemed a bit ashamed to have Jesus find him with such a rowdy group. Eyes downcast, he acknowledged Jesus' greeting with a timid wave of his hand.

Simon started the introductions. Walking around the table with him, Jesus shook each man's hand as he was introduced.

"This is Andrew. He's a fisherman too." Andrew was a small man with a scraggly beard.

"And John..." He was a man of medium build, not as large as Jesus' cousin John. He looked a bit cleaner than the others.

Next came Philip. "Philip is also a fisherman. I hope to persuade him to come back to the Sea of Galilee with me," Simon said.

"And here is Bartholomew. Sometimes we also call him Nathaneal. Don't ask me why." Bartholomew smiled as he took Jesus' hand.

"Now here's somebody you may not want to meet," Simon said in jest. "He's a tax collector, and his name is Levi the publican, but we call him Matthew." Jesus laughed as he took Matthew's hand.

"And this is Thomas. He's the twin brother of big James down at the end of the table. we're always arguing with Thomas because he won't believe anything until he sees it." Thomas did not seem as pleased to meet Jesus as the others. Reluctantly he took Jesus' hand, but he was scowling.

"Now we come to Mark," Simon said as they approached a handsome, smiling young fellow. "When we're not here at the tavern, we're usually at Mark's house. His mother is very tolerant of us."

"She loves all my friends," Mark said.

Judas was next. obviously this was another antisocial person like Thomas. Instead of shaking Jesus' outstretched hand, he simply raised his right hand in greeting and looked away.

James, the twin brother of Thomas, a large, rugged looking man, the larger of the two Jameses, was much more friendly.

Between the two Jameses sat Jude. "Jude is as much an optimist as Thomas is a pessimist," Peter said. "He believes anything is possible."

"I'm pleased to meet you, Jude. And I agree with your philosophy," Jesus said as Jude smiled broadly.

Finally came the younger, smaller James, Jesus' cousin, who had tried to avoid his eyes earlier. Now Jesus made him feel at ease by saying, "I know James.

He's one of my favorite cousins. How are you, James?"

James smiled and took Jesus' hand. "Fine, Jesus; how is your mother?"

"She's adjusting quite well, thank you. Stop in and see her if you can."

"I Will. I will," said James, glad to do something to redeem himself in Jesus' eyes.

And so Jesus and Simon enjoyed a goblet of wine with Simon's friends, and made small talk for an hour or two. Finally Simon stood to say goodbye to each of his friends individually. Jesus waved goodbye to all of them and stepped to the doorway to breathe in some fresh air and enjoy some sunshine. He had no taste for dark and dank places like this.

On the way back to the Temple, where they parted company, Simon told Jesus that his friends all liked him and that several asked to meet with him again.

"I told them you were a teacher of religion. And even though most of them are not very religious, several expressed interest in learning more from you."

"That's fine with me if we don't have to meet at the tavern," Jesus said. "Perhaps I can arrange a place for us to meet at the Temple school."

And so Jesus and Simon parted at the entrance to the Temple compound ...Simon promising to pursue his new and better life ...Jesus urging him to pray daily for the strength to do so.

As it turned out, Jesus was able to arrange for use of the Temple school dining hall.

A week or two later, Simon Bar Jonah visited Jesus at the dormitory, and they made final plans for the first meeting of the twelve. Both men agreed the tavern wouldn't be the right atmosphere. And while Simon thought some might be reluctant to come to the Temple, he was sure he could persuade them.

On the appointed day, Jesus arrived at the dining hall a few minutes early. He had scarcely had a chance to sit down when the big burly Simon burst through the door, followed by the other eleven. Jesus was pleased, and not a little surprised, to see that they had all washed, combed their hair and beards, and were wearing clean although threadbare garments. Jesus suspected this was Simon's influence at work.

After greetings all around, Simon said, "Our friends here want to learn more about sin."

Chuckling, Jesus said, "I would think they had plenty of experience with it." They all laughed.

They could see this was a man of good cheer, the kind of person they would like to have as a friend.

And so Jesus began, "Genesis gives us the law with a lot of 'shalt nots', but in Deuteronomy we find a much more positive approach which we call the Shema, or the summary of the law...'Hear, O Israel! The Lord is our God, the Lord alone. Therefore you shall love the Lord, your God, with all your heart and with all your soul, and with all your strength!'[1] This is the first and greatest commandment. And I say, it is just as important to love your neighbor as you love yourself."

Jesus detected a murmur of agreement as he continued. "The key word is love. If you love God, you cannot worship idols, you cannot worship worldly goods, you cannot worship money or other humans. If you love God, you will thank him daily for everything you have, everything you know, everything you can do. In other words, you cannot be a prideful person.

[1] Deuteronomy 6:4,5

If you love your brothers and sisters, you won't envy them. You'll share what you have with them without a trace of greed or gluttony. You won't envy them or covet anything they have.

If you love God, you won't get angry with your fellow man. You'll be a person of peace, not of violence. Yes, love is the key to avoiding sin. And it's important to remember that when you love God and your brothers and sisters, love cannot be lust. A man can love a woman, treat her with kindness and tenderness, marry her, and share his bed with her. He can be strongly physically attracted to her, but if he loves her there can be no lust.

Finally, when one loves God, he will put the talents God has given to good use. He'll work hard at his education, and later at his trade, profession, or craft. A Godly man cannot be a slothful person."

Jesus continued, "I've given you my interpretation of the scripture, based on the summary of the law from Deuteronomy. Now I'd like to hear your thoughts. Let me read the Shema from Deuteronomy again...

'You shall love the Lord your God with all your heart, and with all your soul and with all your strength.'

What do those words mean to you? Anybody?"

The younger James raised his hand. "It means we should not put anything ahead of God."

"Very good. Now let me ask you another question. Tell me about something you love very much ...something you might have put ahead of God at one time or another."

Matthew was quick to answer. "I love what I call the good life ...good food and drink ...all of the pleasures of this world ...and yes, that includes a good woman at my side in the small hours of the night."

"Would you say that, at this very moment, you love this so-called 'good life' more than you love God?"

"I'm afraid I do," Matthew admitted.

373

"Then you need to keep repeating the summary of the law to yourself until you believe it and practice it. Now, another question ...how does one best express his love of God?"

There was silence in the room, and so Jesus answered his own question. "The best way for a person to express his love of God is by treating his fellow man with love ...all of his fellow men. That means no fighting, no taunting, no hatred, no mistreatment of another person in any way."

The twelve men looked at each other in disbelief. What had they gotten themselves into here? No debauchery? No fighting? Even the scripture was full of war and fighting and killing. Life would be pretty dull if they listened to this man, but somehow they were all drawn to him and secretly wanted more from him.

After the hour ended, it was the larger James who asked, "Can we meet with you again, Jesus?"

Simon quickly supported the idea, but Thomas questioned it, saying, "I don't know. I'm not sure I'm ready to be religious."

Seeming to ignore Thomas, Jesus said, "we can meet here at mid—day on the first day following the first Sabbath of every month. Those who want to come, please do. Those who do not care to participate, we will certainly understand and respect your right to stay away." Jesus was delighted that most of them expressed a desire to come back on a regular basis.

As it turned out, all twelve came to the next meeting. Jesus suspected Simon had twisted a few arms. But the twelve met with Jesus every month, and grew spiritually in a way they had never dreamed possible. From this small beginning, Christendom was born.

## CHAPTER 18 — THE ESSENES

It was Jesus' custom to visit his mother Mary every time he had a monthly three or four-day holiday. He felt bad that she had only Achim the cat for company. But each time he mentioned this to Mary, she reminded Jesus that it was he who told her, "You will never be alone. The Lord is with you."

The third or fourth time Jesus spent a holiday with Mary, she said, "Please don't feel that you have to visit me every time you have a few free days. I'm sure there are places you'd like to go and things you'd like to see other than Nazareth."

And so, when the next holiday came around, following the first Sabbath of the month of Adar, Jesus sent his cousin, young James, back to Nazareth with a message for Mary saying he had decided to take her advice this one time and explore the shores of the Dead Sea.

The journey from Jerusalem to Qumran on the Dead Sea was difficult. But the little donkey Jesus had named Judas (because the man Judas was also a bit of an ass) was a sturdy fellow, and the cart Joseph had built was possibly the strongest cart ever to come out of Galilee.

It was spring, and the first part of the journey was very pleasant. Wild primroses added delightful color to the rolling green hills, and cowslips punctuated the meadows.

After a day and a half, however, travel became more difficult, over hilly, rocky terrain. Descending the final hill, the Dead Sea appeared below in the distance; and a little town, apparently Qumran, also came into view. There was no question how the Dead Sea got its name. It was a murky brown, its beaches of mud instead of sand. And the vegetation around it was scrubby and scraggly like the dry growth of the desert, unlike the olive and date groves and lush plant life in the parts of Judea Jesus had traveled through to get here.

He had no idea where he would stay in Qumran. He had heard there was a small inn, but decided to wait to arrange for accommodations until he had done a little exploring. Just outside of town, there was a monastery, home of a fundamentalist Jewish religious sect called the Essenes. These monks were said to be either the authors or custodians of important Jewish writings[1], many of which were over 300 years old. The Essenes kept these scrolls protected in a series of eleven caves on the banks of the Dead Sea near Qumran. Included in these sacred writings was a scroll reportedly written by Isaiah called the Rule of the Community. This, Jesus had heard, was the basis for Essene teachings and discipline. All of this fascinated him, so he decided to seek out the Essenes first, before looking around the town.

---

[1] Known today as the Dead Sea Scrolls.

The Essene monastery was on a steep hill overlooking the town and the sea ...too steep, in fact, for the donkey and cart. And so Jesus fed the donkey some grain, gave him water to drink, and tied him to one of the scraggly cedar trees that dotted this wilderness. He then made his way up the steep hill. As he approached the main building, presumably a place of worship, he could hear the chanting of the monks at prayer. And so Jesus sat down on a stone step to wait. After what seemed like hours, about fifty men filed out silently. They were clad in white flax robes that covered their heads as well as their bodies. At the rear of the procession was a tall man in blue robes tied at the waist with a white rope, apparently the high priest. He noticed Jesus and approached him smiling, his hand extended. "My name is Wadi of Murrabah," the priest's voice was rich and deep. "I am the leader here. What brings you to our home, stranger?"

Jesus explained that he was both a student and a teacher in Jerusalem, and his curiosity about the Essenes and the writings they held sacred, had brought him here to Qumran.

"Normally we do not welcome outsiders," Wadi said. "But since you have come such a distance over such difficult terrain, I will make an exception in your case. Be advised, however, that our brothers are highly disciplined, living a life of self—denial. Much of what you hear and see here should not be revealed to the outside world lest we be persecuted by Jews of other persuasions. Do I have your promise?"

"You do," Jesus answered.

"Come then, and you can see my brothers tilling the fields."

As the two men followed a path around a hill, a field appeared, certainly more fertile—looking than anything else Jesus had seen in the Dead Sea area.

"God has given us several springs which furnish us with a good fresh water supply," Wadi explained.

"We use it to irrigate our fields, as well as for our laundry, bathing, cooking, and baking."

Apparently the monks had gone directly from prayers to their farm work. They did not look up.

Jesus suspected that Wadi saw him as a potential recruit for the brotherhood. As they stood there watching the working monks, he told Jesus that the Essenes had escaped from worldly temptations to live the monastic life in absolute purity of body and soul. This purity, he explained, was symbolized each day at noon when the entire community went to a little lake formed by one of the springs for the bath of purification. This bath, Wadi continued, represented a spiritual washing away of all the stains of sin.

Prior to the washing, he continued, the Manual of Discipline also prescribed the confession of sins in the presence of the whole community. The confession was then followed by a ritual sharing of bread and wine. The chanting which Jesus had heard was part of this ritual.

As Wadi talked on enthusiastically, Jesus learned that self—denial and celibacy were basic principles of the monastic life. "We meticulously observe the Mosaic Law, the Sabbath, and ritual purity. We believe in the immortality of the human soul after divine punishment for sin." The Sabbath is reserved for day—long prayer and meditation on the Torah." Wadi was glad to have such a good listener.

"How does one become an Essenian monk?" Jesus asked. Wadi's eyes twinkled. Perhaps this obviously good man was indeed a worthy recruit for the order.

"The process begins with a year of probation. Postulants then receive their Essenian emblems, but they cannot participate in meals or other activities with the other monks for two more years. These two years are spent in study, self—denial, and self—discipline. Perhaps you noted a few men in the procession with uncovered and shaved heads. These are the postulants. When they are finally qualified for membership, they are called upon to swear piety to God, justice toward men, hatred of falsehood, love of truth, and faithful observance of all the tenets of the Essene sect."

"It sounds difficult." Jesus frowned as he said this.

"It certainly is, but the rewards are great. I must tell you I have it in mind to try to encourage you to stay here with us and become a postulant. But first, I must tell you more about the Essenian life."

"I'm flattered, but I'm afraid I couldn't be a candidate," Jesus explained. "I'm already committed to a course of study and teaching at the Temple in Jerusalem."

Wadi was clearly disappointed. "But let me tell you more anyway."

"I'd appreciate that." Jesus was truly curious, and he was pleased that Wadi had judged him to be worthy of the monastic life.

"No sect of Jews takes the demands of piety more seriously than do the Essenes," Wadi continued. "We subject ourselves to a discipline as rigid as a soldier's, perhaps more so. All of our goods are held in common. Every moment is accounted for, from morning prayers which begin just six hours after sundown, to evening benedictions after our second and last meal of the day. Our priests, myself included, are true sons of Zadok[1]. We were excluded by the controlling priests of the Temple because we did not accept some of their revisionist teachings.

The world as we see it is divided into two hostile camps ...the forces of truth and righteousness and the forces of darkness, or in other words, the forces of evil. We believe that God appoints a Prince of Light and a Spirit of Darkness, and that those two are continuously waging war for men's souls. Good men must constantly battle the Spirit of Darkness with the help of the Prince of Light. We believe that, one day, a Messiah will come to aid in the triumph of truth and righteousness."

---

[1] Zadok was a chief priest under King David.

"Our mission," Wadi continued, "is to prepare the way for the coming of that Messiah. This great day might be years away, or it could occur at any moment. Meanwhile, we'll be ready, with purified souls and strong bodies, to serve God in whatever way the Messiah directs."

"How did your brotherhood get started?" Jesus asked.

Wadi was delighted that Jesus was so interested, and he enthusiastically launched into a long history of the Essenes. In essence, he said that the Essenes, like the Pharisees, originated from the Hassidim, also known as the pious ones. The Essenes emerged as a distinct group apart from the Hassidim about 200 years ago. The first priest of the Essenes was named Zadok. Zadok believed the Temple had been so defiled that those who were true to the Law could no longer worship there. Zadok, also known as the Teacher of Righteousness, eventually denounced the authority of the Temple and its priests; declared its rites, and even its calendar and holidays, invalid.

And so Zadok took a small group of followers and went into the wilderness near the Dead Sea to establish their monastery at Qumran.

Wadi's historic discourse was so long, darkness was falling before he finished. Suddenly, Jesus remembered he had not made arrangements for a place to stay the night. He stood to leave saying, "This has all been wonderfully interesting, but I must feed my donkey and find a place to stay the night."

"Nonsense!" said Wadi. "You'll stay here with us. I'll send one of the monks to care for your donkey and make a place for him in our stable. You'll spend the night with us, and then join us for morning prayers. Just one word of caution ...before prayers, no words are spoken between us. We'd appreciate it if you would respect that custom."

"Of course," Jesus said.

"Also ...the accommodations I can offer you are very spare, just a cot in a small cell."

"I'm used to little more," Jesus said.

And so, after the evening meal, where Jesus enjoyed meeting and talking with several of the monks, Wadi took him on a tour of the monastery ...the scriptorium, the workshops, the meeting rooms, the kitchen, and the bakery. Particularly fascinating was the monastery's huge stone cistern, which collected the water to supply the monks' needs as well as the irrigation system for the surrounding fields where the Essenes grew grain for their bread, fruits and vegetables for their table, and straw and hay for their livestock.

"Unlike most cisterns that collect rain water," Wadi said, "this one holds pure, clean water because it is spring—fed."

The tour ended at Jesus' room, one of many tiny cells lining a long hall. It was not unlike his room at the Temple school ...a narrow cell, with a cot, a small table, and a basin of water.

It was still the middle of the night when Jesus heard loud bells, summoning the monks to morning prayer. Remembering the high priest's invitation to participate, he quickly washed and dressed. Leaving his room, he found he was just in time to join the silent procession to the place of worship. One of the monks motioned for Jesus to fall in place at the end of the line, after the postulants.

The ritual was quite different from the one Jesus knew at the Temple or his home synagogue in Nazareth. Instead of emphasis on the law, there were continuing prayers and an address by Wadi Murrabah. The theme was the importance of humane treatment of one's enemies as well as his friends. Jesus liked that.

After the prayers and chanting of psalms, the monks filed out, chatting and gesturing vigorously as they went to their appointed jobs just in time to see the sun rise. Some went to the fields, a few to the scriptorium, where they carefully copied sacred texts in beautiful calligraphy[1], a few to the kitchen, a few to the bakery, some to the pottery kilns.

Jesus was persuaded to spend at least part of the day observing these skills before starting on his long journey home. Soon after sunrise he was attracted by the aroma of baking bread, and he decided to visit the bakery. A friendly monk in white garb explained the baking process, and cut off a small piece from a hot, fresh—baked loaf of a crusty, sweet, whole grain bread rich with currants. Jesus had never before tasted anything like it.

At the fifth hour of the day he was invited to join the Essenes in their ritual bath of purification. He had never seen others naked before, and felt selfconscious about his own nakedness. I've inherited that feeling from Adam and Eve, he thought.

---

[1] Many believe the Dead Sea Scrolls were written here.

Following the baths there was a very light meal of clear soup and two kinds of fresh bread ...plain and the multi—grain currant bread Jesus had sampled earlier. The meal began in silence until the high priest invoked the Lord's blessing. The monks were permitted to talk during meals, but idle chatter was frowned upon. Tradition dictated that conversation at meals be limited to spiritual thought and the scriptures. The breaking and sharing of bread was, for the Essenes, a holy act.

Jesus was very impressed with the Essenes.

As the hours slipped away from him, he could see he wouldn't have time to get very far before nightfall. Wadi sensed this also and persuaded him to spend one more night, starting for home after the first bells of the morning.

"Your donkey is in good hands in our stable," Wadi said. "He's getting good food and water, so why shouldn't you stay for one more night?" Jesus smiled and said, "I should be very grateful. Thank you."

The next day he reluctantly said goodbye to the high priest and the several new friends he had made in the brotherhood.

On the way back to Jerusalem, he realized that this unique group was thoroughly Jewish, even though alienated from the Temple and its rituals. The Essenes, he had learned, were also alienated from the Pharisees, who lived a much easier life. Jesus had learned much in two days from those strictly disciplined men, much that he would use frequently in his future teachings, despite the disapproval of the elders and rabbis.

Obadiah, the elder at the Jerusalem Temple who reminded Jesus the most of Achim, was clearly displeased that he was a day late getting back from Qumran. Indeed, the fact that he went to Qumran at all was a source of Obadiah's disapproval. Had it not been for Rabbi Hillel, Jesus would not have been allowed to go.

Both Jesus and Obadiah had arrived early for the council meeting. "Where have you been?" Obadiah asked angrily. "You're late returning from your foolish journey."

"I know you don't approve, sir, but I learned a lot while visiting the Essenes, and I found it difficult to tear myself away."

"You can learn nothing from them but heresy!" Obadiah growled. "And then you compound your disloyalty to the Temple with your disrespect for us shown by your tardiness."

"I meant no disrespect," Jesus said humbly. "Please tell me what I must do for penance."

"Only a court of elders or a rabbi can tell you that, and I'm not about to tell anybody about your transgression. I advise you to keep silence as well. If the others know that you approve of those traitors, you could be expelled from the Temple school."

With that, Obadiah turned away, busying himself with some scrolls at the other end of the room, before Jesus could thank him. Apparently, like

Achim, this old curmudgeon was not a bad sort after all.


A week later, it was time again for a meeting with Simon Bar Jonah and his eleven friends. During the meeting they discussed repentance and God's forgiveness.

After the meeting, big James stayed behind and asked Jesus if he could have a word with him.

"Of course."

"Master, I have committed a serious sin. Last night I drank too much wine and went with a harlot to her room over the tavern. (By this time some of the twelve had begun calling Jesus "Master". It was a name that was to stick as long as they were together.)


"Are you married, James?" Jesus asked.

"Yes." James could not look Jesus in the eyes.

"Then indeed it was a serious sin. Have you done it before?"

"Yes. But I never felt this guilty before. Since we've been meeting with you, I've been trying to live the kind of life you've been teaching us."

"But the wine intervened."

"Exactly."

"Then let this be a lesson to limit your intake of wine to a few goblets. Wine is a gift from God when used wisely, but it becomes a tool of the devil when used to excess."

"I will remember. I will," James pledged, falling to his knees and clasping Jesus' hand in both of his.

"Get up on your feet, James," Jesus said. "But you must ask the Lord God for forgiveness."

"Must I talk to a priest?"

"Not necessarily...unless it makes you feel better. You can talk directly to God. Do you remember David's repentance after he committed adultery with Bathsheba?"

"Yes."

"Do you remember his prayer of repentance?"

"I'm afraid I don't."

"You'll find it in the 51st Psalm.

'Have mercy on me, O God in your goodness.

In the greatness of your compassion, wipe out my offense.

Thoroughly wash me from my iniquity, and cleanse me from my sin.

For I acknowledge my transgression and my sin is before me always.

Against you only have I sinned and done what is evil in your sight.

That you may be justified in your judgment.

Indeed I was born in iniquity and in sin did my mother conceive me.

Behold you desire truth, and in my inmost being you teach me wisdom.

Purge me with hyssop and I shall be clean.

Wash me and I shall be whiter than snow.

Let me hear the sounds of joy and gladness, that the bones you have broken shall rejoice.

Turn your face away from my sins and blot out all my iniquities.

Create in me a clean heart, O God, and renew a right spirit within me.

Cast me out from your presence and take not your holy spirit from me.

Restore me to the joy of salvation, and uphold me within your free spirit.

Then I will teach transgressors your ways, and sinners will be restored unto you.

Deliver me from blood guiltiness, O God, God of my salvation.

And my tongue shall sing of your righteousness.

O Lord open thou my lips and my mouth shall show forth your praise.

You desire not a holocaust. Should I offer it up you would not accept it.

My sacrifice is a broken spirit and a contrite heart. O God you will not despise.'"


"Do I have to learn all that?" James asked.

"It's more important for you to understand the words and pray them with sincerity than to commit the words to memory."

"I'll do it."

"And now James I suggest you say the 51st psalm daily for a while, and then whenever you're tempted."

"All right," James said, vigorously shaking Jesus' hand.

"And God will forgive you and bless you."

Another month went by, and it was again time to meet with the twelve.

Jesus took this opportunity to tell them about the Essenes and their customs ...especially their sacraments of water and bread and wine. He was frank to say that he found their ideas to be most refreshing, even the ideas that people like Obadiah would call heresy.

He knew there was no danger of being quoted to the elders. This group had developed an unwritten law of secrecy. They knew that much of what Jesus preached would be considered blasphemy by the more conservative elders in the Temple. The last thing these twelve men wanted was to get their Master into trouble. They had come to love him and respect him like no man they had ever known.

After the discussion of the Essenes, they moved on to the text of the day ...Leviticus, Chapter 11, on the subject of clean and unclean food. Jesus opened the discussion by reminding the group, "Leviticus tells us we may eat any animal that is cloven—footed and chews the cud, but we may not eat the camel, the rock badger, the hare, or the pig because they are unclean. We are also told we may eat whatever swims in the waters that has both fins and scales. We are told what birds we cannot eat, but Leviticus says nothing about what birds are permitted. of insects, we are ordered that we can eat various kinds of locusts, grasshoppers, katydids, and crickets. In addition, of course, the scripture gives us rules and regulations on the use of vessels and cleaning them."

Thomas, never too bashful to interrupt Jesus with his skepticism, said, "Master, we cannot eat the pig. But once when I was in a caravan with my parents, we passed an Arab camp where they were roasting a pig. It smelled delicious. If God didn't want us to eat of the pig, why would he make the aroma of a roasting pig so appetizing?"

"Good question, Thomas. As I've said before, I believe these rules are man—made and not God—made. If your conscience permits, there can be no sin in violating them." This was to be the first of many times Jesus would share beliefs with the twelve contradicting Jewish law. In time, Simon and his ragtag band of friends would go on to teach this new covenant to others.

## CHAPTER 19 — THE SONS OF THUNDER

As the twelve and their Master got better acquainted, Jesus liked to spend some of his free hours with small groups. On one occasion he took the two brothers, James the elder and John, on a journey to Samaria. Jesus didn't like to play favorites, but John was such a pleasant, thoughtful, unselfish man; he knew John would always have a special place in his heart. John was to become much beloved in the days to come. Jesus liked James too. He liked all of the twelve, except Judas, perhaps, but he was indeed human, so it was natural for him to favor one over the other in his heart. He tried not to show it.

When Jesus, James, and John got to Samaria, they were refused rooms in a Samaritan inn ...because they were Galileans. James said, and John agreed, knowing James was joking, that they should pray to bring fire down from heaven, not only on the inn, but on the entire Samaritan town. Jesus just laughed, suggesting they go on to Sebaste, where he had been tempted by the harlot. "I know some people there," he said, thinking of the man and his wife who had given him water. And so James forgot his fantasy about burning the Samaritan town, and they went on to Sebaste to have a pleasant holiday with Jesus' friends.

Jesus introduced James and John to them as the "Sons of Thunder," telling them of their idea to call fire down from heaven on the inn and the Samaritan town where they had been refused rooms. Their host and hostess laughed about this, for they shared the Galilean hatred of the Samaritans.

"Sons of Thunder, eh?" the Galilean laughed. "I like it." The name was to stick, and eventually include all of the twelve.


Simon and his friends met regularly with their now beloved teacher. It was their custom to sit in a circle, with Jesus in the center, Simon Bar Jonah at his right. On Jesus' left was Andrew, Simon's brother, then James the elder, son of Zebedee, then John the beloved, then the younger, smaller James, the son of Alphaeus. Next was Philip, then Bartholomew, then Matthew, then Thomas, Simon the Cananean, and Jude. Completing the circle, on Simon Bar Jonah's right was Judas.

It was a colorful scene. Since their redemption from their life of sin, the twelve had taken pains to keep their bodies and their clothing clean. Their beards and hair were clean and well—trimmed. And most of them had discovered a liking for new and colorful clothing. They looked much different than on the day Jesus first met them in the tavern. Simon, however, wore brown and Jesus wore white.

Most of their clothing was made by family members ...wives and mothers, who dutifully put their hands to the distaff and spindle to make yarn from wool or flax. Wool and raw flax provided the threads used to make clothing for common men. Flax was finely woven into linen for the rich. And so, most of the twelve chose wool for their garments for the cooler months, raw flax fabric for the hot weather.

Most of the twelve had persuaded their mothers and wives to use colorful dyes for the outer garments they wore over their white tunics. The cloth or rope girdles or cinctures they used to tie around their waists were often dyed in contrasting colors.

Looking around the circle on this particular day, Andrew wore an earthy yellow. His mother had extracted the dye from ochre iron ore. James the elder favored the deep blue of the indigo plant. John wore a simple light gray with a wide beet red girdle around his waist. Philip favored green, the dye for which his wife obtained from the plants in her garden. Bartholomew liked the red from berries, while Matthew chose the deeper red of beet juice. Thomas was not one for color. He usually wore black derived from charcoal, but did condescend to wear a deep red rope around his waist. Young James wore a brighter green, made by mixing ochre and indigo.

*Joseph Radder*

Simon Bar Jonah wore brown with a white rope at the waist. Jude changed colors almost every day. Noticing this, Jesus called him "the chameleon". Simon, the Cananean, wore black with a white cincture. Judas also wore black without even a touch of color at the waist. His girdle too was black.

Jesus couldn't explain why, but in his heart he didn't trust this man Judas. He never looked the others in the eye when he conversed with them, which was infrequently. Usually he was a very serious, quiet man.

He didn't even laugh at the others' jokes. Perhaps all these things together were the reason for Jesus' distrust.

Since Jesus knew he would not be with the twelve much longer before his promised visit to John the hermit in the wilderness, he decided to use their next meeting to impress a mental picture of each of them on his mind. To help this along, he asked each of them, in turn, to tell something about himself.

Jesus called first on James the elder.

"I'm a fisherman," began James, the son of Zebedee, also a fisherman. Jesus, of course, knew this, but he let James continue. "My mother's name is Salome. I fish with my brother John on the Sea of Galilee. We catch a wide variety of good fish; one of the best-tasting, as you know, is the tilapia. We use various types of nets. Simon is the fisherman I admire most. He catches more than any of us ...even more than my father, Zebedee.

"You've told us about fishing, James, but little of yourself," Jesus said. "What have you done in your life to serve God?"

James was, for a brief moment, at a loss for words. Then he said, "One time, using pressure on a man's chest and breathing into his mouth, I brought a dying man back to life."

"Excellent, James," said Jesus. "Now, John, what about you?"

John was normally a quiet and modest person. Talking about himself was uncomfortable for him.

John did not depart from his modesty this day, but he did manage to say that he liked to write.[1]

"As we develop our views on the Torah, and perhaps more importantly, our philosophy on loving one another, I hope you will be able to write them down for us."

"I'd consider it a privilege," John said.

Next in the circle came young James. "I'm the son of Alphaeus," James said. "I've found that I can best serve the Lord through personal sacrifice. When I fast, I feel much better. And I pray a lot. In fact, my knees are sore from kneeling." This was the kind of spiritual talk Jesus wanted to hear. Young James was indeed growing spiritually, much faster than some of the others.

Next came Philip, one of the first to dedicate his life to Jesus. In this meeting he said, "Master, I'm prepared to spend the rest of my life

---

[1]As it turned out, almost thirty years would pass before John, his fellow apostles Matthew and Mark, and Luke the physician from Antioch, were to write their gospels.

helping you spread your teachings among the people."

"That pleases me tremendously," Jesus said, "but the time for that has not yet come. Indeed, I must go away for a while, but I invite you all to meet me in Capernaum on the first day of Marchesvan. There you can help me begin a ministry that could change the world."

This was the first time the twelve had heard Jesus speak of changing the world. They looked at each other. Only Simon seemed to know what their Master meant by this.

Next to speak was Bartholomew, who explained that was his surname. His given name was Nathaniel, but he preferred to be called Bartholomew. Bartholomew said, "Master, Philip and I were talking the other day, and he said that you are the Messiah ...the one Moses and the prophets promised. Is this true?"

Jesus smiled and, as usual, avoided answering this question directly. "If I am," he said, "you will learn the answer in Capernaum."

Bartholomew then yielded to Matthew, who said, "I'm frequently derided in this group, Master, because I'm a tax collector; but they accept me as a person, regardless of my vocation. I'd like to say here and now that I am prepared to give up that vocation to follow you and help spread the good news of your teachings throughout the land."

"Again, I'll say, the time is not right, and will not be right until after we meet again in Capernaum. So don't give up your job yet, Matthew." Jesus was delighted that so many of these men had turned their lives around so quickly.

What Thomas said, on the other hand, was disappointing. "I'm not sure I'm ready to accept all this new thinking, or to give up life as I know it to help you teach it. I want to see more evidence that your theories are right."

"In time you'll know that they are not theories but truths," Jesus answered while thinking ...at least Thomas continues to come to meetings. He hoped that, in time, he'd be able to convince him.

Simon the Cananean tended to agree with Thomas. "As you know," Simon said, "I'm zealous about Jewish Law. I don't object to your interpretation of the Law and supplementing it with your thoughts, but I do object when you appear to reject the Law." Again Jesus trusted that eventually Simon would see the truth.

"My full name is Jude Thaddeus," Jude said when it came his turn to speak. "I'm perhaps as zealous about the Law as Simon, but I do like the positive tone ...the optimism... in your teachings. I believe that anything is possible with God's help...even finding the answers to the most hopeless and desperate causes." Jesus smiled. Even this rigid thinker seemed to understand what he was trying to get across.

Next came Judas Iscariot, the one with the shifty eyes. "I'm not a Galilean like most of you," he said. "I come from Judea ...Kerioth to be exact. I must admit I have a major weakness. I love gold and silver more than life itself. It's appropriate that you have made me treasurer. I will guard your meager funds carefully."

Simon, son of Jonah, was the last of the twelve to speak. "You know me well, Master. But I don't believe you understand that I am still a sinful man ...given to violence and the sins of the flesh. What's more, I lack the faith that many of you have. I cannot be trusted to be loyal. And yet, I see in your teachings, a way out of my sinfulness.

"Here," Jesus thought, "is a truly spiritual man, one who is humble enough to admit his faults and sincerely thirst for redemption." Of all of the twelve, this man was most likely to be their leader when Jesus was no longer with them.

Finally Jesus said, "You may be wondering about me ...what brought me to this point in life. As the

410

son of a carpenter, I was obliged to follow his vocation, but I had an insatiable curiosity about God and religion." Continuing, he told his followers at great length about his experiences, from his boyhood when he stayed behind in the Temple, to his discussions with the elders at the synagogue in Nazareth, his journey with Joseph of Arimathea's trading mission, the time spent with the Essenes, and finally as a student and teacher at the Temple school. He acknowledged that he frequently questioned the Law, and therefore was often considered, by the more conservative rabbis and elders, to be a heretic. He concluded by saying, "My reputation as a heretic is spreading. That is why we must keep our meetings and our discussions secret for now."

With this, he ended the meeting, reminding them that he must go away for a while, and repeating his invitation to meet again in Capernaum. Then he said farewell, shaking each of the men's hands and saying, "If you want to be my brother, have love

*Joseph Radder*

for one another and love your neighbor as yourself."[1]

Before his trip into the wilderness to be with the other John, his cousin, Jesus decided he needed a few days of rest. He could go home to Nazareth, but he wanted to see his birthplace, and so he decided to go to Bethlehem.[2] Young James had reported that Mary was well, and adjusting beautifully to her new life alone with Achim the cat. And so he started out for Bethlehem, promising himself to visit Mary before he went to Capernaum.

First he went to Rabbi Hillel and told him he felt a strong calling to move on, and therefore felt he must leave the Temple school. Hillel was most understanding and promised to pray for him. Next he went around the Temple saying his goodbyes to the other elders and the students.

Bethlehem was much as Mary and Joseph had described it. At the edge of town was an

---

[1] Leviticus 19:17.
[2] Bethlehem, translated from Hebrew, means "House of Bread".

412

inscription on a stone reminding visitors that Bethlehem was the birthplace of King David. Jesus was pleased to be a member of the House of David. And while he decried David's violence and debauchery, he admired his gifts for music and poetry. He remembered the story of David and Goliath, wondering how David could rationalize even such a justifiable killing in light of the Lord's commandment..."Thou shalt not kill."

Bethlehem is situated on a ridge in the rocky hills just south of Jerusalem. It is surrounded by lush green hills, olive and date groves, even though it is not far from the wilderness bordering the Dead Sea.

Eventually he found the caravansary where he had been born in the stable. Not revealing his identity, he obtained permission from the innkeeper to visit the manger. This innkeeper was a friendly fellow, obviously not the same one who had refused his parents lodging some 29 years past.

*Joseph Radder*

There were lambs in the stable on the day Jesus visited. This was easy to understand, since the meadows surrounding Bethlehem were home to many shepherds and their flocks. On his way into town, Jesus had observed these shepherds tending their sheep. And he noticed they had constructed high stone walls to protect the sheep. The walls were topped with thorn branches to keep out the wild animals, but there was an open gate. Jesus was impressed when told that the shepherds would lie across these entryways at night, acting as human gates.

"One day I will lay down my life for my sheep," Jesus thought.

As he knelt in the stable, thanking his heavenly Father for his parents Mary and Joseph, and for the mission God had made clear to him, he recalled the stories his mother had told him of the mysterious, brilliant star in the east the night he was born. It had attracted shepherds and kings alike to the manger.

With a shiver Jesus recalled how the evil Herod had asked the visiting Magi to return after they had found the babe, and let him know its whereabouts so that he also could adore the new-born King. But they went back to their Eastern Kingdoms by another route, knowing Herod planned to murder the child.

As the birthplace of King David, Bethlehem had been a sacred Jewish city for hundreds of years. Jesus wanted to explore its historic sites, such as the tomb of Rachel, Jacob's wife and the mother of the first Joseph and Benjamin. In his exploration of the town, Jesus learned that Bethlehem was once home to the scripture figures Ruth and her husband Boaz. Thinking of Boaz reminded him of the slaves Boaz and Ram who had served him so faithfully on the trade mission to the east. He said a prayer for both of them.

Bethlehem was not only the birthplace of David, but the place where he had been anointed king of Israel some 1,000 years past. About 200 years later, the prophet Micah proclaimed that one day a descendant of David would be born in Bethlehem to return the Hebrews to glory and power.

After thoroughly exploring all of the historic sites, he decided it was time to leave. For a fleeting moment, he toyed with the idea of visiting Mary once more before going to the wilderness to meet John. But his better judgment told him Nazareth was at least four days away. On the other hand, the wilderness bordering the Dead Sea was much closer. And so, reluctantly, he decided to go directly east, praying along the way for Mary's welfare, and vowing to visit her one last time before going to Capernaum.

Even though the roads were rough and the hills steep, the sturdy donkey cart and the faithful donkey named Judas, served him well. This trip reminded him of his journey to Qumran, even though that took him over a road some miles to the south.

The rocky road called the Wadi Qilt followed a valley through the sparsely vegetated mountains.

There was one entire day when Jesus did not see one other living soul. Truly, this was a godforsaken place.

In the desolate flats, the harsh desert created by the evaporation of the Dead Sea was also known as the wilderness of Judea. It had but two oases.

Jesus couldn't believe his eyes when one of these came into view. The first things visible were tall palm trees. As he got closer, he could see a beautiful clear blue lake. Could this be one of those mirages he had heard about? It was soon evident, however, that <u>this</u> oasis was real. He said a prayer of thanks because it had been at least an hour since he had given the last of his water to the donkey. He would have liked a drink himself but, characteristically, he gave up his share to the animal. Now his throat was so parched he felt he couldn't have endured another mile. But again, God was with him, bringing him to this oasis just in time.

417

There were a number of people around the lake, both Arabs and Jews. They were watering their animals and filling their goatskin water bags. Some of the children were wading in the cool lake.

Once Jesus had attended to his donkey, he didn't wait to fill the water bag, but fell to his knees at the lake's sandy shore, putting his face in the cool water and drinking his fill. Then he splashed water on his clothing to ward off the scorching heat. The others there paid no attention, because they too had experienced the heat of the wilderness and many had done exactly as Jesus was doing. As he sat in the shade of a palm tree, his back against the trunk, he told a man resting against the next tree how he had suffered from the freezing cold in the Himalayan pass.

"Why must man suffer these extremes of heat and cold?" the man asked.

Jesus had the answer. "If the earth were perfect, the afterlife in heaven would not be as great a reward. The man, a Jew, understood and nodded in agreement.

Jesus knew that heaven was a perfect place, neither hot nor cold, neither sunny nor cloudy, neither windy nor calm. The perfection of heaven was something impossible to explain to men, and so he didn't try.

After a reasonable rest at the oasis, Jesus was on his way again.


The next day he arrived at the banks of the Jordan River, just north of where it flowed into the Dead Sea. According to John's directions, his encampment was only a few miles north of here. And so Jesus started in that direction, following the river.

Soon the brown water of the Dead Sea turned into a beautiful blue–green. The river flowed from north to south, but somehow the brown sea backed up into the river for a mile or two. The prevailing winds probably had something to do with it.

In time, Jesus saw the smoke of a campfire, and after he walked toward the smoke for a while, he could make out the figure of a man bent over the fire, roasting an animal on a spit. The aroma was marvelous, and especially so since Jesus had eaten nothing but dates, figs, and olives for three days.

"John! John!" Jesus cried.

"Jesus!" John looked up, revealing a big grin. He was clad in wild animal skins. "You're just in time for a feast. I caught a wild goat this morning. He's going to make a fine dinner for us."

"I can tell by the aroma," Jesus said, walking closer and then embracing John. "But I thought you lived on locusts and wild honey."

"I usually do," John beamed. "But tonight is special. I had a feeling you'd be along today."

The crusty brown roasted meat had a flavor not unlike lamb, and both of the men ate more than they should have. They talked for hours over the fire, but then John dozed off and so did Jesus. It had been a long day.

# CHAPTER 20 — WITH JOHN AND AT CAPERNAUM ON THE SEA OF GALILEE

That night in John's wilderness camp, Jesus lay in his tent and thought about the stories his mother, Mary, had told him regarding John's birth, about a year before Jesus was born. According to Mary's account, Elizabeth, a much older cousin, was terribly depressed because she had never borne a child and now she was too old to be a mother. Then suddenly, Elizabeth had told her, an angel named Gabriel announced to Zechariah, Elizabeth's husband and a priest, that Elizabeth would give birth to a son filled with the holy spirit. The child, the angel said, should be named John, and he would grow to bring many Jews back to God. Zechariah, as Mary had told the story, had been unable to believe this. After all, Elizabeth was very old. And so, as punishment for his disbelief, Zechariah was struck dumb.

Gabriel told him he would not speak again until his son was born.

Six months later, Gabriel appeared to Mary, telling her she would bear a son, to be named Jesus, who was destined to reign on the throne of David. Jesus, of course, had never revealed this story to anybody.

Now, on his makeshift bed in John's camp, he felt the time was close at hand when he would be guided by the Father to reveal that he was indeed the Messiah.

Continuing to recall the story of John's birth, Jesus remembered that when John was born, Zechariah did speak again, saying, "His name is John!!" This had been a surprise to all because nobody in the family had ever had that name, and it was customary to name children after their forebears.

It was a habit of Jesus' to pray each night until he fell asleep, but this night, accompanied by the sound of buzzing locusts and chirping crickets, he fell asleep thinking about the story of John's birth.

In the morning, John gave Jesus some tea made from boiled thornbush. It was bitter, but certainly effective in chasing away any lingering sleepiness.

Later they would have a simple meal of locusts and honey. During this meal John told Jesus about the pilgrims who arrived daily at his camp. "They are from many tribes, and even some Sadducees and Pharisees come," John continued. "Apparently my reputation has spread as far north as Capernaum and as far west as Emmaus. I don't know why my message is so popular. There are many other prophets and preachers wandering through Judea, but for some reason they seem to want to hear me."

Certainly, Jesus thought, God must be guiding these people here. After all, John's appearance was enough to scare people away. His hard, lean body, clad only in camel skins, his scraggly beard and his unkempt hair were more frightening than attractive. "What do you preach?" Jesus asked.

423

"I teach them to love one another," John said. "I tell them if they have two coats, to share one with somebody who has none. And he who has food should do likewise."

"Again, the message of love from Leviticus,"[1] Jesus said.

"That's right!" John spoke much louder than necessary. His booming voice echoed off the rock in the nearby mountains. "Love your neighbor as yourself."

"My only problem," John continued, "is that these pilgrims think I am the Messiah. I tell them that I am not. Then they ask if I am Elijah reincarnate. Again, I say no, and tell them that I baptize them with water, but he who is coming after me is mightier than I and he will baptize them with the holy spirit and with fire."

"And who will that be?" Jesus asked.

"It will be you, Master, for you are the Messiah." Strangely, John had picked up this title,

---

[1] Leviticus 19:18

Master, without having known his twelve friends, who had originated this way of addressing Jesus.

"All right, John, I can tell you now, binding you to the strictest secrecy, that I am indeed sent by the Father."

John fell to his knees before Jesus, but Jesus lifted him to his feet and said, "Please, John, worship the Father, not me. My time has not yet come."

As they talked, they could see people coming over the hill in the distance ...some on camels, some in donkey carts, some on foot. They wore the colorful linens of the rich, the dyed flax of the middle class, and the gray or brown flax of the poor.

Reaching the foot of the hill, they followed the serpentine banks of the Jordan, through thickets of tamarisk, willow, poplar, cane, and oleander, many of which were entwined with vines and spiked with brambles.

But no matter how difficult it was, they came ...to hear the words of the man who was here to prepare the way for the Lord.

As Jesus listened to John talking to them, he noted that there was nothing he said that went against the principles of the Torah, and he marveled at the verbal abuse these people took from John. He called them vipers and warned them that they must repent in order to flee from the wrath to come. Indeed, he was the first "fire and brimstone" preacher.

One by one, they knelt down in the water as John took some of it in his two hands from the river and poured it over their heads, saying, "I baptize you with water in the name of the Lord, and cleanse you from your sins. Go and sin no more."

The baptized seemed to be in a state of utmost bliss as they stood with dripping garments and walked to the shore. There were no exceptions ...men and women, young and old, rich and poor, Sadducee and Pharisee, each obviously felt he had been touched by the Lord through John and his purifying water.

That evening, Jesus told John about the Essenes and their rite of purification by water... so similar to the ritual John called baptism.

"I'm sure that the Essenian rite and my sacrament of baptism were both inspired by the Lord," John said.

"There's no question about that, John," Jesus said.

Following the mid—afternoon meal, this time some of the roast goat from the day before, some berries sweetened with wild honey, and more of the thornbush tea, Jesus said, "John, I have something to ask of you."

"I would do anything for you, Master."

"I need to be baptized by you."

"You need to be baptized by me? It would be fitting only if you were the baptizer and I was the baptized."

"No, John," Jesus said, "I need to be baptized by you. Let it be so. It is fitting we should do this to fulfill the prophecies."

And so, in the morning, before the people arrived, John performed the rite. When Jesus emerged from the water, a white dove flew down to him and he heard an inner voice saying, "You are my beloved son, filled with the holy spirit. With you I am well pleased."

For several days, John preached to different groups of people and baptized them as Jesus sat on a hillside watching and listening.

One evening, after the people had left and the two had finished their meal, Jesus said, "John, you tell the people they must eat no bread and drink no wine, but I say eating and drinking is no sin unless it is done to excess. We will go to Capernaum and make the blind see and the lame walk, we will cleanse the lepers and make the deaf hear. And we will raise up the poor. These acts will be much more important than rules about food and drink."

John could see the truth in this, and from that day forward he emphasized the lesson of love from Leviticus, de—emphasizing the rules for living.

Long discussions continued each evening around the campfire.

Finally, one morning, Jesus said, "John, I must leave you now to see my mother, on my way to meet my followers in Capernaum. Thank you for your hospitality, and letting me share in your ministry; but above all, thank you for the gift of baptism. Keep it up, John. It's a great work for the Lord that you are doing here."

As the two embraced, the big, burly John had tears in his eyes. And as the donkey cart took Jesus back down the road alongside the Jordan, he turned back for one last look before he rounded the bend in the river. John was wiping his eyes.

Jesus was able to celebrate his thirtieth birthday in Nazareth. His reunion with Mary was a joyous one. Yet his heart was heavy because he knew this was probably the last time he would see her on earth.

For his birthday feast, Mary cooked all of his favorite foods, baked his favorite breads, washed his clothes, and mended his garments. Each evening Jesus would read to her from Joseph's treasured scripture scrolls.

"You must visit the elders, and your old students at the synagogue, while you are here," Mary said. And so Jesus took half of one of his days in Nazareth to see his old friends.

In the council room at the synagogue, everyone was overjoyed that he had come to visit them. Even old Achim had a big smile on his face, and he hugged Jesus even longer than the others did. It warmed Jesus' heart that he had apparently won the old curmudgeon as a friend.

The students were no longer meeting in the olive grove, but had been instructed to come back to the synagogue school, all of them but Rebekkah. Their rule against women students, Jesus was sorry to hear, was still rigidly enforced.

That evening, when Jesus told Mary about his synagogue visit, she was not surprised to learn that he had spent more time with the students than with the elders. "You always did have a special empathy for young people," she said.

Achim the cat, acting as though Jesus had never been away, curled up at his feet and purred contentedly, as if to listen with Mary to the scripture stories.

On Jesus' last day in Nazareth, Mary prepared another meal, even more festive than his birthday dinner. First, there was a soup of beef broth, vegetables, and barley. Then succulent leg of lamb, roasted a crusty brown. Mary had spent much of the day turning it on the hearth. There was a special bread, made of several grains and currants, similar to the bread Jesus had enjoyed at Qumran. Its aroma, as it baked in the stone oven, was tantalizing, making Jesus anxious for the meal to begin. Finally, there was a honey—sweetened cake and some wine Joseph had been saving for years, for just such a special occasion.

After dinner, they sat at the table and talked for a long time. Jesus considered telling her what was ahead of him, but he thought better of it. Finally, he put his hand on Mary's, looked into her eyes and said, "Blessed are you among women, dear mother. I thank God every day that he chose you to bear me."

Mary wept, but they said no more. As Jesus kissed her goodnight before retiring, she had a terrible feeling that, after he left for Capernaum in the morning, she would never see him again. Even Achim the cat seemed to sense that something was wrong.

Soon after he got up in the morning, bathed, and packed his belongings for the trip to Capernaum, Jesus was surprised to find Simon, son of Jonah, John, and Andrew knocking at the door.

"We came to tell you we cannot meet you in Capernaum," Simon said. "We've decided to go back to work fishing with James and Zebedee.

Jesus was crestfallen. "Follow me," he said, "and I will make you fishers of <u>men</u>."

The three disciples looked at each other. The magnetism and the persuasive powers of this man were incredible. Never before had they met anyone with such powerful influence over them.

Finally, after a long silence, Simon said, "Let us think about it." And so Jesus left them alone for a time to reconsider their decision.

After about an hour, the three came back into the house. Speaking for John and Andrew as well as himself, Simon said, "All right. We'll go with you. But how will we live without our income from fishing?"

Jesus was delighted, and he embraced all three, saying, "Don't worry. God will provide."

Not long after they reached Capernaum, Jesus started preaching, first to small groups, which grew larger by the day. Finally they moved to the shore of the Sea of Galilee, where the thousands of people who came could see him by sitting on a lakeside hill. The crowds continued to grow until they crowded the shore, and Jesus was forced to do his teaching from an offshore boat. Almost everybody who came to hear him brought a gift. Some brought bread, some brought fish, some cheese, some meat, some vegetables, some sweets.

Some of them even brought clothing. Simon beamed as he said, "Indeed, God has provided for us."

By this time, all of the twelve were together again, and there was more than enough to feed and clothe all of them.

A considerable number of the people who came to hear Jesus were women. As it turned out, three of these women ...Joanna, the wife of Herod Antipas' steward, a second woman named Susanna, and a former harlot named Mary Magdalene, whom Jesus had met in the village square and turned from her sin... these three provided the financial support that was needed. They asked everyone who came to the hillside for money, as well as their gifts. And they set up a treasury, and allocated small allowances to each of the twelve for their basic needs.

In the evenings, Jesus stayed at Simon's house in Capernaum. Similar to the house in Nazareth, where Joseph and Mary had raised Jesus, this house was made of stone without mortar. The stones were held together by a plaster—like coating, both inside and out, which was made of clay and lime. These walls kept the house relatively cool in summer and warm in the rainy winter season. The roof was thatched with reeds, sticks, straw, and clay. A door from the dusty street led directly to an inside courtyard. Here, Simon's wife had a hearth for cooking, with an oven for baking. Adjacent to this courtyard was a large room for living and dining. Off of this, were two bedrooms furnished with straw mats. The only sources of light for these rooms were small windows under the thatched eaves. Another outside door from the street opened to the fish market, where Simon's wife sold his daily catch.

Even though Simon had arranged for another fisherman to supply the market, his wife disapproved of his new vocation. "Fishing," she said, "is a much more reliable occupation than following some dreamer and his ideas." She didn't hesitate to say things like this in front of Jesus, which caused him to smile and Simon to react with embarrassed anger.

Each day Jesus and Simon would leave the little house and meet the other eleven on the shores of the sea. While Jesus preached to whoever came, the twelve would help the three women collect the gifts of the people. And they would talk to those people who were troubled, as vicars of the Master.

At the end of each day's sermon, Jesus would ask the assembled multitude, now numbering as many as five thousand, to join him in a prayer he had taught them...

"Our Father who art in heaven, Hallowed be Thy name. Thy Kingdom come, Thy will be done, On earth, as it is in heaven. Give us this day, our daily bread, And forgive us our trespasses, As we forgive those who trespass against us. And lead us not into temptation, But deliver us from evil, Amen."

It was the custom of the twelve to lead the multitude in a response to this prayer...

"For thine is the kingdom,

And the power,

And the glory forever and ever,

Amen."

Following this he would ask the sick and the disabled to come forward for healing prayer. The ill, the infirm, the blind, the lame, would form a long line and then a semicircle. Jesus would go from the left of this semicircle and move to the right, putting his hand on each person's forehead, saying a prayer. The twelve would stand behind the people being prayed over, for they would often fall back in sort of a faint. Sometimes the healing was immediate, but more often than not it took time. Many returned daily to tell Jesus how he had healed them. And, of course, word of this spread quickly through Galilee.

Sometimes there would be so many to heal, Jesus would have to stay far into the night. But he never tired, never stopped, until he had ministered to the very last person to come.

All of Jesus' teaching was not confined to the shores of the Sea of Galilee. Soon he was invited to speak in the synagogue at Capernaum. He was accepted there because he had been careful not to contradict the Torah, but to supplement it, interpret it, and amplify it. In one of his synagogue sermons he said, "Do not think I have come to abolish the Law and the prophets. I have come not to abolish them, but to fulfill them."

Back at the seashore one day, Jesus surprised everyone, including the twelve, by leaving his usual place in the boat and climbing to the top of the mountain. Everybody turned around as he began to speak in a resonant voice from the mountaintop...

"Blessed are you poor, for yours is the kingdom of God.

Blessed are you that hunger, for you will be satisfied.

Blessed are you who are weeping, for you will laugh.

Blessed are you when others hate you, exclude you, insult you, and denounce your name as evil on account of the Son of Man. Rejoice and leap for joy in that day.

*Joseph Radder*

Behold your reward will be great in heaven.

The ancestors of the prophets treated them in the same way.

But woe to you who are rich, for you have received your consolation.

And woe to you who are filled now, for you will be hungry.

Woe to you who laugh now, for you will grieve and weep.

Woe to you when all speak well of you, for their ancestors also treated the false prophets in the same way."

As he concluded this sermon on the mount, he blessed them all by raising his right hand in the air, bringing it down vertically and then horizontally to form a cross. Then he turned and left the mountain. Nobody knew what that sign of the cross meant. But they would soon.

Later that day, Simon said to him, "You are the Messiah, the son of the living God."[1]

Jesus replied, "Blessed are you, Simon, for flesh and blood has not revealed this to you, but my heavenly Father. And so, I say to you, you are Peter, and upon this rock I will build my church."

---

[1] Matthew 16:16—18.

*Joseph Radder*

## EPILOGUE

When Jesus awoke in the upper room, he was alone. He remembered sending Simon, now called Peter, and the eleven ahead to the Garden of Gethsemane, where they would have their final rendezvous before he would be betrayed by Judas and denied by Peter.

He must have been asleep at the table for a long time, for he had dreamed of his entire adult life leading up to this moment—from his 13th birthday to his revelation as the Messiah to those closest to him.

The rest of the story is recorded in the four gospels of the New Testament. Millions have read it over the past 1900 and more years, and millions more will read it in the centuries to come. Each reader will give it a slightly different interpretation.

It is <u>this</u> writer's belief that the world's problems would disappear if all of mankind would

443

accept Jesus' teachings and live by them. Those teachings can be summarized in one word ...LOVE.

# BIBLIOGRAPOHY

American Judaism in Transition — Gerhard Falk

University Press of America

Apocryphal New Testament, 1901

David McKay, Publisher

A Young Man's Jesus — Bruce Barton

Pilgrim Press —1914

Cruden's Complete Concordance — Alexander Cruden MA

Alexander Cruden

Encyclopedia of Judaism — Wigoder

Mac Millan

Hammond's New Supreme Atlas — 1940

Garden City Books

Hidden Jesus — Donald Spoto — 1998

St. Martin's Press

Historic India — Lucille Schulberg

Time—Life Books 1968

Jesus and His Times — 1987

Readers Digest Association Inc.

Jewish Knowledge — Ausubel 1964

*Joseph Radder*

Crown Publishers

Know Jewish Living and Enjoy It — Golomb 1981

Shengold Publishers

Life of Jesus — Craven

Craven

New American Bible — 1970

World Catholic Press

New American Catholic Bible

Benziger Bros. — 1961

Origin of Species and Descent of Man — Charles Darwin

Random House — 1849

Second Jewish Catalog — Strassfield — 1976

Jewish Publishing Society of America

Standard Reference Encyclopedia — 1966

Funk & Wagnall's/Wilfred Funk Inc.

The Man Nobody Knows — Bruce Barton — 1924

Bobbs—Merrill Co.

The Saints Preserve Us — Sean Kelly & Rosemary Rogers

Random House — 1993

446

The World Christ Knew — Canon Anthony Deane — 1953

Michigan State University Press

Two Years Before the Mast — Richard Henry Dana

Random House

When the King Was Carpenter — Maria Von Trapp —
1976

New Leaf Press

*Joseph Radder*

## ABOUT THE AUTHOR

*Young Jesus, The Missing Years* is Joseph H. Radder's first full—length book. For the past twenty years he has been writing articles for magazines and newspapers. Earlier in his career he was creative director and then president of a leading western New York advertising agency. After retiring from this position in 1980 he operated a small agency for eight years, retiring again in 1988 to devote full time to writing. He has two other books in draft form which he hopes to publish in the near future.

Printed in the United States
989800002B